GIRL,
ALWAYS
AND
FOREVER

Sasha Lane

First Published in Great Britain in 2019 by Sasha Lane.
This paperback edition is the first edition.

ISBN: 978-0-9934562-3-7

Other titles by Sasha Lane:

Girl, Conflicted

Girl, Unhinged

Girl, Unconventional

Prologue

I open one eye with difficulty. It takes a second or two before the blurry image that greets me comes into focus. I survey the carnage and wince inwardly. Too many Prosecco bottles line every surface, all cork-less and empty.

How much did we all drink last night? And where is everybody?

I try to picture in my mind the last thing that I remember. My heart sinks. I remember shots. Lots of shots. And Simon, drunkenly shimmying across the lounge.

Sophie was dancing all night. She wouldn't sit down.

I was…drinking.

With difficulty, I attempt to lift my face from the furry surface it's embedded in, to enable my other eye to open too, but it's futile.

What am I lying on?

Why am I face down?

Why am I alone?

I feel like I've woken up in a dream. Slowly I prise my face from the material it's suctioned to and force myself up until I'm resting on my forearms. I realise, confusingly, that I'm on my sofa, still wearing a sparkly purple dress, with the spare duvet covering me.

Weirdly I do not appear to have a headache and I don't feel like I have a hangover, despite all the evidence around me suggesting that right at this moment I should feel like I've died and woken up in hell. I try to swallow but my tongue feels stuck in place. Mmm, maybe some water wouldn't go amiss. My whole body feels sluggish and heavy, like I've doubled in size overnight. In a panic, I quickly pat my arms and do that thing where you wrap your little finger and thumb around your other wrist to make a circle. My finger and thumb still touch, just, and I sigh, relieved. I'm still the same size as I was yesterday – nothing freaky has happened to me overnight.

Maybe I drank so much Prosecco last night that my mind and body are simply numb.

Maybe I'm not hungover because I'm still drunk.

Why, again, were we drinking Prosecco in copious amounts last night?

'Oh noooo.' I groan loudly, squashing my face back down into the comfort of the sofa cushion.

It's all coming flooding back to me now. No wonder I feel numb.

The large volume of Prosecco and the carnage around me can only mean one thing:

Today, I am forty years and one day old.

'So, how's my forty-year-old girlfriend doing?' Joe smirks as he hands me a mug of coffee. I'm still sprawled on the sofa but am now at least on a sideways slant, propped up on my elbow, rather than face down. I lift my heavy arm and take the mug from him, careful to balance the cup appropriately and not tip the coffee all over myself, which could potentially happen this morning.

I scowl and take a sip. 'Why are you making a big deal of it?'

'Of what?'

'Of *me* turning forty.'

'I'm not.'

'It doesn't mean anything.'

'I know.'

'Nobody cares about being forty.'

Joe bites his lip in a failed attempt to conceal his smile.

I push myself up to a seated position and take another sip of coffee. 'And what's so funny?'

'You seem to be protesting a little too much.'

'About?'

'About no one caring about you turning forty. It seems to me like you care.' Joe raises his eyebrows. 'At least a little bit.'

I suck my teeth. 'You're wrong.' I gulp my coffee, thinking that there's every chance I might throw this back up shortly. 'I don't care at all.'

Joe nods. 'I see.'

'Yesterday was just another day; like today is just like any other day,' I state, feeling the layer of coffee sloshing around on top of last night's gallons of Prosecco.

'Of course.'

I try to ignore the mockery implied in Joe's tone.

I swing my legs off the sofa – with some difficulty, as the spare quilt seems to have wrapped itself around me, mummifying me. 'So, I'm going to get in the shower and then cook Sunday lunch.'

Joe laughs out loud. 'Now I know you're bothered about turning forty.'

I glare at him, trying to ignore the Prosecco hangover that seems to have been awoken by the strong caffeine injection and is now dancing a salsa in my head.

'Emma, I love you, I really do. But you've never made Sunday lunch in the last six years of us living together, and honestly, given that you consumed my body weight, let alone your own, in alcohol last night, I'm thinking today might not be the best day to buck that trend.'

We lock eyes, and I really, really wish that I had some smart comeback to reign triumphant, but unfortunately you cannot argue with the truth. I am not a domestic goddess; my skills in the kitchen are limited to making instant pasta and sauce, or heating up a croissant. My only redeeming feature is that I always have wine in the fridge. Although honestly that could be interpreted one of two ways: yes, I'm always prepared for company, i.e. for a friend to drop in unannounced for a catch-up over a glass, *or* that I have a drink problem. Given my current state of unbalance, the fact that I'm still wearing last night's dress and have no recollection of why I spent the night on the sofa and not in my own bed, plus the collection of empty Prosecco bottles lining every spare surface in the lounge, I think it's safe to say that the jury's still out on that one.

Chapter One

'We're here,' I call, struggling to see over the huge box I'm clutching, which is disguising a massive superhero figure and getting heavier by the second. My arms scream in protest as I pray that I don't drop it at the last minute.

Joe wrestles with the latch to open the gate to Simon's back garden with one hand, while balancing on his knee an equally huge box carrying an identical superhero figure. It's always the same: you have to get identical presents for the identical twins; their demand, no one else's.

James, Simon's husband, pulls open the gate, nearly upending the box Joe is desperately trying to hold on to.

'Oops! Sorry.' James offers a hand while propping open the gate. 'Welcome to the madhouse.'

Simon and James moved to a huge house in a leafy suburb on the outskirts of town about three years ago. Their two-bedroom flat quickly became overcrowded as the twin boys they adopted at two years old began to grow up and need room to run around; plus they needed more room to store all the toys that the twins have. Thankfully they now have a playroom to keep everything in, which means no more remote-controlled cars left on the kitchen floor for someone to trip over (i.e. me) or Thomas the Tank Engine trains left on the sofa for someone to sit on (also me).

Moving to the large house made sense and has benefitted everyone: the kids get a playroom and Simon, in his own words, gets to 'shut the door on all that crap' and keep the rest of the house in a reasonable state of tidiness. It's strange, but even as a bachelor Simon always kept his flat pristine – not the first thing you would associate with an extravagant party animal. But those days are a lifetime ago; well, at least eight years ago (Simon carried on partying long after I gave up my clubbing days), and since he married James, Simon has grown up. Mostly.

I follow Joe, or at least step forward gingerly behind him as we head into the garden, blinded by the huge box in my arms.

'Aunty Emma!' I hear the excited voice of one of the twins, maybe Theo, a split second before I scream as freezing-cold water hits the side of my face with speed and I very nearly throw the huge box that I'm clutching in my strained arms right across the damned garden. As I have no free hand to defend myself or wipe my cheek with, the cold water simply trickles down my face and neck, and creeps under my top and into the crevices of my bra. Brilliant!

I can hear whichever twin it is chuckling.

'Theo!' James tuts. 'Shall I relieve you of that?' James takes hold of the present and smiles apologetically as the culprit of my water dowsing is revealed in all his glory.

'Happy birthday, Theo.' I nod at him warily as he stands there, smartly dressed in dark-blue shorts and a checked shirt, legs astride, clutching a large water gun as if his life truly depends on it. I just hope his identical twin, Fitz, isn't hiding somewhere about to tag-team him and hit me with another water shot.

'Let's allow Aunty Emma to at least get through the door before we attack her.' Simon strides towards me, in a red-striped apron covering what looks like orange Hawaiian shorts and a shocking-pink t-shirt. He has metal barbeque tongs in one hand and a large glass in the other in which a green cocktail is sloshing around.

'Hiya, babe.' He leans in and kisses my cheek. 'Sorry about the welcome. Some dear parent thought large water pistols would be a nice present for seven-year-old boys. I'm about to de-friend them on social media as we speak.'

I nod towards the glass of questionable green liquid. 'What the hell are you drinking?'

'Alcohol, darling.' Simon glances over his shoulder. 'Have you seen how many children are running around here?'

'It's a children's birthday party, Simon.' I roll my eyes. 'It kind of goes with the territory.'

'Yes, well, you might think that you're prepared for fifteen kids in a garden all at one time, playing ball and eating hotdogs, but you're not. In theory it sounds like a good idea – but it's not. Alcohol helps.'

He takes a swig.

As if on cue, high-pitched shouting emerges from the far end of the garden, and out of nowhere a football ricochets off the top of my head. Simon just stands there, open-mouthed with shock.

'Drink?' Joe appears at my side, having also been relieved of the huge present he was carrying, and now, thankfully, armed with what looks like a large gin and tonic.

'Yes, please.' I take the glass gratefully and readjust my hair following the ball impact intrusion.

'I'm so sorry.' A flustered-looking brunette woman with flushed cheeks thrusts a pale, freckled child in front of me. The boy stares sheepishly at his feet. She nudges his shoulder. 'Say you're sorry, Elliot.'

'Sorry,' Elliot mumbles and he looks up at me through amazingly long and curled eyelashes that would make any girl envious. I wonder how he manages to get his lashes to curl so much. I'm momentarily distracted as I stare down at them, contemplating whether I should ask him how he gets them to do that.

Joe clears his throat.

'Oh, um, that's okay.' I smile apologetically, although why I feel the need to apologise, I don't know. 'No harm done.' I pat my head reassuringly where the ball struck me.

And with that, Elliot is shooed away and allowed to continue attempting to control a football with Fitz – or maybe it's Theo. I struggle to tell them apart unless they're together, when the only telltale sign is a slightly differing expression.

I've been here less than five minutes and I've already had water fired at me and a football kicked at my head. I pray silently that this won't be one of those 'things happen in threes' situations, or I dread to think what fate may await me – probably being pushed face down into one of the matching birthday cakes.

Movement in a seated area near the barbeque catches my eye and I see my best friend, Sophie, and her boyfriend, Matt (who also happens to be Joe's brother), sitting in the afternoon sunshine. Sophie is waving over at us while clutching three-year-old Florence, whose dark ringlets catch the sunlight as she's bounced on her mum's knee.

'Are you hungry?' Simon asks before taking another large gulp of his green drink.

'Absolutely,' Joe says. 'What's cooking?'

'Come with me.' Simon taps Joe's arm with the barbeque tongs. 'I've made my specialty.'

I raise my eyebrows at Joe but say nothing as he dutifully follows Simon. Having known Simon nearly all my life and only having witnessed him cook on a handful of occasions, I'm concerned, and intrigued, as to what Simon's 'specialty' will be.

I wander over to Matt and Sophie, sipping my refreshing gin and tonic, while trying not to get my three-inch heels stuck in the grass. It never occurred to me that heels were inappropriate footwear for a garden party.

'Hey.' Sophie stands up, handing a grinning Florence to Matt, before pulling me into a hug. 'You look great. I feel like a mess. I was in such a rush to get ready, as Florence decided to upend my makeup bag all over the bedroom floor as I was trying to apply my foundation. I didn't have time to iron the outfit I was going to wear, so I just had to throw something on.' She flops back down in her chair.

I can't help but smile at the irony of Sophie's words. There she is, in full makeup, applied with expert precision like always. Her chocolate-brown curls bounce with her every head movement. She's dressed from head to toe in an outfit that I could never have put together, regardless of how much time I had. It looks nothing like an outfit that someone would just have had to 'throw on'; Sophie always looks like she's stepped out of *Vogue* magazine, even on her worst day.

I, on the other hand, am conscious of the small stain on my dress caused by a coffee drip from my morning caffeine fix. My own makeup was applied in haste: Joe was calling me as he hovered near the front door, telling me it was time to leave, when I was still in the bathroom having barely applied concealer under my eyes.

If you were an outsider looking in, you could easily think *I* was the busy mum struggling to balance my time and prioritising my child over my own personal presentation, not Sophie in a million years.

'You look as gorgeous as ever.' I smile at Sophie.

'It feels like ages since I saw you,' she says, although I'm pretty sure it was only last week. 'How are you?'

'Much better now I have gin,' I say, taking another sip from my glass. 'It's a bit...' I look round as I pause, trying to find the appropriate word.

'Crazy?' Sophie laughs.

'I was going to say "busy".'

Sophie swishes her hand dismissively. 'You know Simon,' she says. 'Each birthday party for the twins has to be bigger and better than the last one.'

I have a flashback to last year when Simon, in his infinite wisdom, decided to host a *Star Wars*-themed fancy-dress party for the twins' sixth birthday. I spent the afternoon dressed as Yoda under a stifling green rubber mask and I was mistaken for a child about a hundred times.

'I know.' I nod. 'And I have to say that I'm impressed with the whole assault course over there.' I gesture towards the football nets, trampoline and small inflatable bouncy castle that are lined up past the two barbeques full of sizzling food, towards the end of the garden.

'I think the twins are going to be more into sports than Simon was as a child anyway.' Sophie grins.

I flop down onto a wooden garden chair next to Sophie, careful not to spill any of my remaining gin. 'I certainly hope so.' I chuckle.

'Simon wasn't good at sport?' Matt asks.

'Oh, he was. Well, mainly running,' I say. 'Much to the PE teacher's frustration.'

'Simon was fantastic at running – the quickest in the class,' Sophie continues the tale.

'But he wouldn't comply with the school sports uniform.' I giggle. 'So they refused to let him compete.'

Matt raises his eyebrows. 'He refused to comply with the school sports uniform?'

'Apparently the navy-blue shorts and pale-blue sports top didn't truly reflect Simon's personality. He needed something much more flamboyant to get himself in the right mindset to take part in a contest.'

'Flamboyant?' Matt asks.

We turn to see Simon walking over to us with Joe, carrying a plate piled high with food, and we all supress a smile, as Simon has now removed the stripy apron to reveal his bright-pink t-shirt and Hawaiian shorts in all their glory.

'I see.' Matt nods.

Simon places the food down on the table in front of us. 'Help yourselves, darlings.' He pulls a wooden chair over and sits down. 'What are we talking about?'

We all glance at each other as Simon bites into a large hotdog.

'Shouldn't you be helping to entertain?' I ask, tongue in cheek.

'We had a deal: I cook, James entertains.' Simon points to the plate of food. 'I've fulfilled my obligation.'

'Right. And now you get to...?' I ask.

'Drink.' Simon stuffs the remainder of the hotdog into his mouth. 'Who wants a refill?'

'I'll give you a hand,' I say, standing up. 'Is that Prosecco I brought over the other day still in the fridge?'

'Of course. What do you take me for?'

I cock my head to one side. 'Well, given your comments so far today, you can forgive me for asking the question.'

'Tsk. I am not an alcoholic, missy. It's just that the occasion to drink alcohol presents itself so rarely these days that I have to take full advantage.'

'Unfortunately he's right.' Sophie nods.

'Thank you, Sophie.' Simon stands up. 'You see, Em, when you're a parent the problem is that you always have the children with you, and once you've got them all ready for bed and actually asleep, the mere sniff of an alcoholic beverage immediately puts you into a coma.'

'We wouldn't change things, though, would we, Simon?' Sophie blows a kiss at Florence, who's still snuggled on Matt's knee.

Simon feigns deep thought, then grins. 'Of course not, honey.'

'Well, as inconvenient as that may be, at least your liver is having some time to recuperate from all the years of drinking shots until three a.m. every weekend,' I say.

Simon grins. 'Ah, those were the days. In fact, we did re-enact them not so long ago when someone here' – he winks emphatically – 'turned forty.'

'Oh God, let's not remember that. Come on.' I loop my arm through Simon's. 'Let's find that Prosecco.'

As we walk back across the garden to the house, one of the twins comes charging over. 'Daddy, Daddy, Daddy.' His blue checked shirt and navy shorts – which are identical to his brother's, so I have no idea whether this is Fitz or Theo – are crumpled from playing, and his brow glistens with a film of sweat.

Simon scoops him up and plants a sloppy kiss on his forehead. 'Hey, Fitz, are you having fun?'

Ah, see, definitely can't tell them apart.

'Yes, Daddy, this is the best party ever.' Fits grins and looks up adoringly at Simon, and my heart melts a little.

'Will you come on the trampoline?' Fitz asks excitedly.

'The trampoline? I'm afraid it's not for grown-ups, Fitz.'

He frowns, still looking adorable. 'Oh.'

'Do you want to go on the trampoline, though?'

'Yes, please, Daddy.'

'You go.' I swish my hand at Simon. 'I'll get the drinks.'

I watch as Simon walks away, still clutching Fitz but spinning him upside down while he laughs and screams.

Inside, the house is quiet, and the kitchen cool, which is welcome after the intense sun outside. I realise that I forgot to put sunscreen on in my haste this morning before we left the house, which I'll probably regret later when my skin is the colour of a pink grapefruit. I keep reading magazine articles that tell you to protect your skin as you get older and to use products with SPF in them every day, and I have every intension of doing this – along with the long list of other good suggestions, such as weekly face masks and daily foot moisturising. Honestly I don't know how we're expected to find the time to do all of this stuff; I'd never make it out of the house.

I open the fridge door and enjoy the blast of cold air on my face as I collect the chilled Prosecco bottle. As the fridge door closes I hear children's laughter from the garden and I smile to myself. It occurs to me, and not for the first time, that Joe and I are the only couple here without a child. It's not unusual: we attend birthday parties, christenings, Christmas nativity plays, and are always the childless couple. Simon and James have the twins; Sophie and Matt have Florence; even my work friend Jenny has recently returned to work in the shop having taken maternity leave following the birth of her son, Darcy.

Don't get me wrong: Joe and I are never made to feel like the odd ones out by anyone, and we absolutely want to be invited to these things. I'm not sure if I do feel left out, or if I'm indeed bothered about it at all. I guess I sometimes wonder why I'm not ready to dive in and be included in that parental group, and whether I ever will be. Joe and I have discussed having kids over the years, but for whatever reason, it's never felt like the right time. I realise there probably is no right time to introduce a baby into the dynamics, and you can feel as prepared for it as possible but the reality is that you're as prepared for parenthood as you are for nuclear physics – you simply have to work your way through it, trying a variety of methods until you get the right result. I guess if I wanted to have a baby then I would have made the time for it.

'There you are.' James's voice snaps me out of my thoughts. 'Simon is looking for you.'

'Oh.'

'There's a table tennis tournament going on in the garage and he's elected you as the umpire.'

I roll my eyes. 'Dear God.'

James chuckles. 'I know.'

'He knows I'm rubbish at that. Table tennis is far too fast for me to concentrate on – the ball just pings all over the place.'

'Don't panic.' James takes the Prosecco bottle from me. 'It's only seven-year-olds, Emma; you'll be lucky if they can hit the ball.'

'Ah. Right.' I nod. 'Of course.'

'I'll keep this safe for you.' He puts the bottle back into the fridge and I follow him out into the garden.

As it turns out, six- and seven-year-olds are far more competitive than you may think, varying levels of sporting skills aside. Three arguments and the threat of a physical fight later, and we call it a draw, and Simon and James lead everyone across the garden to sing 'Happy Birthday'.

Theo and Fitz are presented with two cakes in the shape of Spiderman, exactly the same, except one has 'Theo' piped on it in thick blue icing and the other 'Fitz'. Large candles, which I would personally describe as fireworks, blaze in the centre of each cake. I'm pretty sure that's a massive health and safety breach, but no one else seems to care as we all gather around the blazing cakes and sing at the top of our voices. Theo and Fitz simultaneously squeeze their eyes shut and then blow out their fireworks, and everyone erupts in a round of applause.

'Fancy giving me a hand cutting the cakes?' Simon asks.

'Sure.' I take Fitz's cake from James and follow Simon back into the house.

'Here.' Simon holds out a huge knife as I lower the cake I'm clutching onto the kitchen worktop, careful not to drop it. 'You cut, I'll bag.' Simon cocks his head to the right, where some very posh-looking party bags are lined up – I didn't even notice them when I was in the kitchen earlier.

'Wow – they look…expensive.'

Simon sighs emphatically. 'Don't ask. Nobody tells you that when you have children, one of the most pressurised situations will be deciding what to include in the birthday party bags.'

'The children's parties from our youth were very different, weren't they?' I laugh. 'The party bag contained a piece of birthday cake, some crayons and a box of Smarties.'

I start dividing each cake up carefully.

'Welcome to my world.' Simon scoops a chunk of birthday cake into a blue napkin, then places it into a bag. 'If you put a box of Smarties and crayons in a party bag in this day and age, your child will be blacklisted until they're thirteen.'

I chuckle. 'Oh dear. I hope Sophie knows what she's got herself into with Florence.'

'Don't worry, babe, I'll warn her.'

I shake my head and continue slicing cake.

Not long after, the parents start gathering up their children and Simon hands out the party bags as people filter towards the garden gate. Sophie wanders over to me with Matt, who's carrying a sleeping Florence in his arms.

'We're going to make a move and head home,' she says. 'I think the bouncy castle has well and truly exhausted Florence, which probably means she'll wake up from this powernap with renewed energy and keep us up until midnight!'

'Good luck with that.' I smile as Sophie and I hug goodbye.

'I feel bad leaving Simon and James to tidy up after everyone.' Sophie surveys the carnage that remains. Paper cups are strewn across the lawn, and empty plates are stacked up on the garden tables and chairs. The bouncy castle wobbles in the late-afternoon sunshine.

'Don't worry,' I say. 'You get this little one home.' I kiss Florence on the forehead. 'Joe and I will help with all this – he could use the practice washing up.'

Matt raises his eyebrows at me.

'Okay.' I bite my lip. 'That was a lie. It's me who never does the washing-up.'

'The washing-up?' Sophie smirks.

'Or the cooking.' I nod. 'But, hey, at least I do the weekly food shopping, so we won't starve.'

Sophie laughs. 'You order it online and someone brings it to your doorstep!'

'So? The end result is the same: we *have* food. Honestly, Soph.' I cock my head on one side. 'It's called time management. Nobody goes to the supermarket themselves anymore.'

She shakes her head at me. 'Bye, Emma.'

Sophie and Matt walk over to Simon to say their goodbyes and I can still hear Sophie chuckling to herself.

I don't see what's so funny. All these years that Sophie has been trying to get me to use modern technology, and now I'm doing it, she finds it amusing. If I'm honest, I was against online food shopping originally, as somehow it felt lazy to make some poor delivery man bring my food to my door. But actually, I like the fact that I can do it in my pyjamas, and I spend far less money each week as I no longer wander the aisles aimlessly picking up each and every thing that catches my eye. And now no one knows how many bottles of wine I buy, as they're not lined up, clinking in my trolley for everyone to see. Not that I'm an alcoholic, it's just –

'Em?' Simon's voice interrupts my thoughts.

'Yes?'

'Joe's got my Marigolds on. Fancy picking up a tea towel?'

'Of course.' I nod, dismissing the image of Simon in a pair of yellow rubber gloves.

After grabbing a few plates from the table nearest me, I head back to the kitchen. Joe and I go about the task of washing three hundred pots, while Simon and James get the twins bathed and in their pyjamas, ready for the evening ahead. I find bin liners under the sink and go back outside to collect up the paper cups and discarded napkins, leaving just the trampoline and bouncy castle to sort.

As the clock strikes seven p.m. Joe and I finally put away the last of the clean cutlery and we wearily say our goodbyes.

'Thanks so much for helping – in fact, *doing* the cleaning up. We really appreciate it.' James hugs me.

'No problem. I have a large glass of wine with my name on it chilling in the fridge at home.' I smile.

'Thanks, honey.' Simon also hugs me goodbye. 'You two are stars.'

We climb into the car, Joe driving, of course, due to my gin consumption – although that bottle of Prosecco never made it back out of the fridge. A short time later, we arrive back at our rented flat overlooking the park that runs at the back of the flats. In what feels like a previous life, about seven years ago, Joe and I separated, and I left the house that we shared at the time and moved into the flat alone. Thankfully we got back together later that year and Joe moved into the flat with me, and it's been our home ever since. It's only seven thirty but I'm already feeling tired.

'I'm going to get changed into something more comfortable,' I say, taking off my heels.

'I'll get us a glass of wine.' Joe walks toward the kitchen.

I change into my dressing gown and go back through to the lounge, where Joe is already on the sofa looking at something on his iPad.

'Come here.' Joe pats the sofa next to him. 'I've got something to show you.'

Intrigued, I sit down and pick up a glass of red wine from the coffee table. 'What's this?'

Joe tips the iPad towards me and I see a picture of a lovely detached house on the screen. It looks idyllic. I raise my eyebrows.

'I was wondering if you're free tomorrow?' Joe smiles.

'Are you asking me out on a date?' I say coyly.

Joe laughs. 'I thought you might like to go and view this house?'

I stare at the screen. 'Are you serious?'

He shrugs. 'I made an appointment for two p.m. I thought we could grab a late lunch afterwards.'

'I'd love to!' I squeal.

We've been talking about buying our own place for the last six months and have been scrolling through pages of properties for sale online, but we haven't found anything that we've fallen in love with. Liked? Yes. Viewed? Absolutely – in fact, it feels like we've trawled around hundreds of houses. But we have yet to find a house that we can see as our forever home. Looking at the image on the screen, I can actually feel a little flutter of excitement in the bottom of my stomach.

'It looks perfect,' I say, kissing Joe on the lips.

'I thought so too.'

'Why didn't you say anything?'

'I saw it the other day on my way home from work.'

'You saw it?'

'I got diverted due to some roadworks at the bottom of the hill and I ended up driving past it on the way into work. Then I stopped to get a better look on my way home.'

'And?'

'And I think this one might be the one.'

A grin spreads across my face.

'Want to see more?' Joe scrolls through the pictures of the inside of the house as I snuggle next to him. 'There are four bedrooms.'

'Really?'

'Yeah. Maybe you could get that dressing room that you keep going on about, and I can get a home gym.'

I'm glad he suggested a dressing room for me, and not the gym.

I take another sip of wine. 'I can't wait to see it.'

'Well.' Joe takes the wine glass from my hand. 'Why don't we have an early night, and then tomorrow will be here really quickly.'

He takes me by the hand and leads me through to the bedroom. Untying the belt on my dressing gown, he slowly slips it from my shoulders and kisses me softly on the neck. A tingle makes its way down my spine and I wrap my arms around Joe's shoulders.

In the eight years that we've been together (admittedly a little on and off initially) Joe's had this effect on me the instant he touches me. It's never faded; in fact, our love life has only got better and better.

'I love you,' Joe whispers as he lays me down on the bed. He removes his clothes, and I lie back and feel the warmth of his toned body on top of me as we slowly make love.

Chapter Two

I wake unusually early for a Sunday morning; it's only seven twenty-five on the bedside clock, but I'm excited. We're going to see the house today, *the* house. For once I'm awake before Joe; he's still sleeping peacefully beside me. I slide out of bed and pull on a pair of jeans and a t-shirt that I discarded on the floor yesterday morning before we went to the twin's birthday party, and I tiptoe out of the bedroom and through to the kitchen.

I'm pretty sure that the pastry shop on the other side of the park opens on a Sunday morning, so I decide to take a stroll and get coffee and pastries for breakfast.

I pull on a pair of pumps and slip quietly out of the front door. Once outside, I have to squint against the morning sunshine until my eyes adjust – it didn't occur to me to pick up my sunglasses. The warm summer air feels fresh and it's really pleasant as I walk through the entrance to the park. It's been an exceptionally hot summer and the flowers are in full bloom. The park is covered in different colours, and floral scents fill the air as I follow the winding path down past the tennis courts, passing only the occasional dog walker.

I reach the patisserie and thankfully I'm right and it is open. The smell of warm, buttery pastry is overwhelming as I open the door and walk in, inhaling the scent deeply. I'm spoilt for choice with the huge selection of freshly made pastries, and I note a hint of frustration from the young girl serving behind the counter as I 'um' and 'ah', trying to make the difficult choice between a chocolate croissant and an apple strudel.

'I'll go for the strudel,' I say finally, 'and an almond croissant (Joe's favourite). And a flat white and cappuccino to go, please.' I smile, and the girl sets the coffee machine grinding as she pops the pastries into a small pink box.

A few minutes later, I'm strolling back through the park, balancing two takeaway coffees in a cardboard cup holder in one hand and the pink box containing the pastries in the other.

I reach the external door to the block of flats and realise a problem instantly. I have no free hand to swipe my key-fob against the door security to let me in. I balance the pink box carefully on top of the drinks and reach into my pocket with my free hand for my keys.

'Morning, Emma.'

I jump, upending the pink box, which is swiftly caught by my neighbour, Mr Evans, an elderly man whose fast movement to prevent my pastries from landing upside down on the ground is quite a surprise.

'Sorry, sweetheart.' He hands me back the box. 'I didn't mean to scare you.'

'No harm done,' I say.

'Here, let me help you.' He opens the door and we make our way slowly up the two flights of stairs.

'Enjoy your Sunday,' I say as I reach my front door, and he disappears into his own flat.

I then realise I'm faced with the same problem. I bend down and rest the cup holder on the floor as I retrieve my keys again from my pocket. Once the front door is unlocked, I crouch down in a sort of mid squat position, trying to pick the drinks back up. I'm just thinking that I really must do more yoga when the flat door opens fully and Joe appears, dressed in jogging bottoms and a t-shirt, a look of amusement on his face.

'What *are* you doing?' he asks.

I stand up. 'I thought I'd get us a nice breakfast.' I hand him the coffees. 'I got pastries.'

'Thank you.' Joe holds open the door and I walk in past him.

'I hope you like your almond croissant shaken, not stirred.'

'Sorry?'

I shake my head, smiling. 'Never mind.'

We sit at the breakfast bar and I tuck into the apple strudel.

'You were up early,' Joe says, pulling off a chunk of croissant.

'I'm excited about the house viewing,' I say, taking a drink of extremely nice coffee. 'I have a good feeling about this one.'

'Me too.' Joe nods. 'Nothing against renting this flat, but I can't wait to actually *own* our own house. I realise that might make me sound boring and sensible, but...'

'It doesn't make you sound boring and sensible, it makes you sound like a grown-up. Which is something I struggle with, as I still feel like I'm twenty, but I want it too. I want us to make a home.'

'We must try not to get too excited in front of the estate agent when we see the house.'

'You're right.' I nod, unconvincingly. 'We must stay perfectly calm.'

'I love it!' I squeal, unable to contain my feelings, the minute the estate agent has stepped outside to allow Joe and I to look around the house on our own. We've already had the perfunctory 'This is the kitchen', 'This is the master bedroom' etc., during which Joe and I remained suitably nonchalant.

'Let's go and look upstairs again.' Joe takes me by the hand and we practically run up the stairs like kids.

I go back into the bathroom to admire the huge walk-in shower, while Joe heads towards the main bedroom, which is to the back of the house and overlooks the tree-lined garden. I follow him there a few minutes later and laugh at the scene before me.

Joe is striding around the room, a tape measure in one hand, a small red pencil and notebook in the other.

'What on earth are you doing?' I ask, eyebrows raised to the sky.

'If we're serious about this house then we need to make sure that our furniture will fit in,' Joe says, striding past me, tape measure still thrust out in front of him.

'If it doesn't fit then we'll just buy new stuff,' I say.

Joe rolls his eyes.

'What?' I chuckle.

'That can't be your answer to everything.'

'Sometimes it's the easiest answer,' I protest jokingly.

'And we're going to pay for new furniture on top of a new house, how?'

I stick my tongue out playfully. 'Spoilsport.'

'Are you going to help me or not?' Joe asks.

'You looked like you had it all in hand.'

'Just grab this and walk to the other side of the room.' Joe hands me the end of the tape measure.

'You're very sexy when you're demanding.' I grin, and Joe rolls his eyes at me for a second time.

Once all the immediate measuring has been completed, Joe starts to relax a little and we walk from room to room in the upstairs of the house.

'Oh my God. We have to get this house.' I stare out of the window in the room that will potentially be my dressing room, at the roses in the garden, and immediately drink in the tranquillity. I can visualise the summer barbeques that we'll have on the grey-slate patio. The log burner in the far corner is a perfect addition to the garden, and one we will have to replicate unless we can wrangle a deal and get the owners to leave it behind.

'So, you definitely like it?' Joe stands behind me and slips his arms around my waist, pulling me closer.

'I love it.' I can feel the huge grin plastered on my face. 'Can we move in now?'

'I'll see what I can do.' Joe nuzzles my neck.

'Can we definitely afford it?' My heart sinks a little at the thought of not being able to have this perfect house. It seems too much to think that I could live here, we could live here, in this beautiful home.

'We can afford it.' Joe releases me from his arms. 'I'll go and speak to the agent downstairs.'

He leaves me staring out of the bedroom window. I inhale deeply and hold my breath, just for a second, as I strain to listen. Joe's footsteps descend the stairs and I hear muffled voices.

I exhale. This could actually happen. This could be our home.

I tiptoe quietly back into the master bedroom and into the en suite. Inside is another walk-in shower, which smells like a spa, and I close my eyes, imagining the hot water running over my head. I can see Joe sprawled on the bed on a Sunday morning as we watch rubbish television in bed and drink coffee.

'Emma?' Joe calls, and I practically skip downstairs to find him.

He's chatting with Susan Moore, the estate agent, tape measure back in his hand (I mean, who brings a tape measure?) as he measures out where our sofa could go. I grin as I watch him flit around the room excitedly.

'I think we need a new sofa, Emma.' Joe stands, rubbing his chin thoughtfully.

'Really?'

'Yeah, ours is too small. We need something more…us.'

'I'm glad to see that you're coming around to my way of thinking.' I smirk, and now it's Joe's turn to stick his tongue out at me.

We spend the next half an hour going from room to room planning the décor. It occurs to me about fifteen minutes in that I'm an actual grown-up. I mean, I do realise that I'm forty, but I spend most of my time feeling like I'm still a teenager, and yet here I am, planning soft furnishings in what will hopefully be our forever home.

I'm not sure when, or how, I got here, but I like it.

Friends and family have been going on about me turning forty for ages, and in all honesty I think they were more excited by it than I was. I don't know if it's the whole 'turning forty' thing, or simply that I'm in a good place emotionally, but I'm happy, really happy, and I feel more comfortable in my own skin than I ever have.

I'm forty, in a long-term, loving relationship and moving into the house of my dreams. I'm not sure it gets much better than that.

Chapter Three

'So, did you get the house?' Simon bounces in his chair like a child.

Sophie, Simon and I are having coffee, a rare occasion when it's just the three of us together. It's the Wednesday evening following Joe and I viewing the house on Sunday. We put an offer in first thing on Monday morning and it was accepted that afternoon. I think it's taken us both a day or two to realise the enormity of things and the fact that this is happening for real.

I grin. 'We got the house!'

'Oh, that's brilliant,' Sophie says excitedly. 'Matt says Joe really loves it.'

'He does. I do. It's perfect.'

'So when's the big moving-in date?' Simon is still bouncing. 'And more importantly, when's the housewarming party?'

'There will be no party,' I say calmly. 'We're forty, not twenty. This isn't our first home where we don't mind if people spill wine and crush tortilla chips into the carpet.'

'When have I ever spilled wine at your flat?' Simon says indignantly.

I take a sip of my flat white coffee. 'Our Christmas gathering last year.'

'Oh.' Simon averts his gaze.

'And it was mulled wine, which is red. My carpet is beige.'

'Sorry about that. I think I got too much into the Christmas spirit.'

'Christmas *spirits*.' Sophie giggles.

'Yes, well, anyway, moving on.' He kicks Sophie under the table, making her giggle even more. 'Back to the big moving date.'

'I don't know.' I shrug. 'Maybe two to three months. We only have to give sixty days' notice on the flat, but it depends on how quickly the solicitors move, and the people we're buying from are obviously buying another house, so we're at the bottom of the chain. We're not in a major rush, though.'

'Will you miss the flat?'

'I'll miss the view. I love looking out over the park.'

'It's very exciting,' Sophie says.

'Looking at a lovely new house and imagining living in it *is* exciting,' I say. 'Loading your entire personal possessions into cardboard boxes is not.'

'Yeah, I remember that.' Simon nods. 'You don't realise how much crap you have until you have to pack it all up and move it.'

'Exactly!' I finish my coffee.

'How many pairs of shoes do you have?' Simon chuckles.

I huff at him. 'How many pairs of shoes do *you* have?'

He clicks his tongue. 'Touché.'

'This is the last time that I'm moving. I don't care what happens, I'm staying put in that house,' I say.

'It's romantic.' Sophie sighs.

'What is?' I ask.

'It's like a fresh start, moving into a lovely new home together.'

I frown a little. 'A fresh start?'

'Yeah,' she says. 'Like a new chapter in a book.'

I shrug. 'I guess so. I hadn't really thought about it like that.'

'Like starting all over again,' Sophie continues.

I can't help but think that's a really strange thing to say. Why would we want to start over? Joe and I are perfectly happy.

'Honey.' Simon wafts his hand at Sophie. 'It's only bricks and mortar.' He shakes his head. 'You'll still have to pick his pants up off the floor no matter where that floor is.'

Sophie scowls at Simon, but I can't help laughing. 'And who says that romance is dead?'

'I *am* romantic,' Simon protests. 'But I'm also a realist, babe.'

'Then I only have one question.' I look directly at Simon. 'Given that you and James are both men, who picks up whose pants off the floor?'

Simon wags his finger and says in a serious tone, 'Some things should stay private between the two people involved.'

This just makes me laugh harder.

'Do you really need these?' Joe holds up a pair of pink and red Kurt Geiger shoes. It's later that evening and we're standing in the bedroom, surrounded by empty boxes.

'Of course I still need those,' I say convincingly. Admittedly I may not have worn them in the last few months, but still, I may want to wear them in the future.

Joe looks sceptical. 'I don't remember seeing you wear them recently, and you do have, like, a hundred other pairs of shoes.' He waves his arm emphatically at my shoe collection, which lines the inside wall of our wardrobe and is my pride and joy. 'Maybe you could take this opportunity to, um, cleanse your collection?'

I purse my lips. 'Cleanse my collection?'

'It was just a suggestion.' Joe rolls his eyes.

'I saw that, thank you.'

Joe tries not to smile.

'I think you'll find that it's fifty-three pairs.'

He clears his throat.

'And I'll have you know that I *have* worn those shoes recently.' I stand, hands on hips, emphasising my point. 'I wore them to Simon's work thing the other week.' I'm lying, and I can feel my cheeks instantly flush, showing my hand.

I stare at Joe defiantly. He looks right back at me, and I know that he *knows* that I'm lying.

'Okay.' He shrugs, looking away.

'Okay?'

'You can keep the shoes, but you need to start keeping your Friday nights free.' Joe adds more jumpers to the box he's packing.

'How come?'

'There's a regular poker game at The Old Bell and you need the practice. You can't bluff with that face.'

'Not funny.'

I throw a soft pale-blue trainer in his direction and Joe ducks as it hits the wall. He carries his full box out of the room and I can hear him laughing all the way down the hallway to the kitchen.

Chapter Four

It feels like it's taking forever to pack up the flat as our moving date beckons. Despite Joe's attempt to make me 'cleanse' my shoe collection, all fifty-three pairs make it safely into packing boxes. But I do take the opportunity to take some old clothes to the local charity shop, and to chuck most of the contents of the small store cupboard next to the spare room into the boot of my car and on to the rubbish tip. Why I've saved three thousand carrier bags, an old pair of boots (when did I last wear them?) and instruction booklets to electrical items I no longer own, I have no idea.

I vow to be more 'zen like' in future, which in my mind translates to throwing out all the crap that I don't need and haven't used in the last six months and saving my storage space for more important items, such as shoes, and more shoes, or matching handbags. Hmm.

As the boxes pile up each evening and our belongings slowly get divided into 'pack' or 'find an alternative home for it', I decide I've earned a break. After dinner one evening, I head over to Sophie's for a coffee, leaving Joe to mull over the contents of his sweater drawer with a cold beer.

'It's only me,' I call as I knock on Sophie's door.

'Come in,' she shouts, and I open the door, kick off my shoes and head towards her voice.

I find Sophie in the kitchen. 'Hey.' I smile. 'It's very quiet in here. Where's Florence?' I look around. 'And Matt?'

'He took Florence up for her bath so we could have a chat, uninterrupted.'

'Ah.'

'So I thought we would have a glass of wine instead.'

'Better make mine a spritzer – I'm driving. Plus the packing monster won't let up until I've gone through my wardrobe tonight and picked out at least another quarter of my remaining clothes to donate to charity.'

'Wow, Joe's harsh.'

'I know, right?'

Sophie starts to prepare the drinks. 'Why a quarter?'

'What?'

'Why do you have to donate a quarter of your clothes?'

'Oh.' I shake my head dismissively. 'Something to do with the ratio of clothes that I wear. Joe is adamant that it's kind of a pyramid rule: I wear a few items the most, some items frequently and many items infrequently – therefore I don't need as many clothes and someone else could make better use of them.'

'I see.' Sophie tops up my wine with soda water.

'I take it you don't have the same problem with Matt?'

'Ha! No, I think Matt barely notices what I'm wearing.' Sophie hands me a glass.

'I'm sure that's not true, Soph.' I take a sip of my spritzer.

'God help Joe if he tries to cull your shoe collection!' Sophie laughs.

'He's already tried and failed. I draw the line firmly at that.'

I watch as Sophie takes a drink of her wine. I can't put my finger on it, but something feels different than usual, just ever so slightly off-kilter.

'So, what's going on with you?' I ask, watching Sophie's expression closely.

'Oh, nothing much.' She presses her lips together. 'Work, Peppa Pig, bath time, story time, exhaustion.' She shrugs.

I tap my finger on the stem of my wine glass. 'Is everything okay?' I ask quietly, conscious that even though the kitchen door is closed, Matt is just upstairs with Florence.

'Of course.' Sophie smiles and waves her hand at me. 'I'm just tired, that's all – we're tired.'

'Sorry, I should try to do more to help. I am Florence's godmother.'

'You do enough.'

'I can have Florence over more at weekends. Or Joe and I can come over and babysit so you and Matt can go out – you know, for a date night.'

'That's very sweet of you, but honestly, you don't have to.'

'I want to, and Joe would love to babysit – you know how much he adores Florence.'

'Okay, thanks. We might just take you up on that, once you've moved house and you're settled. You've got too much going on at the moment.'

I leave Sophie's house about half an hour later and drive the short journey home.

'Hey.' Joe looks up from the sofa as I put my head around the living room door. 'Everything okay?'

I pause for a moment. The feeling from earlier of things not being right with Sophie hovers in my heart, but I dismiss it. I'm sure she *is* just tired.

'Everything's fine.' I smile. 'Have you given up packing for today?'

'I'm all sorted. You're not. You have work to do.'

'Urgh,' I huff. 'I'll deal with that tomorrow. Right now, there's a bubble bath with my name on it.'

'Okay, Emma, but don't leave things until the last minute.'

I roll my eyes at Joe, which seems to have become a habit recently. 'Sometimes I wish you were like other guys who are disorganised and leave their pants on the floor.' I remember Simon's comments.

'No, you don't.' Joe grins. 'Can you imagine what would happen if I was as disorganised as you?'

'We would live in disorganised happiness,' I say defiantly.

Joe shakes his head at me. 'It would be carnage, Emma.'

'I'll be in the bath,' I say, ignoring his last comment.

As I soak in the perfumed bubble bath, I contemplate what items I can do without when I finish packing the contents of my wardrobe. After careful consideration, I come to the conclusion that I need everything, and Joe will simply have to live with that.

It's late when I emerge from my bath and Joe's already in bed, looking at something on his phone with the bedside lamp on. I slide into bed beside him, feeling exhausted all of a sudden. There are lots of really good things about moving house…well, actually there's just the excitement of finding the house you love; the rest of it is pretty rubbish and involves physical exertion, stress over paperwork and forcing solicitors to work to the timescale they promised but now seem reluctant to follow. Thankfully Joe is a lot more assertive than I am and has been dealing with everything. I've overheard some curt conversations in the last few weeks between him and our solicitor, and now everything seems to be on track.

'I'll miss the flat when we move,' I say as I pull the bed covers over me, 'but I'll be glad when this is all over. Moving sucks.'

'It will be worth it.' Joe snuggles up against me. 'The house is perfect.'

'I know.' I yawn. 'I love it, and I love you.'

'I love you too, Emma.' Joe kisses my head. 'But don't think you're done with your wardrobe cleanse.'

Grrr.

Chapter Five

It's Monday morning and I'm at the shop really early. I have a load of samples to look over before midday, when Marissa Bamford, aka Cruella de Vil, is expecting my response.

I've been working in the clothes shop in the centre of town for the last ten years. It's an upmarket boutique aimed at well-to-do middle-aged women, although recently Marissa has been leaning towards a more 'early thirties' range. For years I worked there with my long-time friend Jenny, and with Lola – the 'three musketeers'. We worked really well together and had a lot of laughs along the way. I really missed Jenny when she was on maternity leave. I'm so glad she came back to work to keep me sane. Lola left a month ago, as she relocated to London with her new boyfriend, and we're currently waiting for Marisa to find her replacement.

My work life has taken a different turn over the last few years. I've progressed from being the girl who fought to dress the manikins (always a challenge) to being asked to review samples and make decisions about new lines to stock. Well, that may sound slightly grander than the reality. Since I completed my fashion qualification a few years ago and was then asked to design an outfit to sell in the store ahead of a visit from the Royal Couple, Prince William and the Duchess of Cambridge, when they came to open a new hospital wing, Marissa Bamford has slowly been asking me to be more and more involved in the running of the shop. I'm flattered, of course, but also still terrified of her. She has a way of turning up unannounced, wrapped in what looks like a cloak, always with bright-red nails that could have your eye out at ten paces.

I love the challenge, though – this is why I wanted to get into fashion. It's great to look at and feel fabric samples, to study colour swatches and review the designs. I don't get to fly to exotic countries to *actually* meet the suppliers, but I love being more involved and that my opinion is valued (I think). I do, unfortunately, still have to dress the manikins.

I'm still engrossed in varying hemlines when I hear Jenny come through the back door into the staff room and call, 'Morning.'

'Through here,' I call back.

Jenny appears through the door from the staff area to the shop floor, where I'm huddled over the counter. 'Hi. Coffee? I need another cup this morning,' she says.

'I'd love one.' I look up. 'Thanks.' I take in Jenny's flushed face and damp eyes. 'Hey, are you okay?'

She nods. 'I'm fine.'

'A tough drop-off this morning at nursery?'

She nods again. 'Darcy is just so clingy. He gets so distressed when I try to leave him.' She shakes her head. 'I feel so guilty.'

'Don't do that to yourself, Jenny. Every parent feels like that when they take their child to nursery. It's good for him to mix with other babies.'

'I know.'

'And they always tell you that within minutes of you leaving him, he's fine.'

'I know,' she repeats. 'But he's only eight months old.'

'So, stop feeling so bad.'

Jenny sighs. 'It's a daily routine. I feel bad for leaving Darcy. I feel bad for wanting to work and have' – she shrugs – 'adult interaction.'

'It's okay to want to work and have friends as well as being a mum.'

Jenny bites her lip. 'I feel like I fail every day.'

I drop the samples I was looking at a minute ago and go over to Jenny. 'Why? Why on earth would you feel like that? I've seen you with Darcy; you're a great mum.'

Jenny sniffs. 'It's really hard. There aren't enough hours in the day. I feel like I'm either a bad mother, or a bad girlfriend, or a bad work colleague.'

Jenny and Scott have been together for about as long as Joe and I have. She started seeing him just after I met Joe. They've not got married either, but they moved in together shortly after they decided they were definitely a couple. They wanted children from the early days, but it took them years to conceive, for no real reason other than sometimes that's the way it goes. They were so excited when they found out that they were having Darcy. Scott is a great guy, and he and Jenny are so well suited.

'When have you ever been anything other than a fabulous work colleague?' I smile, cocking my head on one side.

'How about when I turn up late looking like I've been through a tornado on the journey in?' Jenny raises her eyebrows and I giggle. 'Remember when it used to be me giving you a hard time for turning up looking like hell after you'd had disastrous experiences in your love life and you were unhinged?'

'Oi.' I whack her on the arm. 'Thanks for reminding me.'

Jenny smiles.

'That's better,' I say. 'Don't be so hard on yourself. Nobody gets it right, Jenny. Everyone feels like they don't have enough time to be one hundred per cent perfect at every role they have in life. I struggle with the fact that I don't see my mum enough; I feel like a bad daughter.'

'But she lives in New York?'

'That doesn't make me feel any less guilty that I only see her a couple of times a year.'

'I guess you're right.'

'And look, you're early today.' I point at the clock hanging above the till. 'So I'll make the coffees.'

Jenny laughs. 'I'm only ten minutes early.'

I take Jenny by the hand and lead her to the staff room. 'If I've learned anything in my old age...'

'Emma, you're forty, not ninety!'

'...then it's to enjoy the little wins.'

'And I'm thirty-eight, so we're *not* old.'

'Of course.'

As I make the coffees, Jenny touches up her makeup.

'Are you looking forward to the weekend?' Jenny asks as I hand her a mug.

'The weekend?'

'Doh. You're moving into your new house on Saturday.'

I cringe. 'Yes and no.'

Jenny looks at me, concerned. 'I thought you loved the house.'

'I do.' I take a drink of coffee. 'But if you saw how much stuff is packed into boxes, you'd understand my apprehension.'

'Surely unpacking when you get there is a lot more fun than packing?'

'You'd think. But I'm guessing it gets pretty frustrating really quickly.'

'Why?' Jenny smiles.

'Because apparently, or at least according to Joe, every surface needs cleaning before you can put anything on it.'

'I see.' Jenny drinks her coffee.

I scowl. 'I hate cleaning.'

'Good job you live with Mr Perfect Home-maker.' Jenny nudges me.

'Yeah, there are pros and cons.'

I ponder the moments when I'm told off for leaving my clothes in random places around the flat instead of putting them in the washing basket or hanging them back up – I mean, who does that? Then there are the times when I find Joe in the kitchen wearing nothing but his boxer shorts and a pair of rubber gloves. Hmm…

'Emma?'

'Yes?'

Jenny is smirking at me and I wonder if she can read my thoughts. 'It's time to open the shop,' she says.

'Oh. Right.' I put my empty mug down and push the thought of Joe in just his boxer shorts from my mind as I head to the front of the shop to unlock the door.

I arrive home just after six p.m. and kick my shoes off the minute I walk through the door. I'd instantly regretted my choice of three-inch shocking-pink Kurt Geiger heels this morning (yes, I was trying to prove a point to Joe) and now I groan as my feet hit the wooden floor.

'What smells amazing?' I head towards the kitchen, following my nose.

'It's only spaghetti bolognaise,' Joe says, stirring a pan.

I smile, thinking how fortunate I am to come home to find my boyfriend in an apron, making me dinner.

'I'll pour the wine. Red?'

'Definitely. Unless we packed it all?'

'I most definitely did not pack all the wine. Plates, maybe, but wine? No.'

'I saved two bowls and some cutlery.' Joe points to the cupboard below. 'Dinner will be five minutes.'

As if on cue my handbag starts ringing.

'Whoever this is, they'd better be quick.' I reach inside my bag for my mobile phone and look at the screen. 'Oh, there's no chance of that.'

Joe looks at me questioningly.

'Hi, Mum,' I say into the receiver, and Joe smiles as I take the wine from the cupboard and start pouring it into two glasses.

'Darling, how are you?'

'Great, thanks, Mum. Only we're just about to –'

'I'm calling about the weekend, Emma.'

'The weekend?'

'Yes, darling. You're moving house.'

'I know that.'

'Well, Parker and I thought we'd pop over and help with the move.'

'Pop over? Mum, that makes it sound like you live five minutes away, not five thousand miles.'

'It's actually about three and a half thousand miles, Emma.'

'So not the point, Mum. And anyway, Dad and Margaret are going to help, and so is Joe's mum.'

'Your father is an old man, darling. You don't want him injuring himself lifting overloaded boxes of your shoes.'

I scowl. Why is my shoe collection the focus of everybody? And anyway, my shoe collection is nothing compared to Mum's.

'Aren't you and Dad a similar age?' I say.

I hear Mum tut on the other end of the phone.

'Well, Parker and I are planning to come over to the UK for a break anyway, and to look at some houses ourselves.'

'Houses?' I blurt out abruptly.

'Yes, Emma, houses.'

'Why would you and Parker be looking at houses in the UK? You live in New York.'

'We do right now,' Mum purrs, 'but when we retire, we can live anywhere we want.'

'Retire?'

'Well, darling, as you *have* pointed out, I'm not getting any younger.'

I didn't say that exactly.

Mum continues: 'And Parker has always wanted to live in England, and I…well, I wouldn't mind coming back to live in the countryside, somewhere, you know, quaint.'

By 'quaint' my mother means expensive and exclusive.

'Wouldn't you miss New York, though?' I say as I look across at Joe, who's sipping his wine with a neutral expression on his face.

'Maybe a little at first, but the pace of life is slower in England and I quite like the thought of wandering to my local pub for a traditional Sunday lunch, joining a walking group, maybe having my own vegetable patch in the garden.'

A vegetable patch? I'm astounded. This is my mother, the high-flying, trend-setting, modern woman who has everything – a great job, a fabulous apartment, a collection of eye-wateringly expensive designer shoes and matching handbags, and central Manhattan right on her doorstep – and she wants to give all that up to grow carrots and trample through the countryside? She left the lifestyle of knitted twinsets and baking cakes for the local Women's Institute when I was in my early twenties (after she and my dad separated) and she got a new job and a new life in New York. Apart from when she visits me a couple of times a year, usually unannounced, she has never looked back. She loves New York.

'Is everything okay, Mum?' I ask warily. 'Has something happened?'

'Of course not, Emma. We're just making plans and looking at options.'

I frown. 'Right.'

'So, the weekend?'

'Yep?'

'We'll fly over on Friday. I've booked a room at the Georgian Hotel for Parker and me. We can be at your flat early on Saturday.'

'Right,' I repeat, my mind still swirling.

'Dinner's ready,' Joe says quietly, pointing at the bubbling pans.

'Mum, the spaghetti's ready. I've got to go,' I say.

'Bye, darling. See you on Saturday morning. Send me a text to let me know what time you need us there.'

'Right,' I say for the third time. 'Safe flight,' I murmur as I hang up the call.

I reach for my wine glass and take a gulp.

'What's wrong?' Joe asks as he turns off the hob and begins straining the spaghetti.

'I think an alien has kidnapped my mother.'

Chapter Six

The day of the house move is soon upon us, and I'm woken by the shrill of the alarm clock at six thirty on Saturday morning – a time I don't usually see. I roll over.

'Joe, the alarm,' I say groggily. 'Joe?'

Eyes still closed, I pat the bed at the side of me, but it's empty.

'Morning, sleepy.' I hear Joe switch off the alarm on the other side of me, and I smell coffee.

'Of course I'm sleepy,' I say into the pillow. 'It's still the middle of the night.'

'Complain all you want,' Joe says jovially, 'but my mum, your dad and Margaret, *your* mum and potentially Parker will be arriving here at seven thirty, with Bill and Alan, the removal guys, arriving shortly after.'

I open one eye.

'So unless you want to be physically removed from the house in your pyjamas by Alan the removal guy…' Joe lifts the quilt up. 'No, I stand corrected: specifically a gold, sparkly princess t-shirt and bright-pink lace pants…I suggest you open both eyes and drink your coffee.'

I force myself up to a seated position and take hold of the coffee mug, inhaling the fumes as though my life depends on it.

'Aren't you excited about moving?' Joe asks.

'Yes.' I nod. 'But I wish we were about twelve hours ahead and had already moved.'

Joe chuckles. 'I know, but we've got plenty of people helping us today.'

I take a drink of my coffee. 'Exactly.' I realise I sound ungrateful. 'But I fear that they'll just add to the chaos.'

Forty minutes later I'm showered and dressed in an old pair of jeans and a t-shirt, and helping Joe carry some packed boxes from the spare room to the kitchen when the intercom buzzes.

Joe lifts the intercom. 'Hello?…Okay, I'll buzz you in.' He presses the button, then hangs up. 'Your mum and Parker,' he says, heading to the front door.

Of course. How is it that despite a seven-hour flight yesterday and a five-hour time difference, my mother arrives twenty minutes early?

'Morning!' Mum appears in the doorway, looking radiant in grey slim jeans and a pale-pink sweatshirt, followed by Parker, who's looking equally spritely in beige chinos and a matching polo shirt.

'We brought Starbucks,' Mum announces, handing Joe a cardboard drinks carrier stacked with four large takeaway coffee cups. 'And these.' Mum hands me a brown paper bag and I instantly smell buttery pastry. Okay, maybe having people around to help today has its benefits.

Just as we finish our coffees and croissants the intercom buzzes again, and my dad and Joe's mum file into the flat too.

'Hi, Emmie.' Dad gives me a huge hug. 'Margaret isn't feeling well, I'm afraid, so it's just me today. It's nothing serious, just a cold that she can't seem to shift. She sends her love.'

After a short search for the teabags, which were already packed, I make them a cup of tea with the last dregs of milk from the fridge.

'Thank you, Emma.' Joe's mum takes the cup of tea from me. 'Did you have a good flight over?' she asks Mum, while Dad and Parker make small talk about some sports team or other. It amazes me how easily they all get along, although I guess it's been a very long time since Mum and Dad were married, and over the last few years we have all been together on numerous occasions. I'm grateful that it's this comfortable.

'Oh, the flight was fine, thanks. We arrived just before seven p.m. last night, so we had a quick bite to eat and then an early night.'

'You look fabulous,' Joe's mum continues, looking in awe at my mum. 'You do every time I see you.'

Mum smiles. 'You're too kind, but honestly you should see the lotions and potions it takes to maintain this. It's a wonder they let me through customs.'

I chuckle, having seen the multitude of vitamins, let alone the bottles of face cream and serums that Mum packs each time she visits.

The intercom buzzes yet again, and this time it's the removal guys, Bill and Alan.

As it turns out, we really didn't need everyone turning up to help. Bill and Alan are not the middle-aged, overweight, burly men with beards that I expected (I have no idea why that was the picture conjured up in my head). Bill and Alan are actually very tall, fit-looking men who appear to be only in their late twenties. They load the numerous cardboard boxes quickly into the truck while we all just stand around aimlessly watching them. They deal with the extraction of our large furniture items – bed, wardrobe, sofa – with ease, barely breaking a sweat in the process, and it's not long before the flat is completely empty.

I stand at the large lounge window and stare out at the view of the park. It was this view that attracted me to the flat the second I saw it. I'll miss it.

'Hey.' Joe comes up behind me, sliding his hands around my waist. 'Everything is packed.'

I exhale. 'I guess it's time to go.'

'If you're ready.' He kisses my cheek.

I take one last look through the window. 'I'm ready.'

And with that, we leave the keys on the kitchen worktop and close the door to the flat one last time. With mixed emotions, I climb into my car and turn on the engine. That flat saw me go through a number of changes in my life. I first moved in after Joe and I separated briefly I hit rock bottom a little (okay, maybe completely), before Joe and I got back together, and he then moved in too.

I look up at the building one last time as the removal van starts to move, and Joe, his mum, my dad, and Mum and Parker all follow Bill and Alan in a slow convoy.

As the convoy pulls up outside our new house, I'm reminded of exactly why we have gone through this painful process: this is our home, our forever home. The minute I see it again I feel happy, and I'm smiling before I've even got out of the car. The street looks idyllic. Large, bushy trees line the pavements and each house appears to be nestled behind a well-manicured garden. I hope Joe takes on that responsibility. I've never had anything other than an orchid to keep alive, and that didn't go so well. After the fourth time replacing it, I gave up.

'It's beautiful,' Mum says, coming to stand next to me, holding her hand up to shield her eyes from the warm July sunshine. 'Very homely.'

There's a bang, and we all simultaneously jump, as Alan and Bill fling open the removal van doors to begin the process of unloading our belongings.

'What can we do to help?' Joe asks Bill as he starts to lift the boxes from the van with ease and speed.

'Nothing to do, mate, other than tell us which box you want in which room. Oh, and a cuppa wouldn't go amiss, if you don't mind.'

'Of course,' Mum says, seemingly happy to make herself useful. 'Why don't I go to the shop and get some essentials – milk, tea et cetera. Save you trying to find where you packed them.'

'Thanks, Mum, that would be great.'

'Parker.' Mum beckons him with a swish of her hand. 'Why don't you help this young man' – Mum nods at Alan – 'to locate the boxes marked for the kitchen, so you can find the cups while I'm gone.'

Parker nods in agreement; always a man of few words.

'Emma.' Mum continues her military organisation, although I'm pretty sure this isn't her mission to lead. 'You tell them where the boxes need to go. Michael.' She turns to my dad. 'Why don't you and Joe start unpacking things once they're in the correct room? See, we'll have all this sorted in no time.'

We all stand there; even Bill and Alan have stopped unloading boxes momentarily and are standing to attention.

'Come on then, everyone,' Mum says brightly with a clap of her hands, and we all scurry into our positions as she heads off to her car. I realise as she drives away that the chances of Mum knowing the location of a local shop that sells milk and teabags are zero, and the chances of her using Google Maps to locate it are slim at best, but I'm sure she knows what she's doing. And anyway, I don't think anyone was in a position to question her. She can be very demanding when the fancy takes her.

Joe opens the front door and we all pile inside. Parker heads to the kitchen, ready to retrieve the cups, Dad and Joe head to the lounge, awaiting boxes to unpack, and Joe's mum goes upstairs to unload the more personal items such as clothes and bedding.

I wait at the bottom of the stairs, ready to point Alan and Bill to the appropriate room as the torrent of boxes begins to flow.

A short while later I see Mum's car pull up and she climbs out clutching a carrier bag. I smile as she walks towards the front door.

'What's so funny, darling?' she asks as she reaches the house.

'How did you find the shop? Have you finally learned how to use Google Maps?' I point to the bag.

She rolls her eyes at me. 'Honestly, the youth of today will all curl up and die if the internet goes down.'

'Youth of today?' I grin. 'I'm forty, Mum.'

'Well, Emma, the world did operate before Google became a staple part of everyday life.'

'So...?'

'So, I asked someone, Emma. An actual human being. A nice gentleman walking his Schnauzer was very happy to assist me with directions.'

I chuckle as I take the carrier bag from Mum and we head inside to make a well-earned cup of tea.

It's like we're on a production line. Items keep appearing in front of me from Alan and Bill, and I point and shout directions. People in different rooms in the house keep calling instructions, and occasionally Dad or Joe's mum replenishes us all with a cup of tea.

It doesn't take long before Bill appears with the last box and announces that the bed, sofa and sideboard are the last three items in the removal van.

'Do you need some help?' I ask cautiously, thinking that although women demand equality in every aspect of our lives in the twenty-first century, there's no way I'm going to help lift a giant sideboard when there are three men in the house. It's not that I wouldn't; it's pure science. Physics says that a five-foot-three woman weighing eight stone – okay, nine stone – with short arms cannot lift a huge wooden sideboard.

I'm saved from any kind of equality dispute by Bill simply shaking his head, looking amused, and saying, 'Don't worry, love, we'll have them in, in no time.'

I stand back and watch the two young men hoist my sofa from the van and into the lounge with ease.

'Another cup of tea?' I ask, feeling the need to do something practical.

'Thanks, but we'll be done in a minute, love.' Alan smiles.

I head up the stairs to see what my mum and Joe's mum are up to. I find them chatting away, having unpacked and organised into piles most of our clothes, bedding and curtains.

'Oh, hi, darling.' Mum smiles. 'Are you okay?'

'I'm fine, Mum.' I frown.

'You look a little flushed, Emma. Do you need to sit down?'

'What? No, I'm fine.'

'Well, I know you're not used to all this...' She pauses. 'Physical activity.'

Joe's mum has the decency to look away.

Oh well, that's just great. My own mother thinks I'm ready for the scrap heap.

'Just because I don't jog, or do Pilates, or Zumba, or whatever the latest exercise craze is, does *not* mean that I'm unfit,' I state.

'Of course not,' Mum says in a soothing voice, similar to how I imagine you would try to tame a tiger looking to bite your hand off.

'I actually lift heavy boxes all the time at work, unloading new stock.' That's a small white lie. I usually make the delivery guys bring all the boxes into the storeroom for me and I unpack the items one by one. But that's beside the point, and that knowledge won't quite cement my defence.

Mum opens her mouth to say something, but I'm saved by Joe calling up the stairs.

'Emma? Everything's unloaded.'

I head downstairs to thank Bill and Alan for all their help.

Joe hands Bill a twenty-pound note. 'Have a few beers on us, guys. You've been great.'

Bill and Alan climb back into their removal van and drive off, and the rest of us resume unpacking boxes and finding places for everything, wiping each surface as we go (yes, I had to be reminded of this several times by Joe).

It feels like an eternity has passed. Surely it must be time for bed, I think. I'm exhausted. I wipe the sweat from my upper lip – rather unladylike, and not for the first time today – and I survey the situation.

Curtains, miraculously, have been hung at both the bedroom window and the lounge window – thanks, I presume, to Joe's mum. In the kitchen, every pot, pan, cup and plate has found a new home, thanks to Mum and Parker. Dad and Joe have positioned all the furniture in each room and flattened down and stacked the empty cardboard boxes.

I seem to have run around aimlessly from room to room and made what feels like a thousand cups of tea. All in all, it's been a very productive day.

'Hey.' Joe walks down the stairs as I come out of the lounge and he wipes his brow. 'Are we done for today?'

'Yes, definitely.' I smile wearily. 'Is it time for wine?'

Joe laughs. 'I was thinking more that I'd get everyone a takeaway to say thanks for all their help today.'

'Good idea. I'm starving.'

I gather everyone in the kitchen. 'Joe's going to get Chinese food and we'd love you all to stay and have something to eat with us on our first night in our new home.'

'That sounds lovely, darling,' Mum says, our earlier conversation about my lack of fitness now water under the bridge.

'I'll come with you to help,' Dad says to Joe, and they head to the front door.

A short while later the kitchen is filled with a Chinese feast and it smells amazing. The food covers the entire table, and we only have four chairs, so we all just stand with our plate and fork and dig in, hungrily, from the buffet.

'So what are you going to do with all this space?' Mum asks between mouthfuls of chicken chow mein.

'Space?'

'You have two extra rooms, Emma. You've gone from a two-bedroom flat to a four-bedroom house.'

'Ah, well – '

'Maybe a nursey?'

I pause, a forkful of sweet and sour chicken halfway to my mouth. 'I was thinking more like a gym – for Joe. And a walk-in wardrobe for me,' I say.

Joe hides a smile.

'Oh well, Michael.' Mum turns to Dad. 'Looks like we're not going to be grandparents after all.' She sighs emphatically.

'Mum, we've had this conversation a number of times and you know it's not on our agenda. Why would that have suddenly changed because we have two extra rooms?'

'I was just asking, darling,' Mum purrs. 'A dressing room sounds lovely.'

Luckily for her, she didn't say anything about me and the proposed gym.

We finally make it to bed at ten p.m., after everyone has left and we promised to have Sunday lunch with Mum and Parker tomorrow. In the morning, they're squeezing in a look at villages they might like to live in, before they prepare to fly back to New York early on Monday.

'Are you happy?' Joe asks as I turn out the bedroom light and he snuggles up to me.

'Very,' I say. 'And relieved that it's over. We can now do the rest of the unpacking at a leisurely pace in our own time.'

'I'm not sure that there's much left to do.' Joe says. 'Your mum is like a military sergeant once she gets going.'

I laugh.

'So maybe there's just one thing left to do?'

'And what's that?'

Joe rolls me towards him and kisses me. 'We need to christen our new home.'

As it happens we also 'christen' our new house twice the following morning, which almost makes us late for our lunch date with Mum and Parker. I feel like a naughty teenager sneaking around with her boyfriend as we arrive at the hotel where Mum and Parker are staying. My cheeks are still flushed from our morning in bed, and I'm feeling rather flustered as I check my hastily applied makeup in the car mirror before Joe and I head to the hotel's restaurant.

Mum waves us over to the table where she and Parker are seated. The bottle of wine in the centre of the table looks inviting.

'Hello, darling.' Mum stands to kiss me on the cheek. 'How was your first night in your new home?' She glances at Joe and his expression remains unchanged. I instinctively blush as flashbacks of our lovemaking last night, and this morning, dance through my mind.

'We had a great night's sleep.' Joe smiles at Mum.

'I'm not surprised, after all that lifting and carrying. Even I can feel muscles this morning that I didn't know existed.'

Joe and I take our seats, and I pick up the menu and try to change the subject. 'Have you been to look at some areas you might like to live in this morning? I mean, are you serious about moving back to the UK?'

'Of course,' Mum says.

'We're very excited,' Parker adds.

'But, um, are you actually retiring?'

'Yes, Emma. Parker and I are both looking to retire within the year. I am nearly sixty-three, you know.' Mum winks.

I guess I keep forgetting that. To me, Mum doesn't seem anywhere near old enough to retire. Even though my dad is only a year older than Mum, he retired years ago, and I always think of him as being older than Mum. Maybe it's because he's had some poor health – his arthritis seems to worsen each year that passes – while Mum appears to have stopped aging ten years ago. I swear I have more wrinkles than her.

'Wine, Emma?' Parker asks, holding up the bottle of red wine that I spotted on the table when we arrived.

'Yes, please.'

'Won't it be great, darling,' Mum continues as Parker pours wine into each of our glasses. 'When Parker and I live here we can come for lunch all the time. And we can go to the spa, and shopping. Oh, it will be wonderful to have you close again.'

'That sounds really good, Mum. I'd like that too.'

'I've lived so far away from you for far too long, Emma. I understand that was my choice.' Mum holds her hands up. 'But I do have some regrets about not being around.'

'Everything worked out just fine, Mum.'

'Cheers,' Joe says, holding up his glass of wine, and we all clink our glasses together. 'Here's to doing this more often.'

'Absolutely,' Mum says.

'So, where have you and Parker been looking today?' I ask. 'Do you have anywhere specific in mind?'

Mum reels off a list of villages within about a ten-mile radius of the town, all of which are lovely. I feel awful that I'm slightly relieved that they're all close enough to mine and Joe's house to drive over for a cup of tea, but not so close that you could pop round unannounced to borrow the hoover. I love my mum, and having her around more will be great, and I do look forward to spending more quality time with her, and of course Parker too. But having spent the last eighteen years with Mum three thousand miles away, I'm not sure I'm quite ready for us to be neighbours.

Chapter Seven

'We need to talk.'

It's the following Saturday night, exactly a week after we moved in, and Joe is hovering in the living room doorway. My stomach flips at his words. Why? I don't know. I mean, we're in a strong, loving relationship and have been for six years, but I'm pretty sure that in the whole history of relationship conversations none of them that started with 'we need to talk' ever ended well.

'Emma?'

I swallow and look up at Joe, not quite able to meet his eyes.

'It's not what you think,' Joe says, still standing in the doorway.

'And what do I think?' I sniff dismissively.

Joe walks over to the sofa and sits down next to me. 'Something stupid and extreme.'

Oh…potentially…

He takes my hand in his. 'It's…um, work.'

'Right.' I nod. 'Work?'

'I've been offered a sort of temporary promotion. An actual promotion.'

Joe has been a data analyst for a large corporation the last few years. He's really taken to it and loves his job.

I smile instantly. 'Joe, that's great.'

He's not smiling with me.

'Why is that not great?'

Joe squeezes my hand and my chest tightens a little as I hold my breath.

'It means working away for a while.'

'What's "working away" and how long is a while?'

'Okay. It means Monday to Friday in London at the Head Office, for six months.'

'Six months?'

'Yes.'

'In London.'

'Yes.'

My chest doesn't loosen at this news; in fact, I think I just feel a bit numb. I look at Joe, who seems to be waiting patiently for me to say something. His body is rigid as he grips my hand tightly.

'That's not so bad?' I say, sounding more positive than I feel.

'It is bad, Emma. It's six months of upheaval. Six months of being away from home, and we've only just moved into our lovely new house. And it would mean starting in two weeks' time.'

'But you are coming back?' I blurt out. 'At weekends, I mean.'

'Of course.' Joe wraps his arm around me and pulls me closer. 'I would leave really early on a Monday morning to get the six thirty a.m. train, and then I'd be back before you finished work on the Friday, so I'd be here when you got home from the shop. They'd put me up in a hotel near the office.'

'Right.' I press my lips together, not trusting myself to speak. A million thoughts are swirling around in my head, and none of them good.

'I know it's not great timing, and six months sounds like a really long time.'

Six months *is* a long time, I think, but I don't say it out loud.

'But it's a really good opportunity for my CV. I would get a further qualification. They could have wanted a number of different people, but they've asked me. And the money is great. We can maybe take a holiday at the end of it. You keep saying that you want to lie on a sunlounger for two weeks and drink cocktails, so let's do that.'

Joe's rambling, which must mean that he really wants to do this. I don't want Joe to be away from home every week. We bought this gorgeous new home to enjoy together, not for me to rattle around in on my own.

It's only for six months.

Who are we kidding? There's no *only* in six months.

I swallow, but my throat is really dry.

'Emma?'

I look at Joe, and against every fibre of my being, I say, 'Okay.'

'Okay, as in you don't mind me doing this?'

'I wouldn't say that I don't mind – of course I don't want you working away. But if this is really good for your career, then you have to do it.'

Joe nods.

'And it's only for six months, right?'

'Right.'

I look up into Joe's eyes. 'I'm pretty sure that we can manage six months of just seeing each other at weekends.'

'It's only really four nights away; I'll have three nights at home with you.' Joe kisses me briefly on the lips. 'I'm more worried about whether or not you'll starve to death while I'm not here.'

'Honestly' – I swish my hand dismissively – 'you make out like I don't cook at all,' I say, feigning hurt feelings and playing along, although my heart feels like a large stone lodged in my chest.

Joe raises his eyebrows and fails to hide his smirk.

'Okay, so I'm not a regular, run-of-the-mill housewife who stays at home making cottage pie and stuff.' My hands go instinctively to my hips. 'I have a career and –'

Joe starts laughing, really laughing, and I bite my lip, not wanting to laugh too.

'Okay, I get it. You're a modern woman.' Joe holds up his hands in surrender. 'You don't need a man to look after you.'

'Too right,' I say, attempting to hold the moral high ground and hold back the tears that are threatening to make an appearance. 'And don't you forget it.'

The rest of the evening is awkward and feels forced. Joe tries to make jokes and I laugh along. He keeps kissing me on the cheek, touching my hair, taking every opportunity to show me that he cares, but my unease just deepens. I'm not okay with Joe going to London every week and staying in a hotel. I want him here with me, in our bed, snuggled up so I can feel the warmth of his body and feel safe knowing he's right there beside me. But now I've said that I'm alright with it, I can't take it back.

We get into bed early and Joe cuddles up to me as I turn out the bedside lamp. It's not lost on me that only seven days earlier we were 'christening' our new bedroom and I was so happy. I thought I had it all, and maybe I did – but just for a week.

Chapter Eight

'So he's going to be away all week, every week, for six whole months.' Sophie takes a slurp of her cappuccino.

It's the following morning and I'm trying to explain the situation to her over coffee and pancakes in our usual meeting place– a coffee shop on the High Street in town which has been the venue of most of our discussions over the years. They sell amazing coffee and even more amazing pastries. Honestly I really don't need Sophie's opinion on this. I already know mine, and it's not good.

'You make it sound like he's going halfway around the world. It's London, Sophie. They have mobile phone signals and FaceTiming and stuff. It's not like we're not going to speak Monday to Thursday,' I protest.

She just looks at me with a despondent expression on her face.

'Anyway, I'm looking forward to having some "me" time to, you know – see my friends, have a soak in the bath with a face mask on, read some books.' I shrug.

'Okay.' Sophie presses her lips together.

I fling my hands in the air. 'Clearly you have more to say on the matter, Sophie, so let's hear it.' I realise I'm snapping at her. 'I'm a big girl; I can take it.'

We sit there in a cloud of silence (well, as silent as it can be with coffee machines hissing and whirring in the background), eyes on each other like animals stalking their prey in the jungle. Sophie is the one to speak first.

'I just, um, think it's hard to have a long-distance relationship.'

I inhale deeply and exhale slowly.

'Joe and I are in a strong, loving relationship.'

'I know that.'

'We are completely committed to each other,' I say.

Sophie opens her mouth to say something else, but pauses, maybe thinking better of it. We drink our coffee and I struggle with the feeling of greyness that seems to have clouded over us. I can't put my finger on it, but it feels like this conversation is about something other than me and Joe and his working away – but what? I stare at Sophie as she downs the last of her drink. She's been acting weird for the last month or so.

'Look, I know that this isn't ideal,' I say calmly. 'And would I prefer it if Joe wasn't going to work away in London for six months? Absolutely.'

Sophie tries to speak, but I hold up my hand to silence her. 'I realise that long-distance relationships are hard, and this will be difficult for me and Joe. But we've been together for a long time and we will make it work.'

Sophie nods. 'I'm sorry. I know that you and Joe are a strong couple, but everyone can be tested.'

'Soph, is, um, everything okay with you?'

Her cheeks flush and she averts her gaze, for only a second, but I notice it. 'Of course.' She swishes her hand at me dismissively, smiling widely. 'Everything's fine. I'm just worried about you, that's all. But you're right. You and Joe will make it work.'

Two weeks pass very quickly, and before I know it, Joe is packing a roller-case for his first week away from me in London. I can't help but feel bereft, like I'm losing him, which is silly as he'll be back on Friday afternoon, which is only four days away, but right now that feels like a lifetime.

I watch him fold shirts and underpants into the case and my chest tightens so much that it feels like it's squeezing the life out of me. An unexpected tear ripples from my eye and I quickly brush it away.

'Hey.' Joe stops folding and looks at me. 'Are you okay?'

'Yes.' I sniff, trying to stay composed. 'I'm just going to miss you, that's all.'

Joe steps towards me and wraps his arms around me, pulling me into a tight hug. 'I'll miss you too, Emma. I love you.'

I squash my face into his shoulder, trying not to cry. I know that I'm being silly. It's a few days and we're more than capable of dealing with that, but for some reason – maybe because I still feel, only three weeks after moving in, that I'm staying in a guest house rather than living in my home – I have the sense that the equilibrium of our life is on a slant. It's not bad, it's just unusual – and I don't like it. A queer, uneasy feeling is hanging over me and I can't shake it off.

Joe kisses me full on the lips and he slides his hand down the back of my jeans and caresses my bum.

'I want you, Emma,' he whispers in my ear. 'I need you right now.' And he slowly peels off my clothes.

As I lie back on the bed and Joe makes love to me, as he has done so many times before, I can't help but feel preoccupied and slightly distant, just going through the motions instead of feeling that instant connection of making love passionately with my boyfriend. Maybe I'm feeling the fear of abandonment, perhaps I'm worried about the time we're going to spend apart, or indeed maybe it's the complete unknown that's got me thrown. Human beings don't like change; and I really don't like the uncertainty of what the immediate future holds for me and Joe, or what lies ahead.

Chapter Nine

'Hey, don't wake up.' I hear Joe's voice through my sleepy fog. 'I'm going to the train station in a minute.'

I squeeze my eyes shut, then roll up to a semi-seated position. 'What time is it?'

'Nearly six a.m.'

'Oh.' I open my eyes and Joe appears in my blurry vision.

He crouches down next to the bed. 'I just wanted to kiss you goodbye.' He leans in and gives me a lingering kiss. 'Go back to sleep.'

I lie back down.

'I love you,' Joe says.

'I love you too.'

'I'll text you when I get there, and we'll speak tonight.'

'Okay.'

'It will be Friday before we know it.'

He turns and leaves the bedroom, and I listen to his footsteps as he makes his way downstairs. I hear the roller-case on the wooden floor in the hallway, and then the front door opens and closes.

Then silence.

I toss and turn for ten minutes, but I can't get back to sleep, so I drag myself from the bed, pull on my dressing gown and head to the kitchen. I flick on my prized coffee machine, even though six fifteen a.m. might be a little early for a caffeine injection.

A few minutes later I stand sipping my fresh 'bean to cup' coffee as I stare out at the beautiful rose-lined garden. A variety of birds hop around the patio and in the undergrowth. It's a lovely morning and a lovey scene, but all I feel is empty.

I sigh, finishing my coffee, and decide that I might as well get to the shop early and make a start on the stock check, which is the first thing on my 'to do' list at work today.

I quickly shower and dress, applying makeup sporadically with a quick sweep of mascara and blusher, before finishing the look with a dark-pink lipstick which matches my skirt.

There's not much traffic on the journey into town, so I arrive at the shop for seven forty-five. I let myself in through the back door to the staff area, thinking that another cup of coffee, unfortunately instant coffee (urgh!), may be a requirement before starting anything.

I reach for the kettle.

'Hello?'

'ARGH!' I turn around as I scream, arms raised, fists clenched, my right leg bent and raised, ready to karate kick my assailant.

'You must be Emma,' says a tall, thin, very young man dressed in a suit, including a waistcoat. He speaks calmly, completely unaffected by my scream or the imminent threat of me attacking him.

He knows my name?

'Who are you?' I almost shout to be heard over the thudding of my heart hammering in my chest.

'I'm Jarrod,' he says, as if that's any kind of explanation.

'And are you a serial killer here to murder me, Jarrod?'

'Of course not.' He looks at me with an expression that I interpret as disdain.

'Then what the hell are you doing in my shop? Other than scaring the living daylights out of me.'

'Oh, did Marissa Bamford not mention it?'

My heart stops hammering and instead it slowly sinks. 'Mention what?'

'I'm your new colleague. I'll be working with you from now on.'

Oh great. No, Marissa didn't bother to inform either me or Jenny that she had hired someone to replace Lola. Charming! And if first impressions are anything to go by, then I hate this man instantly.

'Why are you here so early? It's only ten to eight. The shop doesn't open until nine.'

He looks around, lips pursed. 'I wanted to take a good look at things,' he says. 'To see…well, what can be improved.'

'I see.' So now he's insulting mine and Jenny's running of the shop before he's even met us.

'It's just business.' He shrugs. 'Nothing personal.'

Nothing personal, my arse. He's been skulking around here since God knows what unearthly hour, trying to find something he can score points on with Cruella de Vil, getting me and Jenny into bother. Well, I'm just not going to stand for that. We work hard and do a good job, and I'm not having some preppy child in a suit tell me otherwise.

'And what exactly do you think you've found?'

He licks his lips slowly, which irritates me even more. 'The filing system on the computer could be smarter.'

I suck my teeth.

'And the storeroom needs a complete overhaul.'

Okay, I'll take the computer thing, and that's probably my fault. IT skills are certainly not my speciality, and Jenny does nag me sometimes, or maybe often, to do certain things that perhaps I don't. But I'm not ready to concede to this clown yet.

'The storeroom is perfectly functional,' I state.

Jarrod makes a little sound like a strangled laugh. 'Follow me.'

I scurry across the shop floor after him as he takes long strides towards the storeroom. For the next twenty minutes Jarrod explains to me the logic behind pretty much pulling the entire stock out of the storeroom and putting it all back in a slightly different fashion. It's not ground-breaking, and I'll be damned if I'm going to do it just to massage his ego. I stand by my original statement: 'The storeroom is perfectly functional'.

Despite my continuing and very vocal protests, it would seem that 'perfectly functional' is not what Jarrod is looking for, and we spend the next half an hour in an angry cloud of frustration as Jarrod moves things around in the stockroom in what I see as a futile attempt to make a small room filled with clothes, shoes and handbags into a small room filled with clothes, shoes and handbags. It's the same no matter how you arrange them on the shelves. Twice I narrowly miss being hit in the face by a large handbag as Jarrod flings items around while issuing instructions to me. I'm sweating, and annoyed, and it's not even nine a.m. yet. I don't hold out much hope for a harmonious working relationship with Jarrod if this initial experience is anything to go by.

As I roll up my blouse sleeves, I hear the back door to the staff area open and close, which signals the arrival of Jenny. I only hope that she hasn't had a bad morning with Darcy, or the unexpected arrival of Jarrod could send her over the edge and then who knows what might happen.

'That's Jenny,' I say, leaping backwards out of the storeroom. Thankfully I'm next to the door and Jarrod is penned in at the back of the room behind the new season's footwear collection. 'I'll just go and say hello.' I shoot off across the shop floor to the staff area before he can object.

As I push open the swing door to the staff room, Jenny is just taking off her coat. She turns to me, smiling.

'Morning,' she says. 'Shall I –'

'No time for that.' I hold up my hand as Jenny stares at me. I realise I may look a little unkempt from lugging stock around in a circle for the last thirty minutes. 'New guy.' I point my thumb over my shoulder. 'Beware. Seems he's so far up Marissa Bamford's –'

'You must be Jenny.' Jarrod approaches from behind me before I can finish my sentence.

'Hi, yes, nice to meet you,' Jenny fumbles, looking cautiously at Jarrod.

'I'm the new member of the team.' He grins.

'I was just going to put the kettle on.' Jenny stares at him.

'Ah, lovely. Emma and I have worked up quite a thirst this morning,' Jarrod states.

Jenny looks at me with a confused expression.

'Rearranging the storeroom,' I clarify.

'Oh.' Jenny turns to fill the kettle and goes about making drinks.

'I'll be revising the stock-take spreadsheet,' Jarrod says as he leaves the staff room, and I pull a face behind him as the door swings shut.

Jenny turns back around, frowning. 'I didn't think the storeroom needed rearranging?'

I exhale. 'It didn't, and nor does the stock-take spreadsheet need "revising", whatever that means.'

Jenny hands me a coffee.

'Just leave him to it,' I say. 'He wants to impress Marissa Bamford? Let him carry on. He'll soon realise that there are more important things to do once he actually has to start serving customers.'

'I'm not sure I'm going to like him.' Jenny bites her lip.

'I'm not sure *I'm* going to like him either, but I think we're stuck with him, certainly for the immediate future, so we'd better make the most of it.'

'I guess so.'

'Or take him out for a drink one night and get him a bit tipsy. See what information we can get out of him.'

'Information?'

'There's something not right about him. I wouldn't be surprised if he isn't some long-lost son of Marissa's.'

Jenny chuckles. 'You know she's never been married, and as far as I know, she has no children.'

'Don't be so naive, Jenny.' I shake my head. 'People show you what they want you to see.'

Chapter Ten

Somehow we make it through the day without killing each other; and by that, I mean either me or Jenny killing Jarrod. It's been a busy day full of distractions, and clearly surprises, but as I drive the short journey home the realisation that I'm going back to an empty house hits me. It's my first night alone without Joe. He texted earlier to say he had arrived safe and well, but that's all I've heard from him, and now cooking a meal for one this evening doesn't thrill me. Well, cooking in general is a bit of a turn-off. Joe will be calling me later, though, so at least I'll speak to him tonight.

I pull up at the house and can't help but smile at our lovely home, despite my hideous day. I park the car on the driveway and unlock the front door. I head straight through to the kitchen and pour myself a glass of wine, not even taking the time to remove my shoes – it's a wooden floor; I'll just mop it or something later.

I take a gulp, but it does little to dispel the overall feeling of despair from today. I went to work thinking I would get ahead with the stock take and ease myself through the day, not have the shock of my life as some random man appeared demanding we overhaul everything we've done for the last ten years.

Jenny looked less and less impressed as the day progressed. I'm only hoping that today can be put down to overenthusiasm on his first day and that tomorrow we may see a slightly less uptight Jarrod.

I have another drink of my wine and open the fridge to peruse the options for dinner. It all looks far too much like hard work. Even putting the oven on feels like a challenge this evening. I vow to start cooking proper food tomorrow, and for tonight I grab the soft goat's cheese from the top shelf and close the fridge door, then collect olive oil and a French bread stick from the cupboard to add to my plate.

I go upstairs and change into my pyjamas, before curling up on the sofa with the remainder of my glass of wine and slathering squidgy goat's cheese onto chunks of bread and dipping them in the oil. I switch on the television and find repeats of *Sex and the City*. Perfect.

It's nearly eight p.m. and Joe still hasn't called. I turn off the television and pick up my mobile phone. I check that the volume is still on high and that I haven't accidentally pressed the mute button. Nope, all fine.

I glance at the screen again.

Nothing.

I toss the phone onto the sofa cushion beside me and tap my fingers. Joe sent me a text this morning at about nine thirty to say he had arrived and was at the office. I mean, surely the work day has finished by now?

I pick the phone back up and scowl at it. How many minutes, hours, days, do we waste staring at these damned things?

Bbbrrrring.

My mobile phone chirps to life, and I'm so surprised that I drop the stupid phone on the floor and nearly knock it under the sofa in my haste to pick it up.

'Hello?' I finally say into the receiver.

'Hi, Emma. Are you okay?'

A lump catches in my throat at the sound of Joe's voice. I didn't realise how much I'm missing him already. He sounds so far away.

'I'm fine, thanks. I'd lost track of time,' I lie.

'I'm sorry to call so late. I've just got back to the hotel.'

'You've only just got back to the hotel?'

'Yeah, they wanted to take me for a bite to eat and a beer on my first day. Everyone's so nice.'

'Oh. Well. That's nice,' I say, a little annoyed that Joe couldn't have found the time to give me a quick call or text before heading out with his new work friends.

'Anyway,' Joe continues, 'I've had a brilliant first day. I'm knackered now, though – in need of a hot shower and bed. How was your day?'

'Um, interesting.' I raise my eyebrows, forgetting that Joe can't see me.

'Interesting how?' he asks.

'New guy at work is a pain in the bum.'

'I didn't know there *was* a new guy at work.'

'Me neither. It was a complete surprise. He wears a stupid three-piece suit and looks like he's barely out of school, or maybe that's just because I'm old. Anyway, I'm hoping that it was just first day over-exuberance and he'll be much more likable tomorrow. How about you? At least your new work colleagues are nice?'

'They're all lovely,' Joe says. 'Mark and Karen have really made me feel welcome.'

'So what do Mark and Karen do?'

'Mark is the boss, so I report to him. Karen is working on this project with me.'

'Oh.' I hope Karen is manly and unattractive.

'I'm sorry, Emma, I'm exhausted. I'm going to have to get some rest. I'll call you again tomorrow night.'

'Oh, okay.'

'Goodnight. I love you.'

'Love you too.'

I hang up the phone feeling completely deflated. I was expecting something more from that conversation. I had visions of a romantic chat about how much he missed me already, not a two-minute up-date. I know he was tired, but still.

I sit in silence for a minute and stew, before pressing play on another episode of *Sex and the City*, but I'm barely watching it. After an hour of staring into space, I decide to get an early night. I triple-check that all the doors are locked before I go upstairs.

I stare at my reflection in the bathroom mirror as I put a dollop of my collagen cleanser (a 'must', apparently, now that I'm forty – thank you, Mum) into my hand and rub it despondently onto my face. I think back to our discussions over the last two weeks about Joe working away in London, and I don't recall the mention of anyone called Karen at any point.

I'm sure she's old and unattractive.

She's probably really boring too.

I flop into bed and pull the covers over me. The bed feels cold and empty without Joe's warm body snuggled beside me. I lie awake staring at the ceiling for a long time, before I finally fall into a fitful sleep.

The week ends up being a bit like Groundhog Day. Each day Jenny and I attempt to get on with the day as usual, only Jarrod seems intent on interfering in everything that we do. I'm trying to warm to him, I really am, but he's making it very hard.

The customers love him, which is really annoying. He turns the charm right up with them, and they gush at his every word.

On Thursday, not long before the end of the day, I see Mrs Mangham heading towards the shop. She's a glamourous woman, a similar age to me, I would guess, who is our most affluent customer and also the most demanding one. I step forward ready to greet her, but no sooner has she walked through the door than I find myself elbowed out of the way by Jarrod as he hurries past me to introduce himself.

Jenny stands open-mouthed across the other side of the shop, a half-folded sweater in her hands.

'Good afternoon. I'm Jarrod. How can I help you today?' He beams at Mrs Mangham and I have to ignore the instinct to screw my face up.

'Oh, how lovely. Are you new here?' Mrs Mangham over-pronounces every word. I sometimes wonder if it's painful to be that posh.

'Yes, it's my first week.'

'How nice to see a smart young man.' Mrs Mangham pats Jarrod's arm with her hand.

'What are you looking for this afternoon?' Jarrod's smile widens further than I thought possible.

'An evening dress. Something glamourous.' She purses her perfectly glossed pink lips and flicks her softly curled hair. Is she flirting with him?

Jarrod leaps into action. 'Of course. Come with me. We'll make you the most stylish girl at your event.'

'Oh, girl?' Mrs Mangham giggles as she follows Jarrod eagerly.

61

I head to the storeroom to finish labelling some new stock before the end of the day. Jenny follows me in.

'Is he for real?' she whispers.

'I know, it's vomit-inducing how creepily nice he is to the customers. I mean, you don't have to be like that. We're nice and polite to people.'

'We are.' Jenny nods.

'Maybe he's looking for a cougar.' I smirk and then we both start laughing.

The door suddenly opens and Jarrod appears. We instantly stop mid-laugh.

'What's going on in here?' He looks at us with a stern expression.

I gulp. It's like being caught skiving at school behind the bike sheds by the head teacher.

'I was just finishing pricing up the new stock,' I say, holding up the pricing gun in my hand as evidence.

His eyes narrow as he turns to Jenny. 'And you?'

'I was just collecting these.' She picks up a pair of the new shoes that arrived yesterday. Black, open-toed and patent, with a cute bow. 'I thought Mrs Mangham might like them to go with whatever outfit you're looking at. She only wears black shoes.' Jenny holds them out towards Jarrod. 'I think you'll find she's a size six.'

Jarrod glares at Jenny for a moment before taking the shoes from her grasp. 'How very thoughtful of you, Jennifer. Thank you.'

He leaves and closes the door behind him.

'It's Jenny,' she says under her breath.

'Hey, quick thinking. I thought we were really in trouble then.'

'When he arrived did he say he was in charge?' Jenny asks, hands on her hips.

'Um, no.' I shake my head.

'Then unless I've missed an email or memo from Marissa Bamford telling me otherwise, Jarrod out there' – she points to the door – 'is our colleague, not our manager. So why are we defending ourselves to him and hiding in a storeroom?'

'Good point.'

'Well, no more,' Jenny says sternly. 'From tomorrow, things are going to change.'

I wait until both Jenny and Jarrod have left to lock up the shop. I made out to Jarrod that I was still busy pricing stock when I'd actually done it all, but I wanted him to leave so I could lock up. It freaks me out a little that he keeps getting in at the crack of dawn, so I kind of wanted to make a point and stay later than him. Childish? Maybe, but never mind. It's not like I need to rush home. There's only more cheese and bread awaiting me – I realise I made a promise to myself to cook food in the evening, but there doesn't seem much point when there's still bread and cheese to eat. It will just go to waste.

As I lock the shop door behind me, I realise that it's only six o'clock, so I decide to call in on Sophie on my way home. Joe has agreed to call me at seven thirty every night. We have spoken each evening, but I'm still finding it hard that he's away.

I reach Sophie's house and knock on the door. It takes her a while to open it.

'Hi,' I say as she pulls the door open and I step inside.

Sophie's demeanour is completely wrong. Her shoulders sag beneath her dark curls, and she looks deathly pale.

'What's wrong, Soph?' I ask, immediately concerned.

She walks into the kitchen and I follow. 'Soph?'

She stops and turns to face me.

'Where's Florence?'

'My mum picked her up from nursery. She's spending the night there.' Sophie fiddles with her hair.

My chest tightens and I bite my lip nervously. 'Sophie. What's going on?'

She looks at me warily from across the room.

'Sophie. I love you. But I'm not going to ask you again,' I say sternly.

She gulps. 'You're going to judge me.'

I shake my head. 'I would never.'

'I'm judging me.'

'What do you mean? Sophie, what's happened?'

There's a pause, like the whole world has stopped turning, and then Sophie says the words I never thought I would hear from her lips:

'I cheated on Matt.'

Chapter Eleven

My heart stops, it literally stops, and I can feel my mouth sagging open. I instinctively reach my hand up to my face and my fingertips brush my lips. I'm stunned.

Silence gushes in and fills the room, pushing against me until my chest feels like it's bursting as I hold my breath.

This is big.

Huge.

Unthinkable.

In fact, for a second I wonder if I completely misheard Sophie. My brain is scrambling for some sense. She can't really have said what I think she just said, can she?

'Emma,' Sophie whispers, 'please say something.'

'Jesus Christ.' I exhale, my whole body deflating like a balloon.

'Please say something else.' Her voice breaks.

'Oh, Sophie.'

I rush over to her and pull her towards me. I feel the wetness of her tears against my cheek as I wrap my arms tightly around her and she begins to sob. I cling on to her, needing the support of her body as much as she's holding on to me for dear life. I can feel a nervous tightening in my gut. This is serious, and so wholly unexpected that I blink a few times and pinch my forearm to make sure that I'm not dreaming.

I hold Sophie close until her sobbing subsides a little, and then I release my grasp on her and I guide her over to the sofa.

'Sit there. I'll get us a cup of tea, and then we can talk this through, okay?'

She looks up at me with wide eyes and nods.

I go into the kitchen to make us both a much-needed cup of tea, and also to try to stop my mind spinning uncontrollably before I sit back down in front of Sophie and she starts to talk. I think a large gin and tonic, minus the tonic, might be more appropriate under the circumstances, though; it doesn't feel like a cup of tea is going to cut it.

I stare out of the kitchen window as I wait for the kettle to boil, still reeling from Sophie's shock announcement. I feel numb; there's no other word for it. How the hell did this happen? Sophie and Matt are happy. I know this; I know them. Sophie doesn't cheat – she hates cheating. She loves Matt.

The kettle reaches boiling point and clicks off. I go to take two teabags from the tea container and look down at my hands and realise that they're shaking. I have to pull it together. I need to hear Sophie's side of this, the facts of the situation, to understand what's happened, and then process that information and try to deal with it. I cannot judge Sophie; she's my best friend.

I carry the two mugs of tea into the living room. Sophie is hunched over where I left her on the sofa, staring down at her hands clasped tightly together in her lap. I place the mugs down on the coffee table and sit down gently next to her. I pick up my mug and take a drink. I really wish it was gin.

'Okay.' I take a deep breath. 'Do you want to start at the beginning?'

Sophie reaches forward and picks up her mug. She takes a sip of tea before she says, 'I don't know where to start.'

'Would it help if I asked the questions and you then answered?' I offer.

She nods.

Right. I bite my lip. I have about a hundred questions.

'Who is he?' I say, which seems like the most logical place to start, although this conversation seems to defy logic itself.

Sophie sniffs. 'This is harder than I thought it would be.'

I wait, saying nothing. I need to let her tell me in her own time. Although honestly, I can't imagine a scenario where Sophie would betray Matt with someone she met. The whole thing is unthinkable.

I realise that the frantic inner babbling is my mind's way of trying to deal with things, but I need to quieten my thoughts.

'He's a guy from work.' She looks at me. 'A guy who started with the company about three months ago.'

'What does he do? Do you work closely with him? Is he in your department? Did he hit on you? Sorry.' I hold up my hands. 'I'll try to ask one question at a time.'

'He's one of the senior finance managers.'

'And have you worked with him? Is that how it started?'

'What I'm going to say will sound crazy, but it was an instant connection. I had to greet him in reception on his first day, to show him round and stuff, and the second I set eyes on him something inside me changed. It was like a weird chemical reaction that I can't explain even to myself, let alone anyone else.'

My heart sinks. I'm getting a horrible feeling that this wasn't, as I'd hoped, just some drunken kiss at a work event after one too many glasses of Sauvignon Blanc, but something much more serious. I can't believe I'm about to say this...

'Sophie, did you have a full-on affair with this guy?'

A big, fat tear slides down her cheek and she gulps. Her reaction tells me everything I need to know.

Holy shit.

'How long did this go on for? Oh God – it is over, isn't it?'

'Yes, yes, it's over. It was two months of something stupid and crazy.'

'Define "stupid and crazy".'

Sophie fiddles with her hands. 'We went for a coffee, just an innocent drink, and we...got on. It was just friendly chatting over a latte. I was just being nice to the new guy.'

I bite my lip. A little more than nice.

'And then we met again a week later. He accidentally brushed my hand and there was' – she closes her eyes – 'a reaction, a physical reaction.'

'Accidentally brushed your hand? We're not in the movies, Soph.'

'Accidentally? On purpose? I don't know.'

'So, did you both realise this "physical reaction"? Did you say something? Did he? Who made the first move?'

'I don't want to go into the details.'

'I'm sure you don't, Sophie, but I'm afraid you're going to have to. You can't just tell me that you've cheated on your partner and the father of your child and expect to brush over it like you were telling me your plans for the weekend.'

I can hear my voice escalating and feel my heart beginning to race as a hint of hysteria – no, make that a whole heap of hysteria – creeps in. In the back of my mind I hear mantra, repeating loudly: *Matt is Joe's brother. Sophie is my best friend. Sophie cheated on Joe's brother.*

'I know that,' Sophie snaps back.

I clear my throat and try to take my harsh tone down a notch as I ask, 'Did you sleep with him?' I hold my breath, fearing the answer.

Sophie shakes her head. 'No,' she says quietly.

I have no way of controlling the expression on my face, but I must look unconvinced.

'I *didn't*,' Sophie protests.

'So, you just met for coffee? That's not cheating, Sophie, that's socialising, so I know it didn't end there.'

'No.' Sophie chews her lip. 'It didn't. The coffee led to wine, and then we just sort of kissed.' She holds her head in her hands. 'I'm so embarrassed. It sounds so ridiculous to say it out loud.'

'Was it just one kiss?'

She shakes her head. 'We were meeting up for drinks a couple of times a week, and it always ended with us being…intimate.'

'Intimacy is what you have with Matt; *this* sounds like teenage lust.'

It's my turn to hold my head in my hands.

'I…I ended it as soon as I came to my senses,' Sophie continues, a little panicky. 'When I realised what I was doing, what I was risking, I cut all contact.'

'And where is this guy now?'

'He's going back to the Northern Ireland office next week, so I won't see him again at work.'

'And you're not in contact now?'

'No.'

'When was the last time that you, um, had a glass of wine with him?'

'Two weeks ago,' Sophie says flatly.

I try to digest the wave of information, but it still feels surreal.

'What about Matt? What about Florence?'

'I know, I know. I love Matt. I've made a huge mistake – I know that. I wish I could go back in time and not do what I've done.'

'I thought you guys were happy,' I say, hearing the sadness in my voice.

'We were. We are. I really…I don't know how this happened.'

'Is he in a relationship too, this guy?'

She nods.

I pull my hands through my hair. 'Sophie. You're my best friend and I love you, but what the hell were you thinking?'

'I wasn't thinking; that's just it. I wasn't thinking about Matt, about what I was doing, about the consequences of what I was doing. I wasn't thinking at all!'

I pick up my mug of tea and take a gulp, really wishing it was the gin and tonic, minus the tonic.

'You sound angry with me.' Sophie's voice quivers slightly.

I shrug. 'I'm sorry, Sophie, but I *am* angry with you.'

'I didn't cheat on you.'

'But you didn't tell me for the last two months, so you kind of did.'

'And what would you have done if I'd told you when it was happening?'

'I would have talked you out of it – told you how stupid you would be to risk your relationship with Matt, a great guy who loves you, who's a good dad to your child.'

'You're right. I should have told you.'

'No, Sophie, you should have simply had nothing to do with this guy. You're in a relationship; he's in a relationship.'

'It just happened. You have to believe me that I didn't plan this. I didn't get up one day and decide to cheat on Matt.'

'Then how did it happen? You don't just *have* an affair, Sophie; you make a conscious decision to do that.'

'I know I made a stupid decision, a really stupid decision.'

'I don't get it, Soph. How do you accidentally end up sneaking around with someone who isn't your boyfriend?'

'If I were you, I'd be thinking the same thing. I can't explain it, and I can't expect you to understand because you've never been in that situation. I know that nothing I say can change what I've done.'

'Then help me try to understand,' I plead with her.

She shrugs. 'I can't. I can't explain it any other way except to say that it was a physical reaction. I liked the fact that he paid me attention, that he found me attractive. That I felt like my old self for a change and I wasn't just Florence's mum, juggling trying to be a good mum while all the time feeling guilty for being a working mum. Some days I go to work with two-day-old unwashed hair and simply a spray of dry shampoo and a swipe of lip gloss. I love being a mum, but I'm tired and sometimes overwhelmed, and I feel lost and like I bear no resemblance to my old self. Things just snowballed and got out of hand.'

'That's not an excuse, Sophie. Plenty of people have children and don't cheat on their partners.'

'No, it's not an excuse. But maybe it was an accumulation of things that got me to this point. I didn't realise how I was feeling until it was too late, and I was already going down that road. This isn't about Matt, it's about me.'

'I wish I had known that you were feeling that way. I could have tried to help, to stop you ending up doing something really stupid.'

'I know.' Sophie nods. 'And I realise that this is a shock for you to have to deal with.'

'And how do I deal with it? What do I do with this information, Sophie?'

She looks at me with fear in her eyes. 'You can't tell Joe.'

'And that's the problem, right there. You didn't just cheat on your boyfriend, Soph, you cheated on your boyfriend who happens to be the brother of *my* boyfriend. And I know that I sound incredibly selfish at this moment, but I'm in a really difficult situation now. How am I supposed to keep this secret from Joe?'

Sophie closes her eyes and shakes her head. 'I'm so sorry.'

'Are you going to tell him, Matt?'

Sophie nods solemnly. 'I have to. I know it could potentially destroy everything we have, but I can't live with the lie; it would kill me and end up destroying us anyway. I'll tell him, and soon, but until then you can't say anything to Joe, okay?'

I nod, already feeling slightly nauseous from the weight of the secret nestling in the pit of my stomach.

'Promise?'

'I promise,' I say. 'And what about Florence in all of this?'

Sophie starts sobbing again. 'I'm heartbroken that I've done this to her.' She puts her head in her hands.

I put my arm around her and pull her close. 'I can't say that I'm not shocked by what you've done, but I'm your friend and I'll support you in any way that I can while you sort things out with Matt. I'm sorry if I've been judgemental, but there's no instruction booklet on how to deal with your friend's revelation that she's kissed another man.'

Sophie lifts her head and looks right at me. 'What if Matt can't forgive me?'

'Let's only worry about that if we have to,' I say softly. There's nothing else that I *can* say.

In all honesty, I have no idea what the answer to that question is. Can Matt forgive her? I still can't quite believe that this conversation is real and that Sophie, my oldest friend, has cheated on her lovely boyfriend and the father of her child. It seems so far out of character for her that if a week ago someone had told me I would be having this conversation with her, I would have called them a liar to their face. My brain can't comprehend the outcome if Sophie tells Matt and he ends their relationship. The fallout would be catastrophic, and the reality of that is far too much to take.

I leave Sophie's house half an hour later with a very heavy heart. Once I climb into my car, I find myself just sitting there, staring out of the windscreen at the complete darkness surrounding me. It feels like the sky is darker than usual and the streetlights are dimmed – like darkness is closing in on me. I don't know how long I sit there before finally putting the key in the ignition and starting the engine. My mind must still be numb, and somehow I find myself on autopilot and heading to the one person who I know can help me make some sense of this.

A short time later, I pull up outside Simon's house. The lights are on, so thankfully he must be in. At least I hope he's in and it's not just James home alone with the kids. I get out of the car and stagger on wobbly legs to the front door, aware that to the unknowing observer I may look like I've had a few drinks before driving here, but that couldn't be further from the truth. After tonight's revelations, I've never felt so sober.

I knock loudly on the door and hear Simon chuntering as his footsteps near the other side of the door: 'Alright, alright. Where's the fire?'

The door opens and Simon appears, frowning. 'Em?' His eyes brighten. 'What are you doing here, babe?'

I open my mouth to speak, but nothing comes out.

'Em?'

'Can I come in?' I manage to squeak.

Simon pushes the door open wider. 'Of course, of course.' He ushers me into the house. Closing the door behind us, he turns to face me. 'What on earth is wrong? Are you okay, hun?'

'I'm fine,' I say.

'Is it Joe? Is Joe okay?'

'Joe's fine.'

'Then what is it?'

'Hey, Emma.' James appears in the hallway. 'Want a cuppa?'

Simon wafts his hand towards James. 'I think we're going to need something stronger, darling.'

James glances from Simon to me and nods. 'There's wine in the fridge,' he says. 'I'll leave you two to it and I'll go and check on the boys.'

Simon and I walk through to the kitchen as James heads up the stairs. Simon silently collects two wine glasses and a bottle of chilled wine from the fridge, and we go through to the lounge. I flop down on the sofa, the weight of Sophie's confession hanging heavily on my shoulders. Simon pours the wine and hands me a glass, then sits down next to me.

'Okay. Go. What the hell has happened?'

I inhale, exhale, take a gulp of wine, then just blurt it out: 'Sophie cheated on Matt.'

Simon looks at me, confused. 'I'm sorry, what?'

'I know. It's unthinkable. They seem so happy – they *are* so happy. I don't know how this happened. I don't know what to do,' I state.

Simon takes a second and presses his lips together, apparently deep in thought. Then he says the second thing to shock me to the core tonight.

'It happens.' He shrugs.

'It happens? So that makes it alright? How can you be so blasé about it? What is wrong with everybody? Why does cheating on your boyfriend suddenly seem so excusable?'

'Emma, calm down. I'm not saying that it's excusable; I'm saying that it happens. There are loads of pressures on relationships in this day and age.'

'That's a pathetic excuse.'

'And people meet other people, and there's lust, romance, and they get carried away in the moment. They make stupid mistakes. People aren't perfect, Em, they're flawed.'

I take a drink of my wine. 'I don't know, Si, to me they all seem like convenient excuses to behave badly.'

'Yeah? And how convenient is that excuse for Sophie? How is she doing right now? Given that she's confessed this to you, I'm guessing it's something that she's regretting, not shouting from the rooftops?'

I close my eyes, thinking of Sophie's pained expression as she told me. 'She's devastated. Distraught. Horrified that she's behaved this way, and scared to death that she's going to destroy Matt when she tells him.'

'He doesn't know?'

I shake my head.

'But she's going to tell him?' Simon asks.

'Yes. She says she has to; she can't live with the lie.'

'I'm guessing that she doesn't want you to tell Joe?'

'Not until she's talked to Matt about it.'

'That's hard.'

'I know.'

'When is she going to speak to him?'

'I don't know. She was pretty upset this evening, but she says she needs to find the right time.'

'So until then you have to keep shtum.'

I nod.

'Be careful, Em. Joe might not take too kindly to you keeping something like this from him. Matt is his brother. This could backfire on you, you know – you have split loyalties.'

'I realise that, Simon, but what else can I do? If I told Joe, I'd betray Sophie.'

'That's not a good choice to have to make.'

'And Matt needs to hear it from Sophie, not from Joe, or anybody else, if they're to have any chance of getting past this.'

'Yeah?'

'Wouldn't you want to hear it from the horse's mouth?'

Simon takes a sip of wine. 'Honestly, babe, I don't think it softens the blow either way.'

We sit quietly, deep in our own thoughts, as we finish our wine, and the implications of Simon's words hang heavily in the room.

Chapter Twelve

I spend all of Friday in a nervous state, excited to see Joe later – it feels like ages since he left on Monday morning – but equally fearful as Sophie hasn't had The Conversation with Matt yet and I have to somehow contain the knowledge of her infidelity inside me without accidentally blurting it out at some point over the weekend.

The day at work seems to fly by, despite the fact that I have to dress the manikins twice, as my first attempt in my distracted state resulted in the worst possible fashion expression ever. Even I was shocked that I managed to put an outfit together so badly. Thankfully, I rectified the situation before Jarrod saw it, or God knows what he would have said.

As I drive home, my heart is tight in my chest and an uneasy feeling hovers over me. I can't wait to see Joe later tonight, but Sophie's affair has cast a shadow. I pull up outside the house, walk to the door and unlock it, still in a world of my own.

'Emma, you're home!' Joe exclaims, appearing in front of me. He pulls me into a hug and then kisses me hard on the lips. 'I've missed you,' he says.

'I've missed you too,' I say back, wondering why Joe is home sooner than he should be. I fear that Sophie has told Matt and this is Joe simply flipping out.

He ushers me into the lounge.

'I didn't expect you to be home yet,' I say, trying to keep my voice neutral.

'Sit.' Joe points to the sofa and I slowly take a seat.

'Joe, what's going on? You're acting weird.'

'I have something for you, a surprise. To keep you company while I'm away.'

'To keep me company?'

'Yeah. I realise that you're here, alone, in the house all week and you might like some company.'

I frown at Joe sceptically. Unless it's a maid who's going to clean the house, or a butler to make and bring me food when I'm hungry, then I'm not sure what he could possibly have in mind (and yes, I know a butler is wishful thinking, not a reality).

'Wait there.' Joe's grinning as he leaves the lounge.

I hear rustling, like a cardboard box being moved around, and then the door slowly opens and Joe reappears.

'Oh my God.' The words are a reflex action as I stare, open-mouthed, at him.

Joe is clutching a large, grey, striped cat.

'What is that?' I say, looking up at them both, rooted to my spot on the sofa.

'It's a cat, Emma.'

'I can see that,' I say, 'but what is it doing in our house?'

Joe strokes the top of the cat's head, and it closes its eyes and makes a loud purring noise.

'This is Banjo.' He lowers the cat to the floor. 'I thought it might be nice for you to have another living thing in the house while I'm away.'

This is honestly a huge surprise. If you had asked me a thousand times what would happen the first weekend that Joe came home from working away, bringing a cat back with him would not have featured on my list of answers.

'Where did you get him from – and *how* did you get him?'

'Well, we talked briefly about having a pet at some point once we got the house, and I saw him on one of those animal shelter websites. He was too cute to resist.'

I look down at him and he eyes me warily.

'Anyway, I'd messaged the animal shelter earlier in the week, and I got home a little early, so I went to see him, and I filled out all the paperwork. Don't you like him?'

'Of course,' I say. 'It's just…unexpected, that's all.'

Banjo rubs up against Joe's leg. He is cute, but my thoughts can't help but go to the orchid plant that I have had to replace four times due to unforeseen circumstances – i.e. sudden death. I fear how the cat will fare on those kinds of odds.

I hold out my hand and make a cooing sound, but Banjo just looks at me with what I interpret to be distain. I didn't know cats had varying expressions, let alone the ability to feel emotions and portray them to humans.

'He just needs to get to know you,' Joe says, rubbing the cat behind the ears. Banjo purrs, and I swear he smiles at me with a knowing look while Joe fusses over him.

'What do you want to do tonight then?' I ask.

'Let's have a takeaway and a few beers. I'm knackered after my first week. We can chill out and I can tell you all about it.'

'Sounds great.' I smile.

'And you can tell me what I've missed here.'

I stand up nervously. 'Oh, you've not missed anything. It's been a quiet week. I'll grab us some beers,' I say, keen to change the subject.

'Emma?'

I stop at the door and turn around.

'It's good to be home.'

'It's good to have you back. One week down, three million to go.' Joe nods.

I collect the beers from the fridge and go back to the living room, where Banjo has proceeded to claim my spot on the sofa as his own and is now licking himself contentedly. I hand Joe a beer and sit on the armchair instead.

'Tell me about your first week then,' I say, taking a swig from the beer bottle.

'Oh, Emma, it's been great. I've learned so much, and everyone has been brilliant. I love London too; I mean, I could definitely consider living there,' he babbles.

'Really? I always hate the escalators as you go down on the London Underground. They're so steep you have to cling on for dear life, as one false move and you could start a whole domino effect.'

He laughs. 'I guess so, but the restaurants are amazing.'

'We have nice restaurants here too.'

'I know. I just mean that they're different.'

For some reason this conversation is beginning to annoy me. Joe's been gone for four and a half days and he suddenly wants to up sticks and move to London.

'I didn't realise that you were *experiencing* London so much,' I say, trying to keep the hint of irritation out of my voice.

'It was my first week, Emma. They were just being nice, taking me out each night to help me settle in. I'm sure I'll be eating hotel food for the remainder of my secondment.'

Now I feel bad, and like I've overreacted.

'No, I get it. It's nice that they want to make you feel part of the team.'

'And anyway, I would much rather be spending my time experiencing London with you.'

Now I feel like a complete bitch.

'We'll have to do that,' I say. 'Maybe I can come down on the train on a Friday and we can stay over instead of you coming back home.'

'That sounds perfect.' Joe smiles. 'Now, shall I order the takeaway food? What do you fancy?'

'I don't mind, your choice.'

'A curry it is then.'

After we've eaten the curry, we spend the rest of the evening chilling on the sofa and watching TV. I lie with my head in Joe's lap as he strokes my hair, and Banjo lies in front of me as I stroke him behind the ears. I'm met with a steely gaze if I dare to stop, and I fear that stroking Banjo will now become my new hobby and it will be how I spend all my future evenings while Joe is away.

Chapter Thirteen

I wake, snuggled next to Joe, to sunlight creeping in through the bedroom window. I have no idea what time it is, but before I can move I feel Joe wrap his arm around me.

'This is what I've really missed – waking up with you,' he says, pulling me closer as he begins to kiss my bare shoulder.

I'm instantly aroused from his touch; I guess I've missed this too.

He rolls me over towards him and he pushes himself up to a kneeling position. I look into his eyes and realise that the irritation I felt last night when he was talking about London was actually fear. Fear that I'm somehow missing out on something, and fear of losing him. He's seeing a whole new world in a big city, an amazing city, and he's experiencing that with other people, not me. I guess this situation with Sophie has affected me in more ways than I thought. I now feel vulnerable, and I hate the fact that I feel this way.

Joe half-smiles at me before sitting astride me. He leans down and kisses me, and then we make love. It's slow, and sensual, and it's just what I need to remind myself of what I have. Joe loves me, and as we reach a climax I sink into his arms and wrap my arms tightly around his body. I have nothing to fear, surely?

We shower and dress, and decide to head out for breakfast. Though not before Joe feeds Banjo some disgusting-smelling cat food – I mean, what do they put in that stuff? Banjo doesn't seem to mind, though; in fact, he slurps up his food with speed.

There's a lovely new bistro about five minutes away that I heard about on the local radio on my way into work a few weeks ago. According to the review, it serves the best coffee in town. I've been wanting to try it ever since, so we take a leisurely stroll to the place. It's already busy, but the waitress finds us a table by the window.

I'm starving, maybe from our early-morning bedroom activity, and the whole place smells amazing, a mixture of bacon, pancakes and freshly brewed coffee. I can hear my stomach groaning, urging me to eat. I'm torn between eggs Florentine and pancakes.

'What can I get you guys?' asks the waitress. She's wearing impossibly tight black jeans and a skimpy black t-shirt that barely reaches her stomach, and I stare at her ironed-flat midriff with serious envy.

'The bistro brunch, please,' Joe says, 'and a large black coffee.'

'And for you?' The waitress smiles at me.

I decide on the eggs. I can make pancakes at home, but I have no idea how to poach an egg or make hollandaise sauce. Well, when I say that *I* can make pancakes, I mean I can go around to Simon's house and he and James will make them for me.

'Eggs Florentine, please, and a large coffee too, with milk, though.' I realise that my food choices are perhaps the reason why I haven't got an enviable flat stomach. Oh, who am I kidding? It's not just the food choices, it's the lack of exercise, and the wine consumption too.

'So, what do you fancy doing for the rest of the day?' I ask.

'I thought I'd pop over and see Matt. It feels like ages since I last caught up with him. I'll text him to see if he's going to be in. Do you fancy coming too, to see Sophie and Florence?'

I swallow nervously. 'Um, no, that's okay. I saw Sophie earlier in the week.' I can feel my face becoming flushed. 'I'll let you and Matt catch up on your own, a bit of boy time without us girls.'

'If you're sure?'

I nod. 'I'm sure.'

'Okay.' He takes his mobile phone from his pocket and begins typing.

I don't trust myself to see Matt, let alone see him and Joe together. I know that my face will instantly give away that something is wrong. Not telling Joe about Sophie's affair is one thing, but acting as though everything is fine in front of everyone when I know it's not is quite another. I don't think I can face Matt at all. Sophie is my best friend and I love her, but I can't help feeling incredibly sorry for Matt.

'Emma?'

I look up.

'You were in a world of your own,' Joe says. 'Are you okay?'

'Of course.' I nod. 'Oh, the coffees are here,' I say as the waitress approaches.

She smiles as she places the steaming mugs down on the table.

'I think I'll pop to the supermarket while you go and see Matt. I should have done the online ordering thing and booked my delivery slot earlier in the week, but I forgot.'

'Okay, we'll have breakfast and then head back home. I'll go over to Matt's and just see you back at the house later.'

'Perfect,' I say, and take a sip of my coffee. The review I heard was right. The coffee is amazing. I can't wait to taste the breakfast now.

We eat, and then stroll home hand in hand. Banjo greets us the minute the front door is open, and I have to practically dance down the hallway to avoid falling over him as he slaloms between my legs.

'It looks like Banjo likes you after all.' Joe kisses me on the lips. 'I brought some toys home for him too. They're in the kitchen. See if he'll play with them while I go and see Matt.'

'Okay, then I'll pop to the supermarket.'

'I'll head out now then.'

'See you later.'

Joe gives me a quick kiss, and I watch him leave with an uneasy feeling. It's like the calm before the storm, and I have no idea when the whole world as we know it will implode and we'll all drown under the tidal wave of Sophie's infidelity.

I look down at Banjo, who is sitting at my feet and looking up at me with huge green eyes. Right now he looks like the perfect distraction.

'Okay, Banjo' I say, 'let's see what toys Joe has bought for you.'

I spend the next half an hour throwing a furry grey mouse into the air while Banjo leaps up to an alarming height and captures it with his huge claws, then proceeds to chew it until I prise it from his grasp and we do it all over again.

Once he tires, I drive to the supermarket and aimlessly add items to the shopping trolley without much thought as to what meal they will create. I collect a few bottles of wine as I near the checkout and some more cat food.

The checkout girl seems intent on throwing the food down the conveyor belt to the packing area at speed, with a wide smile fixed firmly on her face. As the food whizzes past me and I attempt to fill the shopping bags, it feels like I'm on one of those reality TV shows where you have thirty seconds to complete the task.

'That will be forty-two pounds and thirty pence,' she says as I'm still trying to get all the food items into bags. I can feel her virtually tapping her fingers on the till as she watches me, still with the wide, fixed smile.

I ignore her stare, and the urge to hurry up, and instead continue at my own pace until all the items are safely packed. I turn to her to pay, and I swear a flash of annoyance washes over her before she quickly regains her composure.

I pay, and then manoeuvre the full trolley, with some difficulty, out of the store and towards my car. For some reason the whole place seems to be on a slant and the trolley wants to go in every direction but the one I want it to. I've broken out in a sweat by the time I reach the car, which is only made worse by my having to lift the full, heavy bags from the trolley and into the boot. There's a reason why I succumbed to Sophie's suggestion of home delivery for the weekly shopping. I must get more organised and start doing that again.

I drive home and start the challenge of trying to get the supermarket bags into the house without letting Banjo out of the front door. (Apparently, with new animals you're supposed to keep them in for a while until they put their scent around the place. It sounds unpleasant, but Joe assured me it's normal and it's just their own scent, it's not that they're going to make the house stink.) It doesn't occur to me until I've had to physically block Banjo from the door three times with my foot, while clinging on to a heavy bag, that I should have just shut him in the lounge while I unloaded the car.

I switch on the coffee machine while I unpack the food, and I resist the temptation to text Sophie to see what's going on at their house. I'm sure everything will be normal while Matt is unaware.

Once the food is unpacked, I grab my coffee and head through to the lounge. I switch on the television, scroll through the list of

---

channels and pick a repeat of the show *Friends*, despite the fact that I will know every word of the episode, having watched the entire ten series at least a hundred times. I sip my coffee as Banjo curls up on the armchair and instantly starts snoring.

It's not long before I hear the front door open and close and the familiar sound of Joe's footsteps. Instinctively, I hold my breath.

'Hey.' Joe pops his head around the living room door.

'Hi,' I croak. I clear my throat. 'How's Matt?'

'Yeah, fine. Sophie had taken Florence to the park, so we just had a beer.'

'Oh, good. So, everything's okay?'

Joe frowns at me. 'Why wouldn't everything be okay?'

'What? No, of course. I was just making conversation.' I wave my hand dismissively. 'What do you want to do for the rest of the afternoon? I bought food, so I can cook something for dinner later.'

Joe smiles. 'I'd love to spend a bit of time here' – he flops down on the sofa – 'just watching some TV. I'm pretty tired after my first week of travelling.'

'That sounds good to me.' I curl my legs up on the sofa. 'It looks like a marathon of *Friends* repeats is on.'

Joe rolls his eyes at me. 'That's not really what I had in mind, Emma.'

'Oh.'

'And we can both make dinner later, yeah?'

It's my turn to roll my eyes. 'Honestly, I can cook some things, you know. I have survived four days of feeding myself while you've been away.'

Joe chuckles. 'I'm not going to ask how much takeaway food you've eaten.'

'None,' I protest.

'Or cheese.' Joe carries on laughing.

'Now that's just being rude,' I say, but I don't argue on that point.

On Sunday we decide to go into town for lunch. An pizza restaurant that opened up a few years ago has quickly become my favourite place to eat. It serves perfect 'Sunday chilling' kind of food.

'We're going to be late,' I say as we get out of the car.

'No, we're not,' Joe says, taking my hand in his. 'We have five minutes to spare.'

'Oh, okay.'

I smile as we start to walk up the hill to the pizza restaurant. I can feel myself salivating at the thought of the hand-made, wood-fired pizzas allegedly made by a world famous chef from Naples, and the scrummy sorbets for desserts.

'What just happened?' Joe says as I fall into him unsteadily.

I look down. 'Oh no! The heel on my shoe just broke.' I stand on one leg like a flamingo, my other leg aloft with my broken shoe hanging pathetically from my foot. 'What am I going to do?' I can feel my cheeks colouring as people look at me as they walk past us.

Joe looks at his watch. 'Well, you can't go to the restaurant like this. We'll have to go home.'

'No,' I say adamantly. 'I've been looking forward to this pizza all bloody morning.'

'It's just pizza, Emma.'

'No, it isn't,' I say. 'It's hand-made, authentic, wood-fired pizza from Naples.'

'So, are you going to hop all the way to the restaurant?' Joe fails to hide his amusement.

'No. I'm going to wait here while you fetch the car, and we will drive to the nearest place that sells shoes, and I will purchase new shoes, and we will come back and eat pizza.'

Joe looks at me for a moment like I'm a crazy person – which, under the circumstances, I do understand.

'Okay,' he says, and he turns around and heads back towards the car park.

I stay fixed to the spot, unable to move, feeling humiliation wash over me as people walking down the street have to move around me like I'm some stupid statue in the middle of the pavement.

It's at this point that I realise, with deep regret, that I'm only a few feet away from a bus stop, and what do you know? A single-decker bus full of people pulls up at the kerb and several passengers get off the bus and also have to walk around me. The rest just stare out the window at me like I'm some animal on show at the zoo. I could literally die.

Thankfully, a few moments later Joe's car appears around the corner. I start to hobble towards it, dragging my leg with the broken shoe behind me. That just makes the situation worse, so I stop, remove the broken shoe, and walk to the car with one shoe on and one foot bare, my head held high, ignoring the stares from people around me and possibly the hysterical giggling from the bus passengers still watching my every move.

'Drive,' I say as I climb into the car and hang my head in shame.

Joe chuckles as we join the queue of traffic. 'Where to then?'

'There's a shoe wholesale place not far from here.'

'Of course you know that.' Joe shakes his head.

'Now is really not the time to chastise me over my shoe collection when I have to throw a pair away.'

'But you get to buy a new pair.'

'Not under the circumstances that I would like,' I say.

Joe simply laughs harder.

I tut. 'Go right at the end of the road.'

We arrive at the shoe wholesaler a few minutes later.

'How are you going to go in there and buy shoes?' Joe asks. 'Are you going in barefoot?'

'There must be a pair of my shoes in here somewhere. I'll look in the boot. We went out the other weekend in your car.'

I climb out, still with one shoe on and one shoe off, and hobble unsteadily to the rear of the car. I open the boot and look down despondently. All that's staring back at me is my old pink wellies that I threw in the car when we moved house.

Great. It's the hottest day of the year so far and I have to put on wellies with my summer dress and plod into a shoe shop to buy sandals.

I shake my head at the ridiculousness of it all, but I have no other choice. I slip off my one remaining shoe and slide my bare feet into the old, pink rubber wellies.

'I won't be long,' I call to Joe, and I walk quickly towards the door to the wholesaler.

Once inside, I hurry to the sandal section, my gaze down and my sunglasses still firmly on. Once in the summer footwear section, I grab the nearest pair of flat gold sandals in a size five, before scurrying back to the tills next to the exit.

'Just these?' The bemused, childlike guy at the till smiles annoyingly at me while looking me up and down. Honestly, he doesn't even look old enough to have left school, let alone be in a position to look down his nose at me, despite my unusual attire.

'Yes,' I state flatly, unwilling to rise to his bait. I realise how ridiculous I look, but I could simply be making a fashion statement. In fact, this sundress/wellies look could be 'in' right now. I'm sure if I scoured the fashion editorials of a few monthly women's magazines I'd find such a look. Perhaps a little more chic and definitely less Bridget Jones, though.

I swish my card over the contactless machine and grab the shoes. Not waiting for him to confirm that the payment has processed, I head swiftly out of the door and back towards the car. I dive into the passenger seat and Joe looks over at me.

'Sorted?' he asks, eyebrows raised.

'Sorted,' I confirm, and I proceed to remove my wellies – with difficulty, as my bare feet appear to have become suctioned to the rubber insoles.

Joe drives back to the car park we vacated only ten minutes ago, seemingly ignoring my wellie fight. By the time we park up, in exactly the same parking space, I've managed to remove the wellies and slide on the sandals (having had to bite through the plastic price tag, nearly chipping a tooth in the process).

'Ready?' Joe looks at me, completely straight-faced.

'Ready.' I nod, and we both climb out of the car.

When we arrive at the restaurant, I'm still a little flustered, and trying to push the vision of me hopping down the street like a pirate, and also trudging into the shoe wholesaler in wellies, deep into the crevices of my memory, never to be seen again.

'I apologise that we're late,' I say. 'We had a…um, delay.'

'Not a problem,' the waiter says, and he shows us to our table. 'Can I take your drinks order while you look at the menus?' he asks as Joe and I take a seat.

'Wine, large,' I say.

Joe looks down at the table in an attempt to keep a straight face.

'Of course. Which wine would you like?'

'Red,' I say, then I realise that I sound flippant. 'Whatever you recommend, thank you.'

The waiter looks at me with a confused expression, but I just look back at him. He appears to think better of questioning me any further, so instead he turns to Joe. 'And for you, sir?'

'A bottle of beer, please,' Joe says.

The waiter nods at us and leaves the table.

'So...' Joe looks at me. 'Tell me something, Emma.'

'Yes?' I say warily.

'How is it that you manage to get yourself into completely ridiculous situations with literally no effort required?'

My mouth twitches. There's no appropriate response to that question.

'It's not like I *want* ridiculous things to happen to me; they just do,' I huff.

Joe shakes his head. 'I'm not sure that you should be let out unsupervised.'

The waiter reappears with our drinks. I take the glass of wine from him before he can place it on the table and take a gulp. He looks at me like I have a drink problem and I've just committed the worst breach of restaurant etiquette.

'It's been a challenging day,' I offer as some sort of excuse, before taking another sip of wine and placing the glass down in front of me.

'Thanks,' is all Joe can say.

The waiter smiles at him. 'Are you ready to order?' he asks.

We both order pizza and a side of potato wedges. I make a mental note to do some exercise at some point to burn off the massive carbohydrate overload.

'Your theory that I should not be let out unsupervised is flawed,' I say.

Joe cocks his head to one side and grins. 'How so?'

'Well, if you have to come everywhere with me, all that will happen is that you'll get caught up in my crazy shit – or worse, crazy things will start happening to you too.'

'Fair point.' Joe sips his beer. 'Maybe it's better if Sophie takes on the responsibility of being your chaperone.'

I stick my tongue out childishly at him.

It seems like no time has passed at all before Joe is waking me at six thirty on Monday morning to kiss me goodbye as he heads off to London again.

'At least you're not on your own,' Joe says, glancing down the bed at Banjo, who is lying across my feet, pinning me to the bed and rendering me immobile.

'I like the cat,' I murmur, my eyes barely open. 'He doesn't answer back, or drink my wine.'

Joe chuckles. 'I'll miss you.'

'I'll miss you too.' I manage to half-prop myself up on my elbow, despite a death stare from Banjo as I rudely awaken him from his sleep.

'Have a safe journey, and text me when you get to the office,' I say.

'I will. Love you.' Joe leans down and kisses me softly.

'Love you too.'

Joe gets up from the bed and I hear his footsteps as he makes his way downstairs and out of the front door. I hear the front door close, and I instantly feel empty. It's weird – I know he'll be back on Friday evening, but his being away from home is harder than I thought it would be. Somehow it feels worse this week than when he left for the first time, last Monday. Maybe because last week I didn't really know what to expect, but this week I know how lonely I'll feel going to bed on my own.

I close my eyes and lay my head back on the pillow.

'Ow!'

My wallowing is short-lived as Banjo thwacks me on the cheek a second time with his huge paw. It would appear that the deep sleep he was in only moments ago is now over and he's ready to get up for the day – i.e. I have to get up and feed him.

He thwacks me again and we lock eyes.

'Okay, Banjo, for this relationship to work we need to have some respect. This is not respectful,' I say.

He simply yawns in my face.

'How was your weekend with Joe home?' Jenny asks as I hang up my coat at work with five minutes to spare before the shop opens at nine am.

'Oh, it was lovely. We had such a nice weekend. We went out for breakfast on Saturday, and we went to my favourite pizza restaurant yesterday. It was great.'

'It sounds like you're kind of dating again, in a funny sort of way.'

'I guess so. We just chilled out on the sofa on Friday night, but it was fun to go out too. Maybe we made more of an effort because he'd been away all week.'

'I wouldn't complain at eating out twice in a weekend.' Jenny sighs. 'Chance would be a fine thing with a baby.'

'Yeah, well, it wasn't without incident.'

Jenny frowns. 'What do you mean?'

I begin the story of my shoe trauma, which is how I will refer to this disastrous event going forward, and Jenny is wide-eyed with disbelief.

'Honestly, Jenny, if you could have seen me…I looked ridiculous, walking on a slant like a pirate with a wooden leg as I tried to make my way back to the car with a shred of dignity.'

Jenny bursts out laughing. 'I would have died!'

'Yes, if that was an option right at that moment then I may have taken it.'

'What happened next?' Jenny wipes tears from her eyes.

'I ended up wearing my wellies.'

Jenny snorts loudly with laughter.

'They were the only thing in Joe's car.' I throw my arms up. 'He gives me grief about my car boot looking like a market stall, but when a crisis hits, I know I have several shoe options to bail me out.'

Jenny is holding her stomach she's laughing that much, and I laugh with her. Then the door to the shop swings open and Jarrod appears, stony-faced.

'What's going on in here?'

Jenny and I jump, and then stare, eyes wide, at Jarrod. Today he seems to be dressed even more eccentrically than ever, if that's possible. He's somehow combined his navy suit with a purple, blue and white striped shirt and a navy patterned tie.

He raises his eyebrows at us in a questioning manner.

'Emma was just telling me about her weekend,' Jenny squeaks, trying to contain her giggles.

Jarrod glances at me, and it takes all my inner strength to keep a straight face.

'Right, well.' He clears his throat. 'There's work to be done.'

He turns and disappears back through the swing door to the shop front.

Jenny pulls a face. 'What's wrong with him this morning?'

'He doesn't like people having fun. He's clearly not, so nobody else can.' I scowl. 'Come on, let's get moving before Captain Miserable comes back in here spreading the joy.'

After what feels like a long day avoiding Jarrod and his bad mood, I finally step through the door at home. I kick off my shoes and head straight upstairs to run a bath. A glass of wine and this month's edition of *Glamour* magazine should keep me entertained in the bubbles for the next hour. I turn on the tap and pour a generous measure of bubble bath under the flow of water.

My mobile phone rings in my handbag downstairs, but I wilfully ignore it. Whoever it is will have to wait. The phone goes silent and I smile to myself.

But as I start to undress, the phone rings again.

Honestly, I wonder how people lived before we became contactable twenty-four hours a day, seven days a week, with no peace. Can't a person ignore the phone anymore without being stalked?

I turn off the tap and walk, half-dressed, down the stairs to retrieve my phone. If this is Simon with some half-arsed trauma, then I might just kill him.

I pull my phone from my bag and my heart lurches. The two missed calls are from Sophie.

I quickly call her back. The phone only rings once before she answers, but I hear nothing on the other end of the line.

'Soph?'

I hear a muffled sound.

'Sophie? Are you okay?'

'He left,' she sobs, almost incoherently.

Oh my God. She told Matt about her affair.

'I'm on my way over,' I say, and instantly hang up the phone.

I'm just about to open the front door to leave when I realise that I'm wearing only a blouse and my knickers.

Damn it.

I run back up the stairs and fling my wardrobe door open in search of a pair of jeans. I find some, half-folded on top of the set of drawers. They'll do, I decide. It takes me three attempts to get myself into the jeans, as the adrenaline hurtling around my body is making my hands shake.

Now fully dressed, I grab my car keys and handbag. Leaving my half-run bath and my chilled-out evening behind, I run out of the door, jump in the car and drive over to Sophie's house as quickly as I can.

When I pull up outside Sophie's, she's already standing in the doorway. I park the car and rush up to the front door. Sophie looks at me with red puffy eyes and I scoop her inside and wrap my arms around her tightly as she collapses, sobbing, against me.

I wait until her heaving shoulders subside before I release my grip on her. Taking hold of Sophie's hand I squeeze it 'Let's sit down, have a drink, and you can tell me everything. Okay?'

She nods, wiping her wet cheeks with the back of her hand.

'You go through to the lounge, I'll put the kettle on.'

'I think I need something stronger than tea.' Sophie sniffs.

'Fair enough.' I nod.

'There's gin in the cupboard.'

'I'll make it a large one.' I say.

I watch Sophie go into the lounge before I head down the hallway to the kitchen. I take two glasses from the cupboard and then open about four more cupboard doors before I spot the gin. Pouring a generous measure into Sophie's glass I then hover over my own. I am driving, but under the circumstances, I think I need something stronger than tea too. I pour in a small splash of gin and then open the fridge in search of some tonic water to dilute it. Topping up both glasses with chilled tonic water I can feel my chest tightening. Whatever Sophie is about to say to me is not good. If Matt left, then things are as bad as they can be.

I carry both drinks through to the lounge where Sophie is curled up on the sofa, her legs tucked underneath her. She looks small and broken and my heart goes out to her. I hand her the stronger glass of gin and tonic, and she takes a gulp as I sit down beside her.

'Where's Florence?' I ask.

'She's staying at my Mum's tonight. I'd planned it. I knew that I had to talk to Matt, to tell him.'

'And where is Matt now?'

She looks up at me with tear filled eyes 'I don't know. He literally threw some clothes in a rucksack and stormed out. I have no idea where he is.' Her bottom lip trembles.

I breath in and exhale, take a sip of my own drink and I look right at Sophie 'Okay. Start from the beginning. Tell me what happened.'

Sophie swallows 'I arranged for Mum to have Florence tonight, so I took her there after picking her up from nursery. I knew Matt would be home early today. When I got home, he was already in the kitchen.' She takes a sip of her drink and I remain silent, allowing her to continue to tell me the details in her own time.

'I didn't really know how to approach it, you know, I figured that no matter how I said it, it doesn't change what I did.'

I nod. I can understand that. You can say it however you want to but cheating on someone is cheating on someone. Sometimes the blunt truth is the best option.

'So, it just kind of came out.' Sophie gulps 'I told him that I'd done something stupid and that I regretted it hugely, and then I said that I'd had an affair.'

I hang my head a little. I'm in unchartered territory here. I love

Sophie; she's my best friend, and I'm always going to be on her side. But she cheated, and I'm struggling with that. I really want to try to understand, and to support her, but I'm conflicted. She's done something that I never thought she would, and I'm therefore not programmed or prepared to deal with that.

'How did Matt react?' I ask, cautiously.

Sophie holds her head in her hand 'He was absolutely devastated. He looked at me like I've never seen him look at me before; like he didn't even recognise me.' A tear streaks down her cheek 'And I can understand that. I look at myself in the mirror too and wonder how I became the person I see looking back at me. He thought I'd slept with the guy, but even when I told him over and over that I hadn't, that I stopped it before it even had chance to get that far, he still didn't believe me.' She sobs.

'Oh Sophie.'

'He kept asking me, over and over, who he is.' She shakes her head 'I told Matt it didn't matter; this is my mistake; it's me who's at fault.'

'That's not totally true, Sophie. This guy knew that you were in a relationship. He's to blame in this too.'

'Yeah, but I made the decision to do what I did. I could have chosen not to.'

'Do you think Matt will find out who he is? Do you think he'll… um, do something to him?'

'You mean hit him?'

I wave my free hand. 'I don't know. Isn't that what men do? It's some primeval thing, I think.'

Sophie takes a drink. 'Not Matt,' she says. 'He's not like that.'

I decide not to push the matter, but I can't help but think that when faced with your relationship having been violated, everyone can be like that, and if I were Matt, punching the other guy in the face might make me feel a little better, if only for a minute.

'So how did it go from there to him leaving?'

Sophie presses her lips together. 'I told him I just got carried away with it all. I was an idiot and in way over my head. I didn't mean for any of it to happen. It was just lust, stupid lust, and I should have known better. I was flattered by the attention. But I told him, it was only kissing, it never went further than a kiss.'

'And what did he say?'

'We argued and I pleaded with him, begged him to forgive me. He says that I've betrayed him, that I've betrayed us, and he can't forgive that – the trust is gone. I sneaked around, and I lied, and he said he never thought that I...I...' The tears are flowing freely now. 'That I would ever do that to him.'

I feel a horrible churning in the pit of my stomach as Sophie's words sink in. Sophie betrayed him, Matt can't forgive her and he left. He's gone.

I hold Sophie in my arms and just let her cry silently. I want to tell her that everything will be alright, that Matt will forgive her and come back, but I can't say that; I *don't* know that everything will be alright, I *don't* know if Matt will forgive her and come home.

'I think you should come home with me,' I say. 'You can't stay here on your own in this state.'

'But what about Matt? What if he comes back and wants to talk?' Sophie looks at me hopefully.

'I'm your best friend; he'll know exactly where to find you. Or failing that, he'll call your mobile.'

Sophie nods. 'You're right; he knows I'd go to you. And thank you. I can't bear the thought of getting into our bed alone tonight.'

'Go and get a change of clothes and your pyjamas and we'll go.'

'Okay.' She gets up and leaves the living room, and I sit there, staring into space.

The genie is out of the bottle now, and there's no forcing it back in. I can't help but fear that the collateral damage from Sophie's confession will spill over and affect more than just her and Matt. We're all involved in this, no matter what, and it's going to be hard not to be drawn into taking sides.

Sophie reappears a few minutes later with a small overnight bag, and I usher her out of the house and into my car. We arrive back at my house a short while later.

'Have you eaten anything?' I ask as Sophie takes off her shoes inside.

'No.' She shakes her head. 'I'm not hungry.'

'Well, you need to eat something,' I say. 'I'll run you a bath and you can have a soak while I get us some nibbles.'

'Thank you, Emma.' Sophie tears up again. 'You're a good friend.'

'You'd do the same for me.'

I half-smile at her and I head up the stairs to the bathroom, where I find my half-filled bath from earlier with a few froths of bubbles clinging to the edges of the water. I roll up my sleeve and cringe as I slide my arm into the freezing-cold water to pull out the plug. The water gurgles down the plug hole and I watch it drain away. I busy myself rinsing and refilling the bath, before going back downstairs. I find Sophie curled up on the sofa.

'Your bath's ready,' I say, sitting down next to her.

Sophie's face is blotchy and puffy from crying and she looks like the life has been sucked out of her. Her usually rich, bouncing curls hang limply on her shoulders and the colour has completely drained from her cheeks.

'There's no rush,' I say. 'Take as long as you need.'

'Thanks.'

Sophie gets up wearily and I hear her heavy footsteps as she makes her way upstairs. Then the bathroom door opens and closes. I run my fingers through my hair and bite my lip, wondering at what point Matt will tell Joe about Sophie, which is inevitable, and when that particular volcano will erupt.

As if on cue, my mobile phone bleeps in my handbag. I want to ignore it, but I can't. Forcing myself up from the sofa, I retrieve the mobile phone from my handbag and continue through to the kitchen. I glance at the screen and my heart sinks; it's a text from Joe.

Hey, how was your day? x

Was it really only this morning that Joe kissed me goodbye and left for his train? It feels like a lifetime ago. I place the phone on the kitchen worktop, unsure how to reply to that simple question. I open the fridge door and take out a bottle of wine. I'm not convinced that wine and gin are a good mix, and mixing any drinks on a Monday night doesn't set a good tone for the rest of the week. But under the circumstances, I don't really care. I pour a small glass of wine and take a sip before picking my mobile back up.

The truth? Or a lie?

I think back to Sophie begging me not to tell Joe. Does that still apply now that Matt knows? I don't know what the rules are now. I don't want to lie to my boyfriend; I never wanted to lie to him or keep this from him. Can *I* tell Joe at this point? It's no longer a secret now if Matt knows. Maybe I can, but not over the phone, and certainly not by text. Instead, I type back:

Long day. Just having a glass of wine to relax. I miss you already. xx

I figure that none of that is a lie; it's just not the whole truth.

The phone bleeps again.

Miss you too. Busy today in the office – only just got back to the hotel. Going for a quick beer with Ed and Karen, then having an early night.

I frown at the phone. Why is he going for a drink with Karen again?

I take another sip of wine. Am I overreacting? Come on, Emma, he said Ed and Karen. Ed must be a guy, so he's not going for a drink with Karen on his own. Unless 'Ed' is short for Edina? I shake my head. You're being stupid, I say to myself. If something was going on between Joe and Karen, he certainly wouldn't be telling you he was going for a drink with the other woman while he's hundreds of miles away and he could easily go for a drink with her and you would never know. Or would he? Maybe he's telling you he's going for a drink with Karen so you won't see her as a threat.

Now I really *am* acting crazy. Come on, Emma, get a grip.

I take a gulp of wine and text Joe back:

I'm having an early night too. Speak tomorrow?

Almost instantly, the phone bleeps.

Sure, I'll call you tomorrow at eight p.m. Night. x

I text back:

Night. x

Although I haven't been asked an outright question and I haven't lied, I can't help but feel like I've deceived Joe with my texts. I didn't tell him that Sophie's here, because then I would have had to tell him why. I sigh and chew my lip, feeling even more conflicted. I'm acutely aware that that this is just the beginning and it's only going to get worse.

I take some cheese from the fridge and put it on a tray along with olives, bread, olive oil and some salted tortilla chips (my staple diet). I carry the tray through to the living room and place it on the table, before going back to top up my glass of wine and pour one for Sophie too.

I've already eaten a third of the tortilla chips by the time Sophie emerges from the bathroom and reappears in the living room now dressed in her pyjamas. The puffiness in her face has reduced a little from the bath and a hint of colour is back in her cheeks.

I switch on the television, but pay no attention to the programme playing in the background as Sophie and I pick at the food. There's very little conversation as we nibble olives, both consumed by our own thoughts.

At ten p.m. I feel a wave of exhaustion and suggest we go to bed.

'Emma?'

'Yeah?'

'Can I sleep in your bed with you tonight?' Sophie shakes her head. 'I don't want to be alone.'

'Of course,' I say.

We go up to bed, and as I turn out the light Sophie turns to me and says, 'I'm sorry. I know I've disappointed you too.'

'I was just unprepared for this, Soph. And I'm sorry too, I'm sorry if I haven't handled it very well.'

'Of course you weren't prepared for this, Emma, and you've been there for me even though I know I've put you in an awful position.'

I swallow down the emotions beginning to bubble again in my chest. 'That's what friends do,' I say.

Sophie sniffs. 'I love you, Em.'

'I love you too.'

I wake early the following morning and note the sound of Sophie's soft breathing as she sleeps. I slide out of bed and get in the shower. It was a fitful sleep; I tossed and turned with Sophie's situation weighing heavily on my heart and mind.

Once showered, I tiptoe downstairs and make a coffee. I've still got plenty of time before I need to get ready to go to work. As the coffee machine busies itself hissing and grinding beans, I decide to prepare breakfast for Sophie. Given that I had to force-feed her last night, I want to make sure she has something to eat before I leave. Thankfully, bacon and bread were two of the items I chucked in the shopping trolley on Saturday morning – perfect.

When the coffee's ready, I sip it and stare out of the window at the birds hopping around the garden. Maybe I should get a bird feeding table. A loud meow to my left signifies that Banjo has awoken.

'Ah, maybe not,' I say, shaking my head at the cat. 'I forgot that you live here now.'

Banjo looks up at me, licking his lips, presumably at the mention of birds. He meows loudly again.

'Okay, Banjo, I get it; it's breakfast time.'

I go to the cupboard and take out a pouch of cat food. Banjo heads straight to his bowl. He headbutts my hand as I bend down to empty the food into his bowl, nearly resulting in the sloppy mess ending up all over the floor.

'Argh!' I jump as I stand back up and Sophie appears in the doorway.

'Sorry,' she says. 'I didn't mean to frighten you.'

'It's fine; I didn't hear you, that's all. Coffee?'

'Yes, please.' Sophie takes a seat at the kitchen table. 'And what is that smell?' She wrinkles her nose.

'Cat food.' I shrug. 'You get used to it.'

She looks at me with raised eyebrows.

'That's a lie,' I say. 'You don't.'

Sophie smiles.

'How did you sleep?' I ask as I place another cup under the coffee machine.

'Okay. I woke a few times. Forgot where I was.'

'You can stay as long as you need to.'

'Thanks, I appreciate that, but I need to pick Florence up from my mum's after work. She needs normality as far as possible, and her usual routine.'

I nod, handing Sophie her coffee. 'Well, seeing as I have a bit of time before I leave for work, I thought I'd make us bacon sandwiches. Sound good?'

Sophie nods. 'Sounds good.'

We eat breakfast, then Sophie has a shower while I apply makeup and pull the hair straighteners through my unruly hair. We leave the house at eight a.m. and make the short journey to Sophie's house.

'I'll call you tonight,' I say as Sophie climbs out of the car.

'I'm okay, Emma. You don't need to keep checking up on me.'

'I know, but I want to. It makes me feel better to know you're okay, so humour me?'

She half-smiles and rolls her eyes. 'Okay, but only to make you feel better.'

I nod. 'Speak later then.'

'And Emma?'

'Yeah?'

'Thanks for last night.'

'Of course,' I say. 'Anytime.'

And with that, Sophie shuts the car door and I watch her go into the house. She turns and waves before closing the front door, and I pull away and continue my journey to work.

'Morning,' Jenny says as I walk through the back door to the staff area at the shop.

'Hey.' I smile, my thoughts still focused on Sophie.

'Everything okay?'

I contemplate telling Jenny everything, if only to unburden myself. I can't tell Joe yet, but I feel like I need to offload and talk through the situation. That would be selfish, though. It's not fair on Jenny to dump all of this information on her, and it's not fair on Sophie if I talk about her private business. (Although I *have* already told Simon, but that doesn't count, surely. It's only Simon.)

'Everything's fine, thanks,' I say. 'I'm just a bit tired.'

That seems to satisfy Jenny. She hands me a mug of tea. 'This should help,' she says. 'Take your time, and I'll start getting on with things before we open.'

'Thanks. I'll be in in a minute,' I call as Jenny goes through the swing door and into the shop.

I take my mobile phone from my handbag and am just about to type a message to Simon when the phone bleeps and a text from Joe appears on the screen:

Hi, really sorry, looks like tonight might be a late one in the office. I'll call you tomorrow after work instead. Have a good day. x

Ordinarily, this text would make me very annoyed, but as I stare down at it, I feel relieved. That's one less conversation with Joe where I have to pretend everything is okay before I can tell him the truth when he comes home on Friday. Given the situation, I barely give it a thought that 'a late one in the office' probably means just him and Karen alone.

Hmm, maybe I'll give that some more thought later.

I quickly type back:

Hi, no worries. Speak tomorrow. Don't work too hard. xx

Now, to Simon:

Hi, can I pop over tonight? Need to talk.

I shove my phone back into my handbag. Simon will have replied by the end of the day. I head out into the shop, hoping it's a busy day to distract me from my thoughts.

Thankfully, the day passes quickly, and as the clock strikes five thirty p.m. Jenny and I lock up and leave the shop.

'I need to get to the nursery to pick up Darcy,' Jenny says. 'See you in the morning,' she calls as she hurries off.

I take my mobile phone out of my bag and am relieved to see a text from Simon:

James is taking the boys swimming. I'll come to you for six thirty. x

I type a message back:

Great. See you in a bit. xx

I walk to my car and turn the radio volume up high as I make my way home with indie rock tunes blasting out. I get home and take a chilled beer from the fridge as I wait for Simon. It's not long before I hear a knock at the door.

'Hiya, babe.' Simon is leaning on the doorframe as I open the front door. He looks me up and down. 'Let me guess?' he says, cocking his head to one side. 'Sophie told Matt that she had an affair and it's not good.'

'How do you know these things?' I say, standing to the side as Simon strides past me.

'You're an open book, hun.'

I sigh. 'I see.' Clearly I do need to work on my poker face.

'Any chance I can get one of those?' He nods at the beer in my hand.

I sweep my hand in the direction of the kitchen. 'In the fridge,' I say. 'Help yourself.'

A few moments later, Simon is sipping his beer as we stand in the kitchen. 'I take it that Matt wasn't feeling very forgiving when Sophie mentioned this other bloke then?'

I shake my head at him. 'Honestly, Simon, sometimes you have a really delicate way of putting things.'

'I'm a realist, Em. I tell it how it is.'

I roll my eyes at him.

'So, back to my question?'

'No, Matt didn't feel very forgiving. In fact, he was so angry about it that he's left.'

Simon whistles. 'Oh, babe, I'm sorry. I didn't think it would come to that.'

'Well, it has, and Sophie is devastated. She spent last night here in bits.'

'Bloody hell.' Simon sighs. 'What happens now?'

'I have no idea,' I say, chewing my lip. 'We're in completely un-chartered territory.'

'Does Joe know yet?'

'No. I figure it's a conversation that we need to have face to face.'

'Probably a good idea.' Simon takes a swig of beer.

'I'm going to tell him on Friday when he gets back from London.'

'How do you think he'll take it?'

I pause for a moment before answering. 'Badly.'

Chapter Fourteen

As it turns out, it takes exactly three days for the volcano to erupt and for my world as I know it to implode too.

I arrive home from work on Friday evening to an unexpected conversation.

'You know, don't you.'

I literally bump straight into Joe as I step through the front door. The look on his face tells me everything. He knows, and he's really unhappy about it. His brow is creased into a deep furrow and he's glaring at me.

I have nowhere to go. I have to tell the truth.

I nod, unsure of the tone of Joe's voice.

'How long have you known?'

Shit. This is the question that I've been dreading.

I've been put in an incredibly difficult situation. I was always going to anger someone, whether by keeping the secret or telling the truth. There was no right answer.

'Emma?'

'Just over a week.' The words slip out quietly.

Joe's lips press into a thin line and I see his whole body stiffen.

'I couldn't...I didn't...It wasn't for me to tell.' I step towards Joe, but he takes a step backwards and I flinch at the physical pain this action inflicts.

'Joe, I –'

'I can't talk to you about this at the moment, Emma. I'm too angry.'

'I know. I get it.'

'No, you don't.'

'Believe me, I'm angry too. I didn't want any of this to happen.'

'But you covered for her, for Sophie.' Joe waves his arms. 'We spent all last weekend together and you never said a word.'

I hang my head.

'We've spoken or texted nearly every day for the last week and you've lied to me, telling me that everything was fine. Everything is not *fine*, Emma.'

'I didn't lie!' I protest.

'You didn't tell me, you kept this from me, so in my eyes you did.'

'Joe, please, try to see this from my point of view. I was put in the middle of this. I wanted to tell you, but Sophie made me promise.'

Joe's hands go to his hips. 'And keeping Sophie's secret is more important than us? Than telling me the truth? We're not supposed to keep secrets from each other, Emma; we're supposed to be better than that.'

We stand, eyes locked. There's nothing more I can say to defend my position.

Joe clenches his fists, then releases them. 'I'll be back later,' he says, stepping past me and grabbing his car keys from the hook on the wall.

'You're going out? Is this how you want to leave things? You've only just got home,' I say accusingly.

Joe turns to face me. 'I'm going to see Matt,' he says flippantly.

'Fine.'

Joe stops for a moment and looks like he's going to say something; then he appears to think better of it, as he storms out of the house and closes the door none too gently behind him, leaving me standing, fuming, in the hallway.

'Well, that wasn't the welcome home I was hoping for,' I say out loud to no one. 'Or how I wanted that conversation to go.'

I kick off my shoes, hang up my car keys and just stand there, feeling completely deflated. In all the years that Joe and I have been together, I can count on one hand the number of arguments we've had. I can't believe that he practically accused me of being complicit in all of this, and that he's had the audacity to walk out. How immature. We're supposed to be adults who talk things through, isn't that what he just said? (I try to delete from my memory the vision of me standing in front of him moments ago saying 'Fine' like a petulant teenager.)

Unsure what else to do, I head into the kitchen and pour the remainder of an open bottle of wine into a large glass. Taking a gulp,

I reluctantly accept that Joe going to see Matt is actually the right thing to do. They've obviously spoken on the phone, and if it were my brother, I would be straight over there too, to make sure he was okay. Wherever 'over there' is; Sophie seems to have no idea where Matt is. She hasn't heard from him since he left other than a text stating he would be in touch to arrange to see Florence, but that was two days ago. Joe didn't seem like he wanted to offer up that bit of information as he huffed out of here.

I take another gulp of wine.

Joe might be being a good brother, but he's not being such a good boyfriend. I don't see him all week, and then he arrives home early and turns on me like this is all my fault before I've barely had a chance to step through the door.

I take another gulp of wine.

How can I be the bad person in all this? Would *he* have wanted to hear that kind of news over a text? Well, maybe that's how Matt told Joe that Sophie had cheated on him, but I was trying to do the right thing and have that conversation face to face. But does Joe appreciate that? No!

I take another gulp of wine.

Well, it's Friday night, so if Joe thinks that I'm going to sit here waiting patiently for him to return then he's got another thing coming.

I tip my glass to my mouth, but realise that it's empty.

Hmm. That means that I've chugged a very large glass of wine in less than five minutes. That's not good. It also means that I'll need more wine.

I turn to leave the kitchen and almost fall flat on my face as I try to avoid tripping over Banjo, who has appeared silently, which seems to be his speciality.

'Bloody hell, you're like a ninja cat.' I shake my head at him, but Banjo just looks up at me and meows.

I top up his bowl with fresh dried food and then pull on a pair of pumps I conveniently left near the door when I wore them yesterday, grabbing my purse out of my work bag along the way. I open the door and step outside. The fresh air hits me like a sandbag and

I realise that I feel a bit lightheaded and tipsy. Clearly, downing a large glass of wine gets you drunk quicker than you think.

I plod, or maybe weave, my way to the local shop. Once there, I head indirectly (via two aisles that I don't need) to the fridges to pick up a new bottle of wine, and then I collect a large bag of cheesy tortilla chips as I head to the checkout. The man behind the till glances at me with a knowing look as though I'm not the first, or last, woman to plonk a bottle of wine and comfort food before him tonight. I feel transparent. I could have simply stood there, taking his knowing look, and paid for my goods and left. However, I'm fuelled by wine and therefore my inner confidence, or attitude, has had an alcohol injection.

'I'm going to meet a friend,' I say smugly.

He raises his eyebrows at this comment, and I realise that I sound like I'm going to sit on a park bench with someone equally as sad as I appear and drink wine directly from the bottle while shoving cheesy snacks into my mouth.

'I meant I'm going to a friend's house,' I say.

He nods politely at me, and I assume he now just thinks that I'm weird.

'That'll be eight pounds thirty, please,' he says, a smile etched on his face.

I swipe my contactless bank card against the machine and roll my eyes, defeated. Why do I sound like a lunatic when I speak to complete strangers? I grab my wine and the large bag of tortillas and leave the shop.

I arrive home, let a meowing Banjo out of the back door, collect my mobile phone from my handbag left in the hallway earlier, and then take up residency on the sofa. I look at the phone. There's no message from Joe. No 'I'm sorry I acted like a dick'. I chuck the phone onto the sofa cushion next to me and pour myself another glass of wine.

I stare at the wine. It's suddenly lost its appeal. My earlier anger has been defused by my jolly to the shop, and now I just feel sad and deflated. I don't want to argue with Joe. I'm not mad at him; I'm mad at the situation. He's not at fault, and maybe he had every right to be angry with me for not telling him. Maybe...

I spend the next few hours wearing a track into the living room carpet as I pace the room, with the occasional break to peek through a small crack in the curtains to look for Joe's car and to check my mobile phone to see if I've somehow missed a message from Joe.

But there's nothing.

No car.

No message.

Just virtual silence.

'Beep.'

I jump as the mobile phone in my hand springs to life and a message from Joe appears on the screen.

I'm going to stay with Matt tonight.

That's it. No 'I'm sorry I stormed out', no kiss at the end of the text. Just a perfunctory message to let me know where he is.

Hmm.

I stare at the screen, wondering what the appropriate response to that is. I decide on:

Okay.

Which, I realise, is only marginally better than my petulant 'Fine' from earlier, so I add:

See you tomorrow.

No kiss.

The wine suddenly looks much more appealing. Why is he staying with Matt and not coming home?

Because he's mad at you, my conscience prods me annoyingly. He's mad at you and so he's punishing you.

Well, that's just fine. Two can play at that game.

I take the bottle of now-barely-chilled wine back into the kitchen and place it safely in the fridge, ready for a potential outing in the not-so-distant future. After letting Banjo back in, I turn out the lights and go up to bed. With an undercurrent of annoyance, I swipe a face wipe angrily across my face, smearing the day's makeup into a horror mask.

I slump into bed, despondent. Why is it that life always seems to be going swimmingly well and then it falls right off the edge of a cliff? I pull the quilt cover tightly around me, feeling completely unloved, and I drift into a disturbed sleep.

I wake at three in the morning to find Banjo, curled up asleep and softly snoring, right across my shoulder with his head under my chin. What a lovely act of feline affection, I think, but then a thoroughly depressing thought occurs to me: that Banjo may, in fact, be trying to suffocate me in my sleep.

The following day, things get worse.

I wake to a further text from Joe, and it's not good.

Going to spend the day with Matt.

There's no kiss at the end of the text; in fact, it's devoid of any emotion.

I huff loudly, causing Banjo, who has moved down to the end of the bed near my feet, to raise his head and glare at me before resuming his sleep.

What am I supposed to say to that? I don't want to be one of those girlfriends who makes ultimatums, but what I want to say is: *You've been away all week, you yelled at me and spent the whole of last night with your brother, so get yourself home so we can start to make up already.* But somehow I don't think that approach would work in this situation; in fact, it would probably make Joe dig his heels in further.

This is new territory for me and Joe. I can't remember another time when we've argued and not at least gone to bed together, if somewhat angry and spikey, but still in the same house and the same bed. Joe has got some nerve staying away and not facing me. It's childish, and I've got a good mind to tell him so.

I pick up the phone and text him back:

I understand that you're angry with me, but ignoring me won't solve anything. We need to talk.

I press 'send', then stare at the phone waiting for his response. It seems to take forever for my mobile phone to bleep.

I'll be home later.

Well, that's that then.

I fling the quilt back, forgetting Banjo snuggled at the end of the bed until he hisses loudly.

'Sorry,' I say, pulling on my dressing gown and folding back the quilt.

I pick up my mobile phone and go down to the kitchen to make a cup of tea. While the kettle boils, I hit Simon's number from the speed dial. He answers after two rings.

'Morning, babe, how's things?' His cheery tone is annoying this morning.

'Joe didn't come home last night,' I blurt out.

'Oh, hi, Simon, how are you? I'm not too selfish to at least acknowledge you in the conversation and make small talk, even if I have no interest in the answers to the questions that I'm asking.' He lays on a sarcastic tone.

I bite my lip. 'Hello, Simon,' I say. 'Is your life wonderful and crisis free with your husband who loves you and your gorgeous twin boys?'

'Well played,' Simon huffs. 'Continue.'

'Joe came home last night, and I was all ready to tell him about Sophie and Matt, but he already knew and he was waiting for me to get home, and he was really angry that I knew and didn't tell him.'

'Oh, babe.'

'He shouted at me, and then left to spend the evening with Matt, but then he didn't come home, and he's spending today with Matt too.'

'And you're unhappy with this?' Simon asks.

'Of course.' I feel like I'm stating the obvious.

'Did he call or text?'

'About what?'

'To let you know he wasn't coming home?'

I wave my hands in the air, forgetting that Simon can't see me on the other end of the phone. 'This isn't about his method of communication, it's about the fact that he spent all of five minutes with me, having a go at me, before disappearing all weekend.'

There's silence on the end of the phone, which I know from years of previous experience means that Simon is about to say something that I don't want to hear.

'Look, Em, I warned you that keeping this from Joe could end up blowing up in your face.'

'Well, thank you, Simon. It must be wonderful to always have the upper hand on hindsight.'

'Emma,' Simon challenges me, and now it's my turn to be silent on the end of the phone, 'all I'm saying is, let him have some space to deal with things.'

'But why can't he understand that it wasn't my fault?'

'Give Joe some time, hun, and he'll probably come to that conclusion himself. But you ramming that point down his throat won't help the situation.'

'So what are you saying? That I should just hang around at home until he feels like coming back?'

'In short, babe, yes,' Simon says. 'You've had some time to process this, but Joe hasn't. Plus, this is his brother; he's bound to be protective of him.'

'Yeah?'

'Yeah. If it was you, Em, and Joe had cheated on you, I'd kill him.'

I smile. 'You would?'

'Of course, babe.'

'Okay, thank you for your perspective on things.'

'I love you, hun.'

'Love you too, Si.'

'Bye.' Simon hangs up the phone.

As it turns out, Joe decides not to come home all weekend. While I understand his need to support Matt – and my need, apparently, to give him space – I can't help but feel hurt that we're so far apart on this.

It's still dark on Monday morning when I hear the front door open and close and then Joe's footsteps as he comes upstairs and goes into the bathroom. I've barely slept, so I'm wide awake as I hear the running water of the shower. Pushing myself up to a seated position, I slide my legs over the side of the bed and reach for my dressing gown. I'm feeling angry and confrontational, neither of which are good at six on a Monday morning.

I head downstairs to make myself a coffee and I take up residence at the kitchen table. Ten minutes or so pass as I tap my finger on my coffee mug, which seems loud in the silence of the room. The stairs creak as Joe makes his way down them and then he appears in the doorway to the kitchen.

I swallow down the last of my coffee and grimace as it's cold.

'I'm off then.' Joe shoves his hands in his trouser pockets.

'Just like that, you're going back to London?' I ask.

'Just like that.'

I look at the floor. 'Aren't we going to talk about it? About why you haven't come home all weekend?'

Joe sighs. 'We have talked about it, Emma.'

'No, we talked for about five minutes and then you left, and all we've had since is one-line text messages. And you're still mad at me.' I look up at Joe and it's his turn to stare at the floor.

He shrugs. 'It's a difficult situation, Emma. Matt is my brother. Sophie cheated on him, and you knew about it and didn't say anything.'

I exhale deeply, trying to hold back the tears that are threatening to escape. 'I was in an impossible situation.'

'I know.'

'I never meant to keep a secret from you.'

Joe swallows noisily but says nothing.

I slide off the kitchen stool and step towards him until we're face to face, just inches apart.

'So, are we going to be okay?' My voice breaks a little.

Joe leans forward and his lips brush mine, barely. 'We'll be okay,' he says. 'I'll see you on Friday.'

I nod and watch as he grabs his roller case and heads out the front door. But the churning in the depths of my stomach is telling me that we're not okay, and this is just the beginning of the fallout.

Chapter Fifteen

Today, work seems like more of a challenge than usual. I'm distracted by how Joe and I left things this morning and I sneak a look at my mobile phone a thousand times, annoyed to see there's no text or anything from him. He's obviously still angry at me, and now that's making me angry at him again. I don't understand why he can't appreciate the situation I was in. I was stuck in the middle through no choice of my own, and it wasn't where I wanted to be. I wasn't comfortable not telling him, but I couldn't.

Jarrod is doing nothing to improve my mood. He's ordering me around like I'm a child again and it's grating on my already frayed nerves. There's no Jenny today to stand between us; it's just me and Jarrod. By lunchtime, I think I might actually explode.

'I'm heading out for an hour,' I call to Jarrod. I fling on my coat, huffing loudly, grab my handbag and let the door bang shut behind me as I leave the staff room and head into the outside world. A Jarrod-free world, if only for sixty minutes.

I know it's childish to slam the door. In my head I can hear the voice of my mother, chastising me like she did when I was a teenager, when I also found the same brief relief from my frustration with her and Dad by slamming my bedroom door.

I march to my favourite coffee shop on the High Street, in desperate need of some 'me' time in my own sanctuary. I feel instantly at ease as I step through the door and inhale the welcoming aroma of freshly ground coffee.

It's busy, as it's lunchtime, so I join the queue and take my mobile phone from my pocket. Finally, a text message from Joe is flashing on the screen. I click into it while I'm waiting my turn.

Hi. Arrived safely in London. All good here. Speak later in the week.

Hmm. Still no kiss at the end of the text, but at least there's some sort of communication. I quickly type back:

Speak soon. x

'Who's next?' I hear the barista call, and I look up to see I've reached the front of the queue.

'A flat white, and a ham and cheese toastie,' I say. I put my phone back into my pocket and pay while my food and coffee are prepared. As I collect my coffee and the plate with my toastie I turn to look for a free table, and then I see him, and my breath catches in my throat.

Matt is sitting at a table a few feet away, engrossed in something on his phone. I haven't seen him since before he found out about Sophie having an affair, *and he moved out.*

I'm pretty sure that he hasn't seen me. I turn and look in the opposite direction, praying for an empty table to instantly appear.

'Emma?'

Too late.

I screw up my eyes, then open them. Hoping I look surprised rather than full of trepidation, I turn back around to see Matt, now standing, at his table.

'Matt? Hi,' I say, my voice an octave too high. 'I was just heading to a table.'

I'm not sure that 'I was just heading to a table' should have been my follow-up to 'Hi', but it was the best I could do under the circumstances. Asking 'How are you?' when I know things are awful doesn't seem appropriate.

Matt looks past me, a little confused, and I glance over my shoulder to see that all of the tables behind me, where I just told him I was heading, are full.

He frowns. 'Are you with someone?'

'Um...' I contemplate lying and saying yes, then just sitting down at some random person's table with them and trying to convince them to play along and act like they know me. But that seems a little too elaborate to pull off convincingly, so I simply say, 'No, I'm not with anyone.'

'Oh, then would you like to join me?' Matt points to the chair across from him.

This feels strange, and unexpected. I'd presumed that Matt was as annoyed with me as Joe is, and would meet any interaction between us with a hostile reception.

'That's fine,' I say. 'I don't want to interrupt you. There'll be a table free in a minute.'

I'm elbowed out of the way by a woman carrying a tray full of giant cups of hot chocolate. She huffs at me as she manoeuvres past me, and I suck in my cheeks. I mean, honestly, it's busy – where does she expect me to stand?

'Come and sit down, Emma, before you end up wearing someone's latte.'

I force a smile, accepting my fate, and I go over to the table.

'Let me help you.' Matt takes my mug of coffee and toastie from me and he places them down on the table while I take off my coat and sit down.

'How are you?' he asks.

'Good, thanks.' I grab my mug and take a drink of coffee before the words 'How are you?' can come out of my mouth and open the can of worms.

'You're okay, even with Joe working away so much at the moment?'

Matt must know that Joe is angry with me; they just spent all weekend together. Which means he knows that Joe barely came home all weekend.

'Yes, fine,' I state a little robotically as I stare down at my toastie, my appetite all but evaporated. 'Does he think I'm not? I'm not surviving on bread and cheese, honestly.' I think of Simon's comment about me living like a student.

'No, no, nothing like that.'

'Oh,' I say, relieved.

'I'm sorry. I don't mean to make you uncomfortable, Emma.' Matt smiles at me softly.

I bite my lip. 'No, I'm sorry. I just wasn't expecting to see you, and I wasn't prepared to see you.' I take in the dark circles under his eyes and the slight crinkles in his shirt.

'I understand; it's awkward. You're Sophie's best friend, but you're also my brother's girlfriend.' He pauses. 'It's nice to see you.'

I put my coffee down and look across at Matt. He looks like he always does – immaculate, like Joe – but today I can see a hint of sadness in his expression. My chest tightens a little. 'How are *you* doing?' I ask.

He looks at me, his head slightly cocked to one side. 'Not good, I guess.'

I inhale deeply. I have no idea what to say next.

'I miss Sophie. I miss Florence,' Matt continues. 'I'm angry at Sophie, really angry, and hurt, and disappointed, but of course I still love her. It's hard: you wake up one day and everything's fine, and then, in an instant, everything changes. It's hard for Florence too. How do you explain the complexities of adult relationships to a three year old?'

I wipe a tear from the corner of my eye. My heart is breaking.

'She's the mother of my child.' He shrugs. 'Being angry at someone doesn't make you stop loving them, it just makes you...angry.'

Instinctively, I reach over and grab his hand. 'Does this mean you want to try to make it work with Sophie? If you miss her?'

He rubs his forehead with his other hand. 'Yes. No. I don't know. I can't forgive her at the moment; it's just too raw.'

'She loves you too, I know she does. So much.'

He presses his lips into a thin line, and he resembles Joe even more.

'She made a huge mistake,' I state.

He nods but says nothing. I release his hand.

'I wish I could do something,' I say feebly.

'You can.' He looks at me. 'Keep checking in on Sophie and Florence.'

I nod. 'I will, of course.'

Matt says nothing.

'*He's* angry at me,' I continue, meaning Joe. 'But you already know that.' I stare right at Matt, trying to read his expression.

His face softens. 'Joe loves you, Emma.'

'He's shut me out all weekend.'

'Joe is overprotective of me; he always has been. Only this time he can't make things better. We're not kids in the playground where he can kick the arse of the boy who's bullying me. He's frustrated because he couldn't do anything to prevent this and he can't do anything to fix it.'

'So he's taking his frustration out on me?'

'He'll come around with a bit of time.'

'Does the passing of time really heal things?'

Matt shrugs. 'I hope so.' He stands up. 'I'd better get going.'

'Okay, well, thanks for sharing your table,' I say, which sounds ridiculous given the conversation we've just had.

'Anytime.' He turns to walk away, and a realisation pops into my head.

'Matt?' I call, and he stops and turns back to me. 'You don't work anywhere near here,' I say, 'and you know this is my favourite coffee shop – I've met Sophie here thousands of times over the years.'

He half-smiles.

'Did you come here hoping to run into me?'

Matt glances down at his feet before looking back at me. 'Take care, Emma,' he says, and then he's gone.

Chapter Sixteen

The day ticks by with no further contact from Joe. This is driving me crazy; I honestly don't know how we can function as a couple like this. Joe's punishing me for Sophie's mistake, and that isn't fair. It doesn't help that our conversations while Joe is working away, are limited to texts and a few minutes of tired chat at the end of the day.

I arrange to meet Sophie for a glass of wine and a catch-up this evening. Should I tell her that I bumped into Matt? I ponder. My conscience gives me a swift kick. Of course! You've done nothing wrong by seeing her boyfriend in a coffee shop, *and* sharing his table, *and* talking about her and Florence. I'll tell her straight away, as keeping bloody secrets is what got everybody into this mess in the first place.

I arrive at the wine bar early and take a seat in a booth by the window.

'A bottle of Sauvignon Blanc and two glasses, please,' I say as the waitress approaches.

She returns a couple of minutes later with the wine and pours a generous measure into each glass.

'Thank you,' I say, and I pick up my glass and take a sip.

Sophie comes bustling through the door and heads over to the table. She's smiling, and I realise that I haven't seen her smile in a long time. I smile back at her.

'How are you?' I ask, standing up to give her a hug.

'A bit better,' she says, taking her seat. 'I spoke to Matt earlier and he has agreed to go to couples' therapy.'

'Really? Well, that's positive, isn't it?'

She shrugs as she takes a sip of wine. 'I guess so.'

'You guess so? Soph, what are you talking about? This is a huge step forward.'

She shakes her head. 'I just can't imagine telling a complete stranger my intimate feelings.'

I take another drink of my wine. 'I get that, I really do, and I'm sure that it won't be easy, but if you want to make your relationship work then you have to give it a try.'

'Oh gosh, I will, Emma. I desperately want Matt to forgive me.'

'Well, if he's agreed to counselling then he must at least want to try.'

Sophie looks sad, and I reach over the table and squeeze her hand.

She gives a little sob. 'Oh, Emma, I so want to believe that everything will be alright, but what if it isn't? What if Matt can't get past this and it's...' Her bottom lip quivers. '...and it's over forever?'

I contemplate this for a moment. As much as I want to tell Sophie that everything will be okay, I can't promise that. I have no idea whether she and Matt will work through things, with the help of a counsellor or not. I want to give her some hope, but the reality is that I don't know what will happen. Maybe now is the time to tell her that I saw Matt at lunchtime. I don't want to give her false hope, but he *did* say that you don't stop loving someone just because you're mad at them.

'You know what, Soph?' She looks at me expectantly. 'If you don't stay positive then you're already giving up, and I think that you and Matt are worth fighting for.'

She nods.

'I saw Matt,' I blurt out. In hindsight, I could have approached this a little more gently.

I see a glimmer of fear in Sophie's eyes.

'It's not bad. It was...well, I don't know what it was.'

'Emma,' Sophie pleads.

'He was in the coffee shop earlier when I went in for lunch.'

'You bumped into him?'

'I guess so. It was really busy and there were no free tables.'

Sophie is looking at me with a confused expression.

'He suggested that I sit with him,' I say.

Sophie looks down at the table and fiddles with her hands. 'And what did he say?'

'Not a lot. Well, he was kind of honest. He still loves you, Soph, but he's struggling with the anger and then the forgiveness part.'

'I know.' Sophie gulps. 'He said as much when he came to collect Florence.'

'Where is he staying? He didn't say, and I didn't think I should ask.'

'He went to his mum's for the first few nights. God knows what she thinks of me. Then a guy he works with put him in touch with someone who was letting a furnished apartment for three months. He's taken that while we try to work through things.'

'That's promising,' I say.

'How?'

'It's short term.' I shrug. 'Hopefully because he wants to find a way to sort things out.'

'What has Joe had to say in all of this?'

I've been dreading this question. I haven't wanted to add to Sophie's burden by telling her that things between Joe and I have taken a turn for the worst following all of this. I told Simon, but I knew he wouldn't let on to Sophie. He wasn't exactly sympathetic, though – his comment 'I told you this could blow up in your face' is still fresh in my mind.

'Emma?' Sophie prompts.

'Joe's, erm, not happy about the situation.'

'What does that mean?'

'Exactly that. He's not happy with you, or me.'

Sophie closes her eyes briefly. 'He's pissed that you didn't tell him, isn't he? He knows that you knew before I told Matt?'

'Pretty much, yeah. When he came home on Friday, he stayed long enough to have a go at me, and then spent the rest of the week-end with Matt.'

'Oh, Emma, I'm sorry! I never meant to drag you into this. I should never have told you.'

'Sophie, it's fine. Well, it's not right now, but it will be. Matt says that Joe will come around with a bit of time, and that it's some over-protective brotherly thing. He says that Joe's simply taking his frus-tration that he can't fix things out on me, I guess because I knew things were broken and I didn't tell him – not that Joe could have done anything to change things.'

I top up both of our wine glasses.

'Do you remember when all we used to have to worry about was what to wear on Friday night to the clubs?' I say, trying to lighten the mood.

Sophie gives a little laugh. 'How did things get so complicated?'

'We got older.'

'I'm glad you said "older" and not "old".'

'Who are you kidding? We *are* old.'

'No, we're not, we're in our prime,' Sophie says adamantly.

'This doesn't feel like my prime,' I say. 'Last week I went to the shop to buy milk and wondered all the way home why the girl at the checkout was giving me a funny look. When I got home, I realised that my dress was on inside out.'

Sophie laughs, nearly spitting out her wine. 'Oh, Emma, how do you do that?'

I wave my hands. 'I don't know,' I say. 'It's not like I *intend* to do these ridiculous things.'

Sophie shakes her head. 'No, I mean how do you always manage to make me smile?'

'Oh.' I think for a moment. 'You're smiling because you're grateful you're not me.' I grin. 'And because I've just made you look down and check that your own dress is on the right way.'

It's nine thirty when I get home and, feeling exhausted, I decide to have an early night. I'm just removing my eye makeup when my mobile phone rings. My heart does a little leap – it might be Joe. I pick up my phone from the bedside table. It's not Joe, it's Mum.

I press the button to answer the call. 'Hello.'

'Oh, darling, hi,' Mum purrs down the phone. 'Those curtains in your bedroom, where are they from?'

I'm momentarily thrown. Can she see me? I hold my phone in front of me, checking to see whether I unwittingly answered a video call.

'Curtains?'

'Yes, Emma, the grey curtains that I hung in your bedroom when you moved.'

'Oh.'

'Parker and I are looking at home furnishings and he couldn't remember what they look like.'

Actually, I'm quite relieved that Parker can't remember what my bedroom curtains look like. That would be exceptionally weird and very creepy.

'Emma?'

'Mum, it's nearly ten p.m.'

'Sorry, I forget about the time difference. We're just having a glass of wine before making dinner.'

'Right,' I say.

'So, where are they from? We'd love a darker grey pair for the lounge.'

I rack my brains, thinking about where I bought all the new house stuff. 'I think I got them online,' I say. 'I'll go through my emails tomorrow and send you the link.'

'That's great, Emma. Thank you.'

'Mum?'

'Yes?'

'Can I ask you something?'

'Of course, darling, you can ask me anything.'

I pause, wondering how to word this without sounding crazy.

'Emma?'

'I always thought that when I was in my forties everything would be easier somehow and it would make sense.'

'I'm not sure that you're making sense now, Emma. That's not a question.'

I sigh. 'Okay, what I'm trying to say is, I thought relationships and life would settle down as I got older – we all got older. But, well, all that seems to be happening is that the challenges are different, but they're still there nonetheless. When does life become more straightforward?'

'Hang on a minute.'

I hear muffled sounds and footsteps.

'That's better; I'm in the bedroom now. What's happened, Emma? Where do you and Joe fit into this?'

'It's hard, him working away,' I say. 'I mean, I knew it would be, but it's harder than I thought it would be.'

'How so?'

I almost don't want to say this out loud, but I know that it's true. 'We feel distant.'

Mum clears her throat. 'I'm not sure that I'm any kind of expert in this subject, Emma. What I can say is that whilst in your forties you may have been in a relationship with a person for some time, all that really means is that you know that person well. You know everything that's fabulous about them, but you know their flaws too. Remember, Emma, nobody is perfect; we're all flawed. Relationships grow and change as much as people do, and challenges come with that. I guess what I'm trying to say to you is that you have to work at a relationship, not necessarily all of the time, but it's always a work in progress. And if it's worth keeping, then it's worth working for.'

I gulp. Does Joe think our relationship is worth the effort? Matt seems prepared to work for him and Sophie – he's agreed to counselling, which is a start. And however much pressure Simon and James are under, I'm never in any doubt of their commitment to each other.

'Emma? Are you okay?'

'I'm fine, Mum. Thanks for listening.'

'Any time, darling. And you'll send me that link, yes?'

'What?'

'The curtains, Emma.'

I roll my eyes. 'Yes, Mum, I'll send you the link tomorrow.'

'Okay then. Goodnight.'

'Bye, Mum.'

I hang up the phone, shaking my head. Bloody curtains!

As I make a cup of tea, I go over in my head what Mum said: *'if it's worth keeping, then it's worth working for'*. Where does that leave me and Joe? He hasn't sent any more texts since this morning. Maybe I should text him. Our relationship suddenly feels hard. Only a few months ago we were buying a lovely house and we were excited to be moving into our new home, starting a new chapter together. But now we don't seem to spend enough time together, and there's this void between us that has formed over Sophie's cheating. What if Joe decides that a new life in London looks much more appealing? What if *Karen* in his office is more fun and less challenging, more cocktails and dancing than a glass of wine and a bowl of pasta? Maybe he's telling *Karen* right now how his girlfriend keeps secrets from him. She's probably nodding along in agreement while she -

A weird screeching noise outside suddenly interrupts my thoughts. What the hell is that?

Banjo?

I quickly go to the patio door and fling it open. It's dark outside and for a fleeting moment fear grips me. What if it's a ploy by a burglar to get me to open the door and they're waiting to pounce on me with a deadly weapon? Someone may have been watching the house and know that I'm alone. What if –

The screeching comes from my left, and I take my mobile phone from my pocket, turn on the torch mode and shine it down to the ground, sweeping it from left to right. The light catches the glowering eyes of Banjo and I instinctively jump. The cat seems to be twice his usual size, fur standing on end, his tail resembling a toilet brush.

'What the hell are you shouting at? Come in the house, silly cat.'

I take a step outside towards him, and then I see it. A fox is at the end of the garden. My heart leaps into my mouth. My instinct is to run, but I need to get the cat into the house and away from the fox. Thankfully, the fox makes my decision for me, and after what sounds like a bark it shoots off under the bushes. Banjo looks poised to charge after it, so I grab him, getting scratched to death in the process, and manhandle him into the house. I shove the patio door closed, and Banjo presses his nose against the glass and meows loudly.

'Why would you want to pick a fight with a fox?' I look down at Banjo, but he ignores me as he begins pacing in front of the door.

'Don't bring that thing back here either,' I say. 'Foxes may be cute, but they have rabies and big teeth.'

Banjo stops pacing and looks up at me with what I interpret to be a 'You're pathetic' expression.

I put a handful of biscuits into his food bowl and pick up the cup of tea I made a few minutes ago. I drink it quickly and leave Banjo munching his biscuits as I head up to bed.

'Stupid foxes in the countryside,' I mutter, hoping the fox decides not to return. I'm sure that they're more scared of humans than we are of them, but I can't help feeling fear when I see one, maybe because we don't see them very often. At least it didn't get hold of Banjo. Do foxes kill cats? I'll have to google it.

I climb into bed a few minutes later, but following the flash of adrenaline from the fox incident, I no longer feel tired. I pick up my phone and stare at the screen. Still no text or call from Joe. I open the search engine. My finger hovers over the screen, then I type *Relationship problems in your forties* and hit enter. I'm met with a long list of articles, none of which look good:

Can your marriage survive the 'Frustrated Forties'?

Forty ways your marriage changes after forty

Couples in their forties should go for marriage MOTs

Couples in their early forties most at risk of breaking up

Great. Are Joe and I destined to break up? We're not officially married, but for all intents and purposes, we live a married life. Are the statistics right? They must be based on something. Why are relationships so at risk for people in their forties?

Against my better judgement, I click into one of the articles. This does nothing to calm my crazy thoughts. But are they crazy, actually, if all these articles are right?

People in their forties should go for regular relationship 'check-ups' to prevent them becoming victims of the 'Frustrated Forties'.

What on earth is a 'relationship check-up'?

This is complete and utter rubbish. I click off the numerous open articles and place the phone by the side of my bed. People in their forties can't all face relationship break-ups. What about all the pensioner couples walking around still happy after a lifetime together? No, I'm not going to get absorbed in online scaremongering. When Joe comes home this weekend, things will be different, better, back to what they were a few months ago. Yes, the power of positive thinking is a much more sensible approach.

I switch off the bedroom light, and then get a fright as Banjo leaps onto the bed. After kneading my expensive bedding repeatedly with his claws, he snuggles down in a ball at the bottom of the bed next to my feet, seemingly none the worse for his fox standoff in the garden.

I'm drifting off to sleep when a thought pops into my mind and prods me like a hot poker. Mum and Dad were in their forties when they split up. Were they victims of the Frustrated Forties themselves, and am I genetically programmed to follow suit and repeat their behaviour?

Chapter Seventeen

I wake early the next morning, and in an attempt to distract my overworked brain from worrying about the signs and pitfalls of the Frustrated Forties, I decide to get up and go to work early. Even Banjo looks surprised as I disturb his usual snoring while I'm climbing out of bed. I shower, dress, down a strong cup of coffee and leave the house, all within forty-five minutes.

I arrive at work, hang up my coat and prepare for a full-on, productive day. Right, what shall I start with? Maybe the stock check?

'Why can't I find anything?' I rustle through the drawer that should contain the stock paperwork. 'Never mind. I'll just use the computer file.'

I press the button to fire up the system and watch as the screen lights up and the annoying circle of doom spins in the centre. I tap my fingers on the desk until the login box appears, and then I enter my username and password.

A frowning face icon appears with a big red cross next to it and a message: 'Incorrect username or password.'

Hmm. I must have hit a wrong key. I type in my login details again and hit the enter key with a little more force.

The frowning face icon appears again, mocking me. Damn it. I look down at the keyboard. Is the Caps Lock on? It isn't. Unable to accept defeat, I type in my details one more time.

I'm greeted by a padlock and a new message: 'User ID locked. Please refer to your administrator.'

I exhale loudly. There's only one person who can be to blame for this. And where is he? Any other time, Jarrod would have been here at the crack of dawn and way before me, but this morning he's nowhere to be seen. How am I supposed to get anything done? And more to the point, why the hell would he change my password?

I hear the door to the staff area open and close. Right. He's going to get it! I stomp to the staffroom and fling the door open.

'Morning,' Jenny says brightly.

'Oh, it's you.'

'Um, yes, Emma, I work here,' she says, looking at me a little strangely.

I glance at the clock.

'Put your coat back on, Jenny,' I say, grabbing my own jacket.

'Why? What are we doing? Emma, are you okay?'

'I'm fine. We're going to have a nice cup of coffee and a pastry, and then we'll come back to work in twenty-five minutes in time to open up.'

'But –'

'We can't do anything, Jenny,' I say, heading out the back door onto the street. 'Captain Annoying has changed my password and locked me out of the system.'

'I see.' Jenny's eyebrows are raised and she pulls her coat back on and follows me out of the door. 'I guess I could do with a strong coffee anyway. Darcy woke me at five a.m., which is the only reason that I'm here early and had the time to apply makeup before leaving the house.'

I glance at Jenny and press my lips together.

'What?' she asks, looking confused.

'You have your cardigan buttoned up wrong,' I say.

Jenny looks down at herself.

'Sorry,' I offer apologetically.

'Shit.'

She starts fumbling with the buttons on her cardigan and I feel bad. I didn't mean to embarrass her.

'I couldn't let you walk around all day like that,' I say.

'It's fine.' Jenny waves her hand at me dismissively. 'Believe me, it could have been a lot worse.'

We both giggle as we head off down the street to the nearest place that sells coffee and croissants.

'What are we going to do about him?' Jenny asks as she pulls a chunk off her pastry and then squashes it between her fingers.

'I think you can order a hitman on the internet if you look in the right place.' I sip my cappuccino and tap my finger thoughtfully on the edge of the cup.

'Really?' Jenny looks at me, astounded. 'You can do that?'

'Yes, you probably *can* find stuff like that on the internet, but no, we're not *actually* going to do that.'

'So back to what we *are* going to do,' Jenny continues. 'I'm not sure how much more of this I can take. If Jarrod picks the wrong day to provoke me, then who knows what I might do when I'm sleep deprived.'

'Don't worry; I'll corroborate whatever story you want if you can make him go away.'

Jenny giggles. 'Hopefully, it won't come to that.'

'I don't understand where he's sprung from. There was no mention of recruiting someone new after Lola left, and then Jarrod just appeared in a puff of smoke.'

'Like Marissa Bamford does.'

'Exactly.' I nod. 'And when I tried to broach the subject of Jarrod's retail experience with her, she just snapped down the phone "Are you questioning me?", and I didn't have the bottle to say "Well, yes".'

'She *can* be scary.'

'Can?'

'Okay, she *is* scary, but she likes you. She values your opinion.'

'No, she *asks* for my opinion and then mostly ignores it.' I drink the last of my coffee. 'Come on, we'd better get back or Captain Annoying will really have something to get upset about.'

We get back to the shop at five to nine and are surprised to find it still empty.

'I hope Jarrod is coming in to work today or it looks like we won't be getting much done. If we can't access the computer then we can't sell anything.'

'Maybe my login will work,' Jenny says optimistically, hanging her coat up.

We go through to the shop front and I turn on the lights while Jenny loads up the system. She taps on the keyboard.

'Nope.' She shakes her head. 'I'm locked out too.'

There's a click and a bang as the back door to the staff area opens and closes. I hold my hand up to Jenny.

'Follow my lead,' I say quietly.

A moment later, Jarrod appears in the shop, looking a little flustered. I take in his slightly-less-than-perfect appearance. His shirt, usually pressed to within an inch of its life, has a few crinkles.

'Good morning, Jarrod,' I say, eyebrows raised and with a hint of attitude in my tone.

Jenny looks at me, wide-eyed.

'Have you been messing with the system? Only we came in early to do a stock check and neither of us could get into the computer. Could we, Jenny?' I turn to face her.

'Um, no. That's right.' Jenny gulps as she brushes croissant crumbs from her cardigan.

I turn back to Jarrod. 'It says that both our passwords are incorrect. Do you know anything about that?'

My hands are now on my hips and I realise that I'm challenging him. And that I've told a little white lie. I didn't come in early to do a stock check, I arrived at work to distract myself from my personal life – but that's beside the point.

Jarrod glares at me and appears to regain his initial loss of composure. He stands up straight and licks his lips before speaking.

'I changed everyone's password. We need to have better security. You probably hadn't changed your password in years.'

That's true.

'Okay, I get that we need to be secure,' I say. 'But you could have just asked me and Jenny to update our passwords ourselves, instead of treating us like children and doing it for us – and potentially causing a massive issue.'

Jarrod sneers at me. 'A massive issue?'

'Yes,' I say indignantly. 'What if you were run over by a bus on your way into work this morning and we couldn't access the system? The business wouldn't function, and we'd have had to close the shop for the day.'

'I drive to work, so getting run over by a bus is highly unlikely, and Marissa Bamford is the overall administrator for the IT system, so she could have reset both of your passwords should such an event have occurred.' He smiles at me, but it doesn't quite reach his eyes. 'Now, shall we all have a cup of tea and start this day again?'

He turns and walks back through to the staff area, and I hear him switch on the kettle.

'Smart arse,' I chunter under my breath.

Jenny gives me a sideways glance.

'Something's not right with him.' I nod towards the door. 'He's off-kilter.'

'Well, I'm not going to ask him what's wrong.'

I shake my head. 'Me neither.'

'Emma?' I hear Jarrod call loudly from the kitchen.

Grr.

Chapter Eighteen

Hi, Em. Just wondering if you're in tonight? Florence would love to visit her Auntie Emma. xx

That's the text I receive from Sophie on Wednesday morning. Of course I reply that I'm home tonight and up for a visit.

That evening, the doorbell rings at exactly six o'clock. I can hear Florence's excited chatter as I walk towards the door.

'Hi.' I greet Sophie with a hug. 'How are you?' I bend down to be on the same level as Florence. 'And how's my favourite little girl?'

Florence giggles. 'Pussy cat.'

'I'm sorry?' I stand up.

'Oh, um, I think she might be referring to Banjo.' Sophie smiles.

As I step back to let them both in, I glance behind me, but there's no cat in sight.

'I may have mentioned that you'd got a cat.' Sophie waves her free hand dismissively; Florence is pulling her along by the other. 'I didn't think she would remember.'

'Cat!' Florence shouts again, and she scurries off into the living room.

Hmm.

'I'll put the kettle on,' I say.

'Ooh, can I have one of your coffees, please?' Sophie asks. 'I could do with the caffeine.'

'Won't it keep you awake all night?'

Sophie rolls her eyes at me and laughs. 'Emma, I have a three year old; I'm already in a comatose state most nights before my head even reaches the pillow. It's a miracle if I can even be bothered to remove my makeup before climbing into bed.'

'Oh. Right. Coffee it is then.'

I switch on the coffee machine and start preparing the drinks. 'You look a little better,' I say. 'How are you doing?'

'I'm okay. It's hard without Matt, for many reasons. It's hard having to look after Florence all on my own. Matt did more than I thought, both around the house and with Florence. It's really hard, though, when he comes to pick her up and she goes to stay over-night with him. I feel completely lost when she's not with me.'

'Wow. What's it like between you when you see each other?'

Sophie shrugs. 'We're civil.'

I bite my lip. There are a million things that I could say right now, but none of them would help to ease the pain that Sophie is clearly in, so instead I take hold of her hand and squeeze it tightly.

She gulps. 'I really miss him.'

'I know you do.'

'What if he never forgives me?' Sophie looks at me tearfully.

I'm saved from any kind of response by Banjo shooting into the kitchen, closely followed by a giggling Florence.

'Cat! Cat!' she shouts as she points at Banjo, who comes to a stop next to his food bowl. He looks back at Florence descending on him and appears to decide that she's not a threat, as he stuffs his face into his bowl and starts chomping his biscuits.

The coffee machine pings, signalling that the drinks are ready.

I take Florence by the hand. 'Why don't we leave Banjo to eat his tea while we go into the lounge and find something fun to do?'

'Cat!' she shouts again, but then she accepts defeat and allows me to lead her out of the kitchen.

'I'll grab the coffees,' Sophie says, looking more composed.

In the living room, I sit Florence on the sofa and go to the cup-board where I keep the princess play mat that I bought her for Christmas and keep here for when she visits.

'Yay!' Florence laughs. 'Pwincess.'

I lay out the play mat, and Florence slides off the sofa and plonks herself down on it. Instantly, she presses every button within reach, and different songs start playing randomly.

Sophie hands me a coffee and we sit down on the sofa. Within seconds, Banjo appears and climbs onto the arm of the sofa next to me, then proceeds to clamber over me and make his way to Sophie's lap, where he curls up and begins purring as she strokes the back of his ears.

'He's so soft and cute,' she says. 'What made Joe buy you a cat?'

I take a drink of my coffee. 'I think he thought it would be nice for me to have another living thing in the house while he's away – you know, something waiting for me when I get home.'

'Ah, that's lovely.'

'You say that, but this week I've woken up to find Banjo in the bed with me, and I mean *in* the bed, not on top of it.'

Sophie chuckles.

'And I decided to do a load of washing – mainly because the clothes basket had reached a critical level of capacity – but when I came home from work last night I found Banjo sleeping in the middle of the clean laundry.'

Sophie looks down at Banjo on her lap and grins.

'He hadn't just slept on a little bit of it either, like one t-shirt or something. Oh no, it was like he'd tunnelled through it all and then rolled around just for good measure, to make sure every item of clothing was covered in fur.'

Sophie laughs. 'Oh dear.'

'I had to do the whole lot of washing again. Plus, I have no idea what they put in that cat food, but it is not a smell that you want to experience at seven in the morning!'

As if on cue, Banjo stretches out on Sophie's knee and rolls over, looking adorable as he allows her to tickle his tummy.

'He seems to like you,' I say, eyebrows raised.

'He's lovely.' Sophie rubs his tummy and Banjo purrs loudly.

'Was it perhaps you, Sophie, rather than Florence' – I glance down at Florence, who is still engrossed in her princess play mat – 'who wanted to see Banjo?'

Sophie looks nonchalant. 'Maybe.'

Later that evening, I get another visitor, proving that I've slipped down the pecking order in my circle of friends and my cat has taken priority.

'Where is he then?' Simon bursts past me as I open the front door.

'Hi, Emma. Lovely to see you. I'm fine, thanks. How are you?'

I say with a hint of sarcasm, repeating the words that Simon said down the phone to me only last weekend.

Simon looks at me with a hint of disdain. 'I can see you're fine, Em; you're right here in front of me. Now, where's Mr Whiskers?' He delves into a carrier bag he's holding and pulls out a packet of cat treats.

'Except he's not called Mr Whiskers. His name is Banjo. And it's nice to know you've come around here to see the cat before me.'

He shakes the packet of treats and Banjo appears from nowhere, like a ninja, and wraps himself around Simon's legs.

'Hello,' Simon coos, bending down to stroke Banjo. 'Would you like some treats, Mr Whiskers?'

'Shall I make you a cup of tea while you and the cat become acquainted? And please don't call him Mr Whiskers; you'll confuse him.'

'You could change his name to Mr Whiskers.'

I roll my eyes at Simon. 'Would you like it if we started calling you by a different name?'

'Actually, yes.' Simon pours cat treats into his hand and holds them out. Banjo immediately dives in and starts eating the treats. 'I would prefer something more striking, like Isaac or Darwin.'

I shake my head at Simon and head into the kitchen to make the tea. While the kettle boils I hear the jingling of bells, and I look back into the hallway to see numerous cat toys strewn across the floor and Banjo chasing a colourful butterfly dangling from a pole that Simon is waving about. Simon's laughing, and I smile. It's actually very cute to watch.

'It seems that my cat is the new attraction,' I say to Simon, handing him a mug of tea a few minutes later. 'He's having a string of visitors.'

'We're just making sure that you're okay while Joe's away,' Simon says.

'That would be more convincing if you were looking at me while you said that,' I reply, 'and you weren't also trying to rub the cat's head while not spilling your tea.'

Simon stands up. 'Come on then, Miss It's All About Me. Let's hear about what's going on in your life, and I'll abandon the loving, affectionate animal you have invited into your home.'

'Simon, if you walk away, the cat will follow you. Trust me. I experience this when I try to go to the bathroom in peace.'

Simon holds up a hand. 'Enough said.'

We go into the living room, and Banjo duly follows. Simon lolls on the sofa with his feet outstretched, so I sit in the armchair.

'Are you coping living on your own?' Simon asks me in a serious voice. 'You're not depressed because Joe's got a strop on with you, are you?'

'Of course I'm fine,' I say. 'Don't be ridiculous. I'm a grown woman; I don't need a man to look after me.'

'Really? Only I saw what you were like when you lived alone when you were single.'

'And how was that then?' I ask, slightly offended.

'Your staple diet was cheese and biscuits, and you counted the grapes in your wine as one of your five a day.'

'There is food in the fridge,' I protest, 'and not just cheese.' I stick my tongue out at him.

'If you say so, hun.'

'I made pasta tonight,' I continue to protest. I realise that I'm being so defensive because Simon is, unfortunately, right. I do remember those days of eating whatever happened to be left in the cupboard or fridge, and I did always have wine, but I'm not going to admit that to Simon.

'Never mind that,' Simon says, drinking his coffee. 'What's going on with Emma at the moment? Is Joe still really mad at you?'

I shrug. 'Honestly, I don't know. We haven't had much contact since he left on Monday morning.'

'How did you leave things?'

'Joe says that we'll be okay.'

'Do you believe that?'

'I *want* to believe that.'

'But?'

I want to tell Simon about my fear of Karen, but I think that I'll sound ridiculous. Somehow my brain doesn't acknowledge that what I'm about to say instead might sound worse.

'Have you read about the Frustrated Forties?' I ask tentatively.

'What's that?' Simon frowns. 'It sounds like some hideous reality TV show.'

'No, it's a *thing* apparently.'

'A *thing*?'

'Yes, I did some research on this, and apparently couples in their forties are getting bored and frustrated with each other and they're breaking up.'

Simon snorts loudly. 'Where have you been reading that crap, Em?'

'It's not *crap*, Simon. You're supposed to go for some sort of relationship MOT.'

Simon howls with laughter. 'Oh, Emma, is that what you're worried about with Joe? You think he's got bored of you?'

I shrug, feeling a mixture of embarrassment and indignation at Simon's reaction.

'Honestly, Emmie, babe, you have nothing to worry about. Joe will get over himself and things will go back to normal, I promise.'

'You think?'

'Absolutely. Now stop taking relationship advice from Dr Google and stay in reality instead, okay?'

I chew my lip. 'Okay.'

'Anything else that I can help with?' Simon sits back and crosses his legs.

'Urgh. I'm hating the new guy at work.'

'Is he hot?'

'What? No, he is *not* hot,' I say.

'Shame. It would have made hating him a little more fun.'

I shake my head at Simon. 'Anyway...'

'Sorry, go on. Why do you hate him?'

'He keeps acting like he's in charge, bossing me and Jenny around, changing things that have worked for years.'

'Such as?'

'He created this whole new over-complicated stock-checking system with all these spreadsheets, and then he changed my password and locked me out of the computer!'

'Why did he do that?'

'He said it was a security thing. He said we need to be more cyber-conscious and aware of being hacked. I said, good look to the hacker if they could have guessed my password, because I forget it half of the bloody time.'

Simon laughs. 'Sounds like he's trying to assert his authority.'

'Exactly. Except he doesn't actually have any. He's not our boss – as far as we know, anyway. It seems to be his mission to make mine and Jenny's life miserable.'

'Maybe he's not getting any.' Simon winks.

'Getting any?'

'You know, at home. His leg over. Whatever you want to call it.'

'Funnily enough, Simon, I realised what you meant by the term "getting any". I was wondering what that had to do with me and Jenny.'

'Sexual frustration.' Simon shakes his head. 'He's venting his sexual frustration at work.'

I raise my eyebrows.

'You mark my words.' Simon wags his finger at me. 'You'll see an instant change in his personality once he gets some action in the bedroom.'

'Is this how the world works now, Si?'

Simon exhales slowly and says knowingly, 'It's how the world has always worked, babe.'

I chuckle. 'So is this how we judge you going forward? If you're in a bad mood, does it mean that you're not getting any?'

Simon shoots me a wanton look. 'Look at me, babe. As if I don't get any. James can't resist me.'

I fall into a fit of giggles. You've got to love Simon's modesty.

Chapter Nineteen

I scowl at my reflection in the bathroom mirror, taking in the grey-ing hair roots and the dark creases beneath my eyes. Whoever said that forty is the new thirty was clearly misguided or delusional, or both. Forty sounds like my mum's age – certainly not the number of candles on my last birthday cake.

I can't quite believe that I've reached a point in my life where I need a 'touch-up spray' to dowse the grey parting of my hair each morning in between hairdresser visits, a time where I need to be conscious of receding gums and overgrown eyebrows – honestly, I'm sure throughout the whole of my twenties and thirties my eye-brows didn't need anywhere near the amount of maintenance cur-rently required to prevent me having a monobrow.

I gently pinch the skin under my upper arm with my thumb and forefinger and I sigh. That's not a situation that's improving of its own accord either.

I rest my hands on the sink and lean in closer. If this is my half-way point, then I dread to think what I'll see in the mirror in ten or twenty years' time. I shake my head to dispel the image of me grey haired and dishevelled, unrecognisable under layers of wrinkles and wobbly bingo wings.

I vow to use my time wisely while Joe is working away. I will ap-ply a facemask weekly, one with collagen or something that dispels the signs of aging. I will go to the weekly running club to become fit and toned and youthful, or at least a bit less squidgy – I'm sure that's achievable in a six-month timescale.

There's still no contact from Joe.

I cave, and decide to text him:

Hi, just checking in.

I type, my finger hovering over the send button. Does that sound too carefree? Should I put a kiss on the end?

I add a '*x*' and press send before I can debate the content of the text any further. Any contact is better than none, and Joe will have to text me back at some point.

When I arrive at work, at eight-forty five a.m., I bump into Jenny outside.

'Morning,' she says brightly.

I don't share her enthusiasm, though. Who knows what the day ahead will bring? It's been a little tense since the whole password debacle, and I've done my best to stay out of Jarrod's way.

Jenny, meanwhile, has been her usual non-confrontational self and has tried her best to encourage a truce by engaging us all in con-versation and camaraderie over a cup of tea and a Jammie Dodger.

As we enter the staff room at the back of the shop, I stop, mid-stride, and turn to Jenny. 'Is that someone singing?'

'It sounds like it.' She tiptoes in behind me.

'Oh my God,' I whisper, 'it sounds like Jarrod.'

Jenny puts her hand over her mouth to hide her giggles.

'He's singing along to Beyoncé,' I say, astounded.

We both stand, motionless, in the kitchenette area and listen to the usually straight-laced and stuffy Jarrod singing Beyoncé's 'Crazy in Love'.

Suddenly, I'm struck by a thought and I press my lips together.

'What?' Jenny asks quietly.

'Bloody hell. Simon's right!'

'What are you talking about?'

'Simon said that Jarrod was being mean to us and exerting his authority because he was sexually frustrated.'

'What?' Jenny looks at me as though I'm a madwoman.

'Honestly, he said we would notice a change when – oh God, this is Simon's terminology, not mine – when he "got some action in the bedroom".'

Jenny bursts out laughing. 'Oh, do you really think that's it? He "got some action" last night?'

'I can't think of any other plausible explanation for how someone goes from being Mr Over-Cautious IT Man to belting out "Crazy in Love", can you?'

'What do you think she's like?'

I purse my lips. 'One extreme or another.'

'Such as?'

'Either she's as tightly wound as him, in which case they spent the evening discussing new ironing techniques before a fumble under the sheets.'

Jenny chuckles.

'Or – and I do realise I'm sounding like a complete bitch, by the way, but we've got to have some fun, given the torture he's put us through.'

'Or?' Jenny prompts.

'Or, she's some sex-crazed dominatrix who's ordered him around the bedroom before handcuffing him to the bedposts.'

We both erupt into laughter. I'm laughing so hard that tears are streaming down my face. Jenny is doubled over, clutching her sides.

The door from the shop to the staff area swings open and Jarrod looms in the doorway. We both instantly stop laughing, and I can feel my heart hammering in my chest as Jarrod looks from Jenny to me and then asks the dreaded question:

'What's so funny?'

That evening, I find myself sitting on the sofa at home dressed in my jogging bottoms, a t-shirt and a pink hooded top. I stare down at my new purple and black trainers that feel so comfortable that I never want to take them off. I glance at my phone – ten past six – and instinctively clasp my hand around the cold metal of my keys. I bite my lip.

It's now or never.

Maybe I'm not destined for now. Maybe I'm okay with never.

I take a deep breath. Eleven minutes past six.

'Oh, come on, Emma,' I say out loud, pushing myself up to a standing position, and I take long, purposeful strides until I'm out of the house and heading towards the car.

I drive to the local cricket club, where the beginners' running club meets. My heart is filled with dread. I hated sports at school, and I've barely set foot in a gym in the last ten years – except on the rare occasion when I've admitted defeat and gone along with

Sophie, only to immediately regret my decision and weak resolve. Yet here I am, rocking up to a running club when my one and only attempt at jogging was about eight years ago and I barely made it to the end of the road and back.

This is the result of my stupid resolution to put my alone time while Joe is working away to good use. Somehow I thought that improving my fitness level was the best way to do this. I'm reconsidering that decision now. I'm thinking I'm fine with being just moderately fit.

Too late now, I realise as I pull into the small car park. My mobile phone beeps as I park the car. I glance at the screen and see a text from Joe. Finally – it's taken him all day to respond to my text:

I'm fine. See you tomorrow.

That's it? Hmm.

I scowl at the phone and decide against texting Joe back.

I lock my phone in the glove box and quickly get out of the car, before I can change my mind about this bloody running club, and I walk briskly towards the small brick building. On pushing the door open, I instantly feel relief as I look around and see people of all ages, shapes and sizes.

My relief, however, is short-lived.

A super-toned girl, in full makeup applied to perfection, bounds into the centre of the room with more energy than a five year old in a sweet shop. Her ponytail swings wildly with the momentum. She claps her hands together loudly, and I die inwardly.

'Hey, everyone!' She grins. 'Well done on coming to "Running for Beginners" tonight! You're awesome!'

I glance around, taking in all the people nodding and smiling back at her in unison.

'I'm Katie, and I'm going to help you through your running journey...'

My running journey?

'...until you reach your own personal goal.'

Oh dear. I think I've made a catastrophic error. I don't think I possess the levels of energy and enthusiasm that it would appear I'm going to need to make it through the next hour, let alone to commit to my personal running journey. I also fear that there may be a drastic difference between what I perceive to be my personal goal and the expectations of Miss Hyper Lycra in front of me.

'Okay.' Katie spins around, making eye contact with everyone in the room. 'Today is the start. It's just three kilometres.'

Three kilometres? Exactly how far is that in real people's terms? Around the block? To the local mini supermarket and back for wine?

'I want you to stay focused and push yourself,' she continues. 'You're going to want to quit, but you are stronger than you think you are. Don't quit on me; we can do this together.'

I'm thinking I want to quit right now, unless when she says 'we can do this together' she means that she's prepared to give me a piggyback halfway around the route.

'And just to help you guys keep your pace and to give you some moral support tonight,' Katie continues excitedly, 'I've got a few friends who are going to join us and be your running buddies.'

Half a dozen people in luminous running gear appear from nowhere and stand among us.

'Now,' Katie states, 'I'm going to assign a buddy to each of you.'

Dear God, I pray silently, please let it be a woman. Please let it be a woman.

'Declan,' Katie shrieks, 'can you buddy up with…Emma.'

She points a long, shocking-pink nail in my direction, and possibly the hottest guy I have ever seen steps towards me. Not many people can pull off the Lycra look, but Declan has managed it in abundance. He looks like he belongs on the cover of a men's fitness magazine.

Well, thank you, god of humiliation. Not only is my running buddy not a woman, but he's also completely ripped and half my age. I must have murdered someone in a previous life, and then murdered someone again.

'Hi,' Declan say warmly to me. He looks even more attractive when he smiles. 'I'm guessing this is your first time at the running club?'

I can feel the heat from my cheeks (burning hot enough to sizzle bacon on) as I try to meet his gaze.

'What gave it away?' I do a stupid little laugh. 'The fact that I look completely unfit, or the terror on my face?' I hope my humour will be a good icebreaker and also indicate to him my inexperience with running.

Declan bites his lip, and I think my heart actually skips a beat.

'No, it's neither.' He shakes his head. 'You still have the price tag on your top and jacket.' He points at my abdomen.

Kill me. Kill me now.

I look down and see a white square tab hanging from the bottom of my top, and another dangling from the sleeve of my brand-new pink running jacket, seemingly confirming that this is true and declaring to the world that I'm a complete idiot.

'Oh, right, yes, well…' I splutter.

'Shall we get going?' This appears to be a rhetorical question, as Declan simply starts walking towards the door and I have no option but to scurry after him.

Once in the car park, I expect to start my 'running journey', but instead I'm ushered to the far end of the tarmac near the edge of the building.

'We need to warm up first,' Declan says.

Of course. Warm up.

'So, we're going for fluid movement. Stretching while moving, not a static stretch.'

I nod, having no idea what this means.

'Just follow me.'

Declan takes me through a number of exercises, encouraging me along the way, until I begin to feel out of breath. I hope the running starts soon, or there's every chance that I won't make it fully around the route and will instead have to call an Uber to collect me at some point.

Finally, we set off, at a leisurely pace. This isn't so bad, I think as we trot along behind a number of runners who are making their way up the road.

'So.' I turn my head to Declan. 'How long have you been running?'

I'm surprised that this one question is such an exertion for my lungs. It hadn't occurred to me that my entire oxygen level would be consumed by saying one sentence.

'I've always been a runner,' Declan answers.

Of course you have.

'I won regional events as a kid,' he continues. 'But I don't have as much time to compete anymore, what with work and everything.'

'Right,' I gasp. Is it me or are we picking up the pace?

'I'm a personal trainer,' Declan continues.

'Right,' is all I can manage again.

'Okay, Emma, we're going to drop the pace a little here.'

Oh, thank God.

'You need to take it steady as we head up the hill. It's a long gradient, so you'll feel it in your calves.'

I can already feel my calves and they're screaming loudly at me in anger. What does a long gradient mean? I look up ahead and see an incline up to what appears to be a steep hill.

Declan starts chatting away again as we start our assent, but this is no time for me to engage in conversation. I don't want to appear rude, but breathing has to be my main focus here.

'Perhaps we…shouldn't…talk,' I gasp. 'Need…to…save…energy.'

'Absolutely. Sensible idea.' Declan smiles at me.

By the time we near the brow of the hill, I feel like I'm barely moving, just dragging myself along the pavement in a pathetic state, gulping at the air. Sweat is pooling pretty much everywhere. I had no idea that I could sweat this much. I can feel liquid trickling down every crevice of my body; I'm sweating in places I didn't think I *could* sweat. Declan is practically walking beside me, barely out of breath, as I shuffle along shamefully.

As I force myself over the peak of the hill, I see a building glowing in the distance; it's just a blur, but it fills me with hope. Hope that I am going to survive. I focus on that glow as the thumping of my heart fills my ears and blocks out whatever Declan is trying to say to me as we make our way back to the cricket club. I watch his lips move but hear nothing, until my feet hit the tarmac of the car park and I instantly grind to a halt. I can already feel every muscle in my body seizing up in protest.

'Well done, Emma!' Declan says with a level of enthusiasm that, in my current state, I have no chance of replicating. 'You must feel great.'

'Mmm,' I murmur. If 'great' means delirious from exhaustion.

'Now for the cool down.'

Bloody hell. I guess it's too much to expect that 'cool down' means lying down in a darkened room and staying still.

Declan hands me a bottle of water and I gulp it noisily.

'Let's start with a shoulder stretch...' he continues.

I force my body through a series of stretches, before Declan finally releases me from the torture with the dreaded words, 'See you next week.'

Yeah.' I nod half-heartedly. 'Next week, absolutely.'

'Don't forget to keep rehydrating throughout the evening.'

'Rehydrating? Yes.' I nod wearily, and take another gulp of water from the bottle as I stumble back to my car.

I lower my aching body slowly and gently into the driver's seat and glance at my reflection in the car mirror. My face is a shade of pink that I've never seen it be before, and if I had then I would have been making an emergency call for a paramedic. My hair, which was combed into a neat ponytail when I arrived here not so long ago, is beyond unkempt. Wispy strands have escaped and are swirling around my head like tentacles.

I stare out of the window. It's completely dark now. I have no idea how long I was running for, or what distance I covered; the three kilometres Katie mentioned seemed much shorter in my head.

Well, Emma, this may have been one of the more stupid ideas that you've had recently, I admonish myself as I turn the key in the ignition and gingerly press my foot onto the accelerator. I contemplate heading straight home, but there's somewhere closer that I can seek refuge and refreshment.

I knock wearily on Simon's door, leaning gingerly against the wall to prevent myself sliding to the ground and just lying there until someone scoops me up with a snow shovel or something.

I hear Simon's cheery tone from the other side of the door. 'Coming.'

'Come quicker,' I mumble.

The door opens. 'Emma?' Simon frowns. 'What are you doing here?'

'Do you have caffeine?' I push past Simon and stagger into the house, ignoring the fact that he's dressed in pyjamas and may in fact be heading to bed.

'Hi, Simon. How are you? How was your day?' Simon says in a mocking voice.

I don't even bother to look over my shoulder at him as I continue to plod awkwardly down the hallway to the kitchen, mainly because turning would involve moving muscles and I don't have the energy for that.

Simon quickly follows me. 'Are you going to explain why you've landed on my doorstep at' – he glances down at his wrist – 'eight thirty-five on a Thursday night dressed like a...' He cocks his head to one side. 'What are you dressed as? And why do you look so dishevelled?'

Continuing with my mission, I stand in front of his very posh 'bean to cup' fandangle coffee machine and press the 'on' button. After exhaling noisily, I tell him: 'I've been running.'

Simon laughs loudly. I just raise my eyebrows at him until he regains some control over his amusement.

'Why? Were you being chased?' He continues to chuckle.

'No.' My tone is dismissive. I stare at the coffee machine as it huffs and puffs and ejects hot liquid into the waiting cup. The simple aroma of freshly brewed coffee instantly breathes life back into my mutilated muscles.

'Em, I love you, you know that, but are you crazy? Why would you be out running alone in the dark?'

'I wasn't alone.' I take the cup of coffee from the machine and blow it before taking a sip of scalding espresso. 'And it wasn't dark when I set off running.'

'Christ. How long were you out there?' Simon stifles more giggles.

'I've joined a running club,' I say indignantly.

'A running club?'

'Are you going to repeat everything I say?'

'No,' Simon says in a sulky tone. 'But why would *you*' – he gestures at me – 'who's had a long-standing fear of the gym, join a running club?'

'I don't know, Simon, maybe to get fit in my forties.'

'Oh dear God, woman, you've literally just turned forty. Please tell me that you're not having a mid-life crisis, and this isn't some more doomed advice from internet research for Fragile Forties or whatever it was called?'

He takes the cup from my hand and takes a slurp of coffee, before handing it back.

'No, it's not, and no, I'm not having a mid-life crisis.' I shake my head. 'I thought it might be a way to pass the time while Joe's working away, that's all. You know, get out of the house instead of sitting in alone, and maybe improve my fitness at the same time.'

'Shame.' Simon sighs emphatically. 'I was hoping for the mid-life crisis, then I would be forced to take you dancing and drink shots all night long like we used to.'

'I think shot drinking and all-night dancing are behind us, Simon. Although a shot of something stronger would be very welcome right now if I weren't driving.'

Plus, when Declan said to hydrate, I don't think he meant with Sauvignon Blanc. I look down at my cup. Or caffeine for that matter. Never mind.

'Yeah, you're right. The fun of drinking excessively is not worth the pain of dealing with two seven year olds with a hangover.'

'I thought you didn't get hangovers?'

'That was before – when I was a seasoned drinker and I'd trained my body through years of exposure to alcohol. Now I'm a cheap date and alcohol intolerant.'

I laugh.

'So, how was it?'

'What?'

'Doh! The running club?'

'Oh. Um, torturous.' I down the last of the espresso. 'And not only because I had to run outside in public when I'm marginally unfit.'

'Marginally?'

I glare at Simon and he holds his hands up in submission.

'But also because the "running buddy" they assigned to me was the hottest guy you could ever wish to meet.'

Simon leans on the kitchen worktop and looks thoughtful. 'Now you're talking. Just how hot was he?'

'Too hot for me to feel comfortable sweating profusely alongside while trying to engage in his small talk.'

'Wow. I might have to join the running club with you.'

'Simon, he's about twenty years old. You're old enough to be his dad.'

Simon looks at me with a hurt expression.

'And might I remind you that you have a husband – James.' I look over to the kitchen doorway, where James is standing, arms folded, with an amused look on his face.

'Oh, hi, babe.' Simon grins over at James, who shakes his head at us – which, I realise, is something he does quite a lot.

'I'm being serious, Em.' Simon thwacks my arm. 'I could do with being a bit fitter myself. James is always trying to get me to play squash with him.'

'Please tell me that you actually mean the game of squash on a sports court and that isn't just a euphemism for something far worse.'

James nearly spits out the glass of water he's just poured himself from the fridge.

Simon purses his lips. 'Now you're just being rude.'

I can't help but giggle.

He wafts his hand at me. 'And do you know that you've still got the label on your jacket?'

I sigh. It's been a long night.

Chapter Twenty

I wake in a crumpled heap, the bedcovers twisted around me and, of course, with Banjo snoring on the pillow beside me, which has become a daily occurrence. Honestly, I have never heard such a noise from a cat. I try to move but my body feels too heavy. Tentatively, I stretch a leg out from underneath the bedding and then instantly regret it as a shooting cramp fires up my calf.

Bloody hell. I thought exercise was supposed to be good for you, yet less than twenty-four hours after my experience at the running club I feel like my body is shutting down completely, rather than feeling energised and euphoric as promised. At this rate it will be a miracle if I can get out of bed.

The alarm clock suddenly springs into action at the side of me and Banjo raises his head and gives me a death stare.

'I'm sorting it, Banjo, just give me a minute.' I reach an arm out towards the bedside table and feel my shoulder muscles burn. Why does my shoulder hurt? You use your legs when you run. I wasn't doing anything with my arms.

I silence the alarm clock and slither my arm back under the quilt. Banjo gives a long sigh and resumes his napping position, which, to be honest, is exactly the position I would like to remain in today.

I fear this morning's getting-ready-for-work regime is going to be challenging given the lack of movement from my entire body. I stare up at the ceiling. Right, come on, Emma. The only cure for this is a hot shower and an injection of caffeine, in that order.

I roll gently onto my side and swing my legs slowly around and off the edge of the bed, using the momentum to get me up to a seated position.

There, that wasn't so bad.

Taking a deep breath, I push off the mattress – and groan like a ninety-year-old woman as I try to straighten up to a standing position. Hobbling to the bathroom, I feel each muscle in my thighs wince with every step. I turn the shower up to the maximum temperature; there's nothing else for it, I'm going to have to stand under the intense heat and boil myself like a ham until some flexibility returns to my body.

Slowly, the red-hot water soothes my body back to life. I stand there for a long time before remembering that I actually have to go to work today. I shampoo my hair and use some lemon-and-ginger shower gel whose aroma, the bottle promises, will invigorate me. I have my doubts; I think it's going to take more than that this morning. I step cautiously out of the shower and wrap my hair in a towel, before pulling on my dressing gown.

Hovering at the top of the stairs, I glance down. This is *not* going to be good. After much 'oohing and 'aahing', I finally make it to the bottom of the stairs and into the kitchen. I glance at the clock as I make an extra-strong coffee and decide there's no time to sip it in the tranquillity of my kitchen. I'll have to gulp it down while I dry my hair, as I need to leave for work in fifteen minutes. I could have put it in a travel mug, but the last time I did that I left the mug in the car for a week and…well, who knew that mould grew so quickly? There was nothing else to do but throw the cup away. Lesson learned, but I haven't got around to buying a new one. I can't stop here and sip the coffee, though, as that would make me late for work, and there's no chance I'll be able to do my usual 'cutting it fine' jog from the car to the shop. At this rate, I don't feel like I'll ever jog anywhere again. In fact, right now that sounds fine to me.

I open a packet of cat food and squeeze it into a bowl. As if by magic Banjo appears from nowhere and rubs his face on my legs. My stomach churns at the smell. No wonder he appeared immediately; you can probably smell that stuff from three streets away. How cats find that appetising I don't know. I doubt I'll ever get used to the strong smell of cat food first thing in the morning.

Thankfully, I make it to work with about three minutes to spare. Jenny finds me offloading my coat and bag in the staff room.

'Ah, you're here. Jarrod is looking for you,' she says with an apologetic expression.

'I'm not late. I'm perfectly on time.'

'I don't think you're in trouble. He wants you to help him with something.'

'Oh.' I walk towards the door to the shop front.

'Emma, are you okay?' Jenny asks. 'You're walking funnily.'

'I'm fine,' I say dismissively. 'I went for a run last night. Don't ask.'

The day goes quickly, but I have mixed emotions about Joe coming home tonight. After our barely seeing each other last weekend and hardly texting all week, I have no idea what to expect when he gets home. Joe sent a text earlier to say that his train was delayed but he should be home for seven p.m. I decide to stop at the supermarket on the way home and pick up something nice for dinner and maybe a bottle of wine. Hopefully, that will set the tone for a better evening, and a less tense weekend ahead.

After wandering up and down the supermarket aisles aimlessly staring into the fridges, I finally choose steak with fat-cut chips and a side salad, followed by raspberry cheesecake, which all sounds very posh but needs little preparation and is easy to cook – potentially. How do you know how long to cook steak for? What actually is medium rare? I pick up a bottle of chilled Prosecco from the wine fridge on my way to the checkout.

It's six o'clock when I arrive home. I'm greeted by a meowing Banjo who seems to want to trip me up along the path. He swipes at me with his paw as I try to clamber past him to the front door with my bag of shopping in one hand and my handbag in the other. As I struggle to get the key into the door Banjo meows persistently at my feet.

I look down at him. 'Anyone would think that I'd left you for days, carrying on like this, not that I left for work at eight fifteen this morning after you'd inhaled a full packet of disgusting-smelling cat meat and a massive bowl of biscuits.'

Banjo just gives me a disapproving look.

The second the front door opens, Banjo charges in. I follow at a slower pace, beginning to feel the muscle tension from this morning creeping back into my legs. I unpack the food and put it in the fridge, along with the bottle of Prosecco, and I take out a chilled beer. This should help to relax my aching muscles, or at least numb them until Joe arrives home and I can open the Prosecco.

I drink the beer and then shower and change into jeans and a t-shirt, before going back to the kitchen to turn on the oven. As I'm reaching into the fridge for a second beer, I hear the front door open and close and I hold my breath.

'Emma?' Joe calls.

I place the unopened bottle of beer back in the fridge and open the kitchen door. Joe is standing in the hallway. He looks tired and his crumpled shirt is half untucked from his trousers.

'Hey.' He cocks his head on one side and smiles at me, showing the dimples that I fell in love with years ago.

'Hey,' I say back quietly.

'I missed you.'

'I missed you too,' I say, stepping towards him.

'I'm sorry, Emma, about last weekend. I took everything out on you, and I shouldn't have done that.'

'No, I'm sorry. I should have handled things differently too,' I say, a wave of relief washing over me.

'I've gone over things a thousand times in my head all week. We can't take sides.' Joe shakes his head. 'The only people who know what goes on in their relationship are the people in it.'

'Agreed.' I nod.

'So, I think going forward we have to respect that, and support both Matt and Sophie but not let their issues come between us.'

'I don't want them to, I really don't. I hate it when we fight.'

'Me too.' Joe pulls me into his arms and kisses me deeply. I kiss him back, enjoying the warmth of his lips on mine. It seems like a long time since we kissed like this, since I even touched Joe, and I can feel the huge void that's been between us disappearing.

'I really missed you,' Joe whispers in my ear as his hand reaches up under my t-shirt and he strokes the curve of my lower back. A tingle shoots down my spine. 'Let's go to bed,' he says.

'But I bought dinner and everything.' The instant that the words are out of my mouth I realise how stupid I sound, mentioning food in the middle of a passionate embrace, and I giggle.

Joe laughs softly too. 'You bought dinner?'

'I thought I should be all housewifey, given that you've been away all week.' I shrug, not adding that I was unsure what might greet me when Joe came home this evening.

Joe laughs harder now and takes me by the hand, leading me up the stairs. 'Whatever it is, we can eat it later, once we've worked up an appetite.'

In the bedroom, Joe begins removing my clothes quickly and with ease as I fumble with the belt on his trousers. In seconds I'm naked. He lays me down on the bed and takes off his shirt, before he lies over me and strokes my cheek with the back of his hand.

'I do love you,' he says as I look up into his eyes.

'I love you too,' I say, and then Joe gently eases himself between my thighs and he pushes himself inside me and we make love. It's fast and frantic, and Joe's lips find mine and he kisses me as we move together, releasing all the pent-up emotions from the last week. I gasp, lost in the moment, lost in Joe, and cling on to his shoulders as we reach a climax.

We lie there, panting, in each other's arms, and then Joe rolls over and lies next to me, and I rest my head on his chest, listening to his rapid breathing as I try to calm my own hammering heart. I feel momentarily light-headed and a little wobbly; maybe from the love-making, but also from the realisation that Joe and I are going to be okay, that we have moved past the awkwardness of last weekend.

'So, what did you get us for dinner?' Joe asks a few moments later, propping himself up on his elbow.

'I got steak, and Prosecco,' I say proudly.

Joe raises his eyebrows. 'Very nice.'

'And cheesecake.'

'Even better.'

'And I'm going to cook,' I continue.

'Maybe you should just pour the Prosecco and I'll sort out the steaks.'

I open my mouth to protest, but think better of it. That's probably a good idea, given that my skills in the kitchen don't usually extend to grilling meat and instead are limited to opening a bottle of wine, using the coffee machine, and occasionally boiling some dry pasta.

'Come on then; I'm starving.' Joe taps my thigh and then rolls off the bed. He opens the wardrobe and takes out some jeans and a sweatshirt.

I nudge my legs around to the edge of the bed. My thigh muscles twinge. 'Ow!'

'What's wrong?' Joe asks, pulling on his jeans.

'Um, nothing,' I say dismissively.

Joe looks at me curiously. 'Emma?'

I suck in my cheeks. 'I went running,' I say.

'You went *running*? Alone? You didn't go out in the dark, did you?'

Well, it wasn't dark when I started running, I think, but I don't say that out loud.

'I joined a running club,' I state.

'You joined a running club?'

Joe looks at me like I'm an alien. Although I kind of understand why, given that in the eight years we've been together I only sort of went for a jog once, I still find myself a little offended.

'You seem surprised,' I say, my eyebrows raised in good-natured challenge.

Joe takes a moment before answering, and when he does his face has a more neutral expression. 'Maybe, but that's great – as long as you're safe,' he says.

'They give you a running buddy, so you're not running on your own, and Simon might come with me next week.'

'Simon? Running?' Joe chuckles. 'Having seen his Hawaiian shorts and bright pink t-shirt at the twins' birthday party, I dread to think what Simon would wear to go running.'

I think for a moment, and then cringe. Maybe Simon just said that in the moment and he won't actually come with me.

'Anyway.' Joe pulls me up from the bed. 'We'd better get you lubricated with Prosecco or you might cease up completely.'

'That sounds like a good idea.' I pull on my dressing gown.

'And I'll make a start on the steaks.' Joe grins.

'Fair enough,' I say.

We have a lovely evening, eating steaks perfectly cooked by Joe and amazing cheesecake while we chat about nothing in particular. No work talk, no Sophie-and-Matt talk, just me and Joe snuggled on the sofa. Until he says:

'I'm sorry, Em, I'm knackered – it's been a really long day. Shall we go to bed?'

We lie in bed, Joe's arm wrapped casually over me, and it's not long before I hear his soft breathing as he falls asleep. My eyelids are heavy too, and as I drift off to sleep my last thought is that, after my earlier fears of what Joe coming home might bring, it's been a perfect night.

I wake in an empty bed and hear the faint sound of coffee grinding downstairs. The room is bright from the early-morning sunshine and I can hear birds chirping outside. I smile as I pull on my dressing gown and pad downstairs. Joe meets me in the hallway, already dressed in shorts and a t-shirt, a mug of steaming coffee in his hand.

'I hope that's for me,' I say.

Joe hands me the mug. 'Of course. I'm going to drive to the country park and go for a run in a minute.'

'Okay.' I take a sip.

'And then maybe call in on Matt on my way home.' Joe shrugs. 'See how he's doing.'

'Good idea.' I nod. 'Maybe I'll check on Sophie and Florence too, and we can meet back here at lunchtime and go for a meal at the local pub?'

See, it's working already, our being supportive of both Matt and Sophie.

'That sounds nice.' Joe kisses me on the cheek.

'I'll text Sophie.' I wander through to the living room and flop down on the sofa. My mobile phone is on the coffee table.

Hi, do you fancy coffee and a catch-up this morning? I text.

I switch on the television and flick to the news while I drink my coffee. The news presenter is talking to a very slim and glamourous blonde about a new way to lose weight. The blonde woman seems very animated, so I turn up the volume.

'You can lose weight easily with the new fasting diet.' She beams. Fasting diet?

'You fast on a couple of days of the week and the weight will just drop off!' she continues, excitedly.

The weight will just drop off? I'm sure it will, because I'll actually be dying of starvation. In fact, that's not how it would go for me. I get angry if I skip breakfast. Forcing my body to fast for days would result in one of two things: either I'd be that angry, having not eaten, that I'd be arrested for murdering the first person who pissed me off or I'd eat them.

'Shut up,' I tell the television, and I press the mute button and go back to sipping my coffee, ignoring the still-animated stick insect as she rambles on.

Joe pops his head around the door. 'I'm off for my run.'

My phone buzzes, and I look down at the screen and read the text message from Sophie:

Sounds great. Meet you at the usual place in half an hour?

'Okay. I'm going to meet Soph, so I'll see you back here at lunch-time.'

'See you later.' Joe disappears and I hear the front door open and close.

I send Sophie a text back:

See you in half an hour. xx

I have a quick shower, pull on a casual navy dress, and apply the bare minimum of makeup required to make me look like a human so that I won't scare children and old ladies in public. Then I grab my keys and head out the door to my car.

I'm in a really good mood this morning, so I turn up the radio and tap the steering wheel to the beat of the nineties' dance tunes.

A short while later, I arrive at the coffee shop where Sophie and I usually meet. I glance around but can't see her, so I make my way over to the counter to order.

'What can I get you?' a young guy with an incredibly strong Scottish accent greets me. At least I assume that's what he says, given that I'm in a coffee shop at the ordering point. In any other circumstances I would have to embarrass myself and ask him to repeat himself (probably about three times, before admitting defeat and just smiling at him and hoping the powers of telepathy would be enough for us to communicate).

'Two cappuccinos, two chocolate twist pastries and...' I stare down at the fridge of drinks in front of me. What can three-year-olds drink?

'Yes?' the barista prompts.

'Um, one of those fruit water things for kids.' I point.

I pay, and then collect the drinks and pastries on a small tray from the end of the counter, before taking a seat at a table for four at the far end of the coffee shop. I'm just about to text Sophie when I see her bustling through the door with Florence in her arms. I wave to catch her attention, and she smiles at me and heads over to where I'm sitting.

'Hi.' She settles Florence on a chair opposite me and then hugs me. 'Thank you for suggesting meeting up. I feel like I've got cabin fever after being stuck in the house for the last few days.'

'Sorry,' I say as she releases me and we both sit down. 'I thought we'd be able to spend more time together while Joe's in London all week, but it doesn't seem to have panned out that way.'

'It's not your fault.' Sophie waves her hand at me. 'I have Florence and couples' therapy, and my mum keeps popping over to make sure I haven't hung myself from the shower curtain rail.' She laughs, but I don't.

'Soph, you're not...' I don't even know how to say the words. It never occurred to me that Sophie could be struggling with things so much that she would do something stupid and hurt herself.

She shakes her head. 'I'm fine.'

I raise my eyebrows at her.

'Honestly,' she says.

I nod. 'I got you a coffee and a pastry,' I say, pushing the plate and mug across the table towards her.

'Thanks, I'm ready for this.' She takes a huge bite of the pastry while simultaneously opening a packet of white chocolate buttons for Florence, pulling a colouring book and a handful of wax crayons from her handbag and placing them on the table, and putting a straw in the top of the fruit water. Multitasking at its finest, and something I can only aspire to.

'Can I do something to help?' I offer.

'What? No, I'm used to doing three things at once.' Sophie laughs. 'Tell me, how you are? How's Joe being with you after last weekend?'

'It's all good,' I say, taking a drink of my cappuccino. 'We talked things thorough and we made up.'

'Oh, Emma, I'm so relieved. I couldn't stand being the reason that Joe was mad at you.'

'I think it's just everything, Soph,' I say. 'I mean, it's hard with Joe away – everything feels more pressurised. It seems like two minutes between him arriving home and going back to get his train. But we're managing, I guess. The clock is counting down, so it won't be too long until he's back home for good.'

'Is he enjoying it? The project, I mean?'

'Yeah, I think so. He says he misses me, but they've made him feel really welcome in the London office, and it's good for his CV. And we're making the most of our time together when he is back.' I blush at my own words, which is silly given that Sophie is my best friend.

She grins at me. 'I'll bet.'

'He'd barely made it through the door last night before he was leading me upstairs to the bedroom.'

'That doesn't sound like talking things through.' Sophie chuckles. 'But that's the best way to make up from an argument.'

'Sorry, I wasn't thinking,' I say, suddenly conscious that Sophie's relationship is on the brink. Here I am boasting that my boyfriend can't wait to get me into bed, and I'm pretty sure that it's going to take more than that for Matt and Sophie to make up, if they can at all.

'Don't be silly, Emma. I want things to be normal between us, I *need* things to be normal. Every other aspect of my life is upside down – you are the one constant that I can count on.'

I reach across the table and squeeze her hand. 'How are things between you and Matt?' I ask.

Sophie glances at Florence, who is busy stuffing chocolate buttons into her mouth, and gently stokes her hair. 'A little better, I think.'

'Really? That's good.'

'We had another therapy session this week, and afterwards he asked me to go for a drink, so we went to the pub across the road and just had a beer and talked.'

'What about?'

'About some stuff that we touched on in the therapy session. About what happens if we both decide to stay together and make a go of things.'

I think back to the conversation I had with Matt when I saw him while grabbing a latte. 'And is Matt open to that?'

'He seems to be. I mean, he says he needs to take things slowly. I guess we both do. I still have to live with what I've done, what I risked, and that's not easy. I still look at myself in the mirror some days and don't recognise the person looking back at me. I find it hard to accept what I've done.'

'At least you can say that you told the truth,' I say.

'What do you mean?'

'He didn't find out that you'd cheated; you told him. You could have said nothing and hoped that he would never find out.'

Sophie shakes her head. 'I could never have done that. The guilt of the deceit would have driven me crazy. Do you think I shouldn't have told Matt? Do you believe that what people don't know won't hurt them?'

'Honestly, I have no idea, Sophie. I always had a very simplistic view of adultery: it's wrong; you don't do it.'

She nods, drinking her coffee.

'But what do I know?'

She cocks her head questioningly.

'I've never found myself in that situation, so I can't be sure what I would do. I know what I *think* I would do, but if this situation with you and Matt has taught me anything it's that I have no experience of this and therefore no right to judge anybody for their actions.'

Sophie smiles. 'Thank you. You don't know what it means to hear someone say that.'

'I'm not saying I approve of cheating,' I tell her. 'But I accept that there are reasons I may not be able to appreciate that make someone do that.'

'I understand.'

'So where does this leave things with you and Matt?'

'We keep going. We have some more sessions, we keep up a dialogue and hopefully we're able to move forward.'

'And have you, um, talked about why, um...?' I look over at Florence, who grins a white-chocolatey grin at me.

'Why I did what I did?'

'Well...yes.'

'I don't know. Maybe I lost my mind for a moment. Maybe I had a mid-life crisis, whatever that is. I don't remember consciously making a decision to have an affair; it just kind of happened. I got carried away in the moment. When I was with that other guy, I was out of my life, out of reality, and it was a weird feeling of escapism – an addictive feeling. I liked how being with him made me feel.'

'I didn't know that you needed escapism, that you wanted to be out of your life,' I say quietly.

'Neither did I until I was, and then I was right in the middle of this parallel life and it was like I was in my own movie, like it wasn't real, and maybe that's how I justified it initially with my conscience. Then reality hit me and I regretted it instantly.'

'I'm not sure if I should be asking you this, but...' I look up at Sophie and meet her gaze. 'Have you seen him since? This guy?'

She shakes her head vigorously. 'No. As soon as I told him it was over, I blocked his number from my phone.'

'I think that's for the best,' I say.

There's a moment of slightly awkward silence between us and I realise that neither of us is comfortable with this conversation. I'm reminded, not for the first time, that it's hard on everybody connected to a couple when their relationship breaks down.

'So, what else is going on with you?' Sophie asks. 'How's that annoying guy at work – Jarrod, is it?'

'Yes, and thankfully he's less annoying.'

'Oh, good. What changed?'

I can't help but giggle. 'Well, if you believe Simon's theory then all it took for Jarrod's personality to do a one-hundred-and-eighty-degree turn was him getting it on with his girlfriend.'

Sophie laughs. 'What?'

'Simon suggested that it was sexual frustration and Jarrod was taking it out on me and Jenny because we're women.'

'Simon has such a simplistic view of the world.' Sophie exhales. 'And usually it rotates around sex.'

'I know, but this time he might have a point.'

'Really?'

'Yeah. It would appear that the minute Jarrod started dating this girl, he turned into Mr Polite and Jolly.'

'How do you know he's dating someone?'

'Because he talks about "we" now and not just himself.'

Sophie presses her lips together. 'I see.'

'I guess everyone needs some kind of validation.' I drink the last of my cappuccino. 'Look, changing the subject a little, you said you feel like you've got cabin fever.'

'Well, it's just that it's only me and Florence, and there's only so many times I can watch *Peppa Pig* before I think I might go mad.'

'Why don't you meet up with my friend Jenny?' I suggest. 'You already know each other pretty well. She's found it hard coming back to work full time and leaving Darcy.'

'It is hard. You feel so guilty leaving them.' Sophie strokes Florence's cheek and Florence giggles. 'But you also desperately need adult company and conversation.'

'I'm sure that Jenny would appreciate spending time with someone who's actually experienced what she's going through,' I say. 'Not that I don't care – it's the complete opposite. But I can only offer my opinion and be supportive; I can't share my experiences, given that I'm not a mum. It might do you both some good to meet up.'

Sophie smiles. 'I think you might be right. I'd love to arrange a playdate. How old is Darcy now?'

'Nine months or so. I'll give you Jenny's number.' I reach for my mobile phone in my handbag.

I leave Sophie an hour later, having promised that I'll pop over one night during the week. Joe's car is already parked outside as I pull up at home.

'Hello?' I call as I step through the front door.

Joe appears at the top of the stairs in just his running shorts. 'Hi. I was just going to take a shower.'

'No worries. I'll be in the lounge,' I say. 'How was Matt?'

Joe looks thoughtful before answering. 'Doing okay, I guess.'

I nod.

'And Sophie?' Joe asks.

'The same.'

'Right, well, I'll be in the shower.'

He closes the bathroom door behind him. Perhaps it's better if our conversations about Sophie and Matt are limited to carefully worded snippets. I kick off my shoes, plod through to the lounge and ease myself down on the sofa, anticipating a muscle spasm at any moment. As I flick through this month's *Glamour* magazine, Joe's phone, on the arm of the sofa, beeps and I see the screen light up.

I freeze momentarily, suddenly overcome with an urge to look. Why? I've never looked at his phone before. I trust Joe. Don't I?

I glance up at the ceiling. I can hear the shower running above me. He'll never know if I just take a little look.

But you'll know. The annoying voice of reason pricks at my conscience.

It might be nothing – simply a text from one of the lads from football practice.

But it might be something.

I don't know Joe's password to unlock his phone, so the only chance I'll have to read the message is when the phone beeps for a second time as a reminder that there's a text waiting.

The shower is still running above me.

Beep.

It's a reflex: I lunge across the sofa and snatch up the phone. There on the screen is the waiting text. I read it. Blink. Refocus. Read it again. Then it disappears from the screen as if it was never there.

But it *was* there, and it isn't from one of the guys at football practice; it's from Joe's new work colleague. It's from Karen.

Hi. I've found a fab Italian for us to try! Looking forward to another week of spreadsheets. X

I feel like I've been punched in the stomach, the breath sucked out of me in an instant. My thundering heart is the only sound and it's ricocheting off every surface around me. I gulp, but my throat is too dry.

The shower is no longer running above me.

I look down at my hand, gripping the phone so tightly the knuckles are white, and I struggle to release my vice-like grip to place the phone back down where I found it on the arm of the sofa.

It's like every sense in my body is amplified. I hear each footstep above me as Joe goes from the bathroom to our bedroom, quickly puts on clothes and then comes down the stairs. I exhale, trying to steady my breathing and relax my facial muscles, as Joe comes into the room.

'What time do you want to go to the pub?' Joe asks, flopping down on the sofa next to me.

'Oh, um, I don't really mind.'

'Emma, are you okay?' Joe frowns at me.

'Of course.' I force a big smile. 'I'm fine.' I hope Joe can't hear the frantic beating of my heart. I reach for the television remote, simply for a distraction, and scroll through the list of channels, paying no attention whatsoever to the screen.

Joe is sleeping with Karen. All this time I've been focused on Sophie and Matt and I've only glanced at my own relationship; I took my eye off things and this is the consequence. I had misgivings about Karen before but dismissed them, figuring I was overreacting because Joe was away in London all week.

Pah! Overreacting? I don't think so.

'Emma?'

'Yes?' The smile is fixed firmly on my face again.

'I can practically see the cogs turning in your head. What's going on?'

I look straight at Joe. I contemplate just blurting it out and asking him right now what that text means. But then I'd have to admit that I'd looked at his phone and that's bad. But not as bad as sleeping with your co-worker! But if I ask him outright, I have no idea what he'll say or even if he'll tell the truth, and how will I deal with his answer? If I say those words 'Are you sleeping with Karen?' out loud then this becomes real, and what the hell happens if he actually admits it right now to my face?

'I'm just worried about Matt and Sophie,' I say, which isn't a lie.

Joe's expression softens and he nods. 'I know, me too. But they seem to be trying to work things out.'

'I guess so.'

'And although I've struggled with it, I've had to accept that people's relationships are between the two of them.'

Unless there's three of them, and one is called *Karen*.

'Sometimes you have to take a step back and let people get on with things, whether you want to or not,' Joe continues, sounding an awful lot like my mother.

I try not to focus on the stupid text I've seen, but it's no use. A vision of Joe and this *Karen* slapper wrapped in a passionate embrace keeps playing over and over in my mind like a bad movie on repeat. I find myself with a devil sitting on one shoulder and an angel perched on the other.

'*You're overreacting.*' The angel sighs at me and rolls her eyes. '*You know that Joe wouldn't cheat on you. You're letting your imagination run wild.*'

Yes, that's right. Joe loves me; he wouldn't cheat on me with Karen or anyone else. I'm just being silly.

A sharp prod from the devil jolts me from my thoughts.

'*You don't know what he's up to in London…miles away…in a hotel.*'

Argh!

'Come on.' Joe taps my leg 'Let's go now, I'm starving after that run.'

We have lunch at the pub, and I feel like I'm starring in my own movie. I listen as Joe chats about nothing much, and I make all the right noises showing him that I'm listening to his every word, smiling throughout, when the reality is that my mind is racing in overdrive as I try to portray the image of calmness and normality instead of a crazed woman on the brink of insanity thinking of Joe with another woman. Joe doesn't seem to notice and after a couple of hours in the pub we head home.

'Shall I see if there's a film on?'

'What?' I glance at Joe.

Joe cocks his head on one side. 'You were miles away.'

'Sorry, um, yes, that sounds good. I'll get us a drink.'

I take my shoes off and walk through to the kitchen, my stomach churning, as Joe heads into the lounge. I find a bottle of red wine in the cupboard and grab two glasses. As I pass the fridge a blurry image catches my eye and I stop in my tracks, facing the fridge door. A photograph of me and Joe at Christmas last year is pinned to the door with a heart-shaped magnet. My head is tilted up towards Joe and he's looking down at me, smiling. We're clinking Prosecco glasses, cheeks flushed, probably from too much Prosecco already that night, and we look happy; we were happy. Are we happy now? Is Joe?

I press my lips into a thin line and hold back the tears that are threatening to come. We *are* happy, and I need to get these thoughts of Karen out of my head. I carry the wine through to the lounge and place the glasses down on the table.

'There's that film you love about that fashion woman on in about five minutes, if you want to watch that?' Joe says.

'Great.' I open the wine and start to pour. 'That sounds perfect.'

I hand him a glass of wine and we snuggle together on the sofa. I take a sip and glance sideways at Joe. He looks at me too and smiles. I smile back. I need to trust the angel and dropkick that devil from my other shoulder.

Chapter Twenty-One

Once Joe has gone back to London on Monday, we exchange texts over the next two days. On the surface, it looks like perfectly normal electronic correspondence between two people in a relationship, but I'm scrutinising every word. Does he mean it when he says that he misses me? Is he secretly with Karen while he's texting me? Are they both having a good laugh about how gullible I am? It's both emotionally and physically exhausting.

Already this feels like a tense week, and so when Wednesday – my day off from work – finally arrives, I decide to have a morning of complete relaxation and pampering to recuperate and reset my overworked emotions. With no alarm set, I still, annoyingly, wake at seven thirty a.m. After scowling at the clock, I close my eyes and try to drift off back to sleep, imagining myself on a sun-lounger at the beach, the sea softly lapping the sand and the sun beaming down on me.

Mmm, I really need a holiday.

I squeeze my eyes closed tightly and go back to my sun-lounger and add a cocktail in too. Maybe a Cosmopolitan. Yummy.

Beep! Beep! Beep! Beep!

A loud noise interrupts my sunny dream, nearly making me spill my imaginary Cosmopolitan. I squeeze my eyes shut again. Whatever it is will go away.

'This vehicle is reversing,' a recorded voice booms loudly outside the house.

Then I hear the scraping of wheels on the pavement. Bloody bin men! Can't they be quiet? It's seven thirty a.m., for God's sake!

I drag a pillow over my head to block out the noise, but it does no good. The moment is ruined. I'm now far too awake to go back to sleep and to the solace of my sun-lounger. I throw the covers off in a huff and roll out of bed.

Right.

I sit on the edge of the bed and tap my fingers.

I know, I'll have a soak in the bath; that will be relaxing.

I get up and head to the bathroom, where I pour a glug of bath oil into the running water and slather a bright-blue clay face mask onto my skin. Then I head downstairs to collect the latest copy of *Glamour* magazine from the front room and a bottle of water from the fridge.

A few minutes later, I slide into the warm, fragrant bath water, instantly relaxing. I prop a rolled-up towel behind my head and open my magazine, ready to take in the latest fashion trends and beauty miracles.

Brrriiiinnng!

The shrill ring of the doorbell nearly makes me drop the magazine into the bath.

'Who the hell is that?' I say out loud.

I'm not expecting anyone. Whoever it is will go away.

Brrriiiinnnng!

The doorbell shrieks persistently.

'Are you kidding me?'

When it rings for a third time, I throw the magazine on the floor, my patience on the brink of running out, and I re-emerge from the bathtub, dripping wet and slippery from the bath oil, and fumble around for a towel. I wrap the towel around myself, chuntering under my breath, and stomp down the stairs and fling the door open, ready to unleash my anger on whoever is on the other side and daring to interrupt my peaceful morning.

A large man in a luminous yellow jacket takes a step backwards and looks at me with alarm.

'Yes?' I snap.

'Um.' He looks around, then up, then down, not meeting my gaze, which I admit may be a little more of a crazy stare.

'What can I help you with? You've rung my doorbell incessantly, so what do you want?' I pull the towel a bit tighter around myself, realising that I sound a bit curt, but I haven't asked him to land on my doorstep.

'Um, well, there's a delivery,' he fumbles.

'Delivery? There must be some mistake. I haven't ordered anything.'

He looks down at the paperwork on the clipboard in his hand. 'Are you Miss Emma Story?'

'Yes,' I say, getting way past the end of my patience.

'Then you have a delivery.' He gestures at a box behind him on a wheelie trolley that's so huge it could practically fit a person standing up. 'Where do you want it?'

The response that springs to mind isn't appropriate. I think carefully before answering. Maybe Joe has ordered something and forgotten to tell me about it. Maybe it's a surprise.

'Just inside, I guess.' I open the door wider to allow him to manoeuvre the giant box through the doorway.

'Right, there you are.' He shoves the box forward, nearly knocking me over in the process, and I swiftly dive backwards to avoid a second impact, clinging to my towel for dear life. 'All done,' he says, rubbing his hands together. 'Just sign here, please.'

He offers me the clipboard, and I reluctantly take it from his grasp and sign my name with a ballpoint pen attached to a piece of string.

'Cheerio then,' he says, and gives me one last, weird look as I close the door on him.

And then I see it. I catch my reflection in the hallway mirror, which was previously hidden behind the open door, and there, staring back at me, is the face of a blue Smurf. The clay mask is dried to my face like a horror mask in all its glory.

Well, that's just marvellous. No wonder he was looking at me like I was a lunatic; I *look* like a lunatic.

I shake my head at my own ridiculousness and turn my attention to the massive box that now fills the hallway. It has my name on it, but to the best of my knowledge I haven't placed an order for anything, and given the size of the box, I'm guessing that I would remember doing so, as it would have made a huge dent in my bank balance.

After a brief inspection I realise that I'm going to need scissors to help remove the vast amount of brown tape that is wrapped around the box. As I return from the kitchen, scissors in hand, I pause as a thought crosses my mind.

What if I open the box and someone jumps out at me, like those people in surprise cakes at birthday parties or a stripper at a stag do?

But why would someone send me a person in a box? Wouldn't they suffocate in there with no air and all that tape?

Is that my mobile phone ringing? It's still early. Who would be calling me at this time? Maybe it's Joe.

I put the scissors down on the floor and head upstairs to the bedroom to retrieve my phone. It's not Joe.

'Hi, Mum,' I say into the receiver.

'Morning, darling,' she says brightly down the phone. 'I've had a text message to say that it's arrived.'

'What's arrived, Mum?'

'My delivery, Emma. The text says it was confirmed as delivered about three minutes ago.'

And then the penny drops.

'You mean that the huge box that's just arrived and is clogging up my hallway is for you?'

'Well, of course, darling. I did mention that I was having a delivery,' Mum says dismissively.

'Um, no, Mum, you didn't.'

'I'm sure I told you when we last spoke.'

I inhale and exhale. 'That's not really the point, Mum. Why would you be having a delivery in the UK when you live in New York?'

I start to walk back downstairs.

'Haven't you opened it?'

'I was getting around to that,' I say, deciding not to mention my hesitation through fear a human being would pop out of the box the minute I released the tape from the edges.

'It's for the house, Emma,' Mum says as though I should know exactly what this means.

'What house? You haven't got a house yet. Have you?' I'm beginning to wonder if I've completely blocked from my short-term memory a conversation with Mum where she explained all of this to me.

'No, Emma, that's also why I'm calling you. We've had an offer accepted!'

'Oh, wow, really?'

'Yes, Parker and I will be residents of the UK within the next three to four months. We'll only be about twenty minutes' drive from you and Joe. Isn't that exciting, darling?'

'Yes, um, of course,' I stutter. I knew this moment was coming, so why it feels like a complete surprise I don't know. Maybe because Mum has lived in New York, on a different continent to me, for so long that I never really thought we would live in the same country again, let alone only a twenty-minute drive from each other. I suddenly feel overwhelmed and emotional.

Hang on a minute.

'How did you know that I'd be home today?'

'A lucky guess. And I knew you could always collect it from the depo if you were out.'

'Collect it from the depo? You do realise that I drive a small hatchback and not a transit van, don't you?'

I'd have liked to have seen the large luminous-jacket man and his clipboard try to get that box in the back of my car.

'Anyway, Emma, I must dash. Love you.'

The phone line goes dead, and I hover, still only halfway down the stairs. This is the strangest morning I've had for a while, if you don't count being woken up by a large cat snoring on your head. I wonder what the rest of the day has in store for me?

As if on cue, Banjo appears by my feet from nowhere, ninja-like as usual, and frightens me half to death.

'Meow!' he shouts, looking up at me impatiently.

'Okay, okay, Banjo.' I plod down the stairs – with difficulty, as he slaloms between my legs and I nearly tread on his tail. 'Breakfast is on the way. Let me just see what's in this huge box.'

I tear off the tape and peer in but all I can see is bubblewrap. I'm tempted to dig further but stop myself. Although my mother thinks it's fine to use me as her storage department that doesn't mean I can rummage through her stuff. Does it?

I see a brochure tucked into the bubblewrap. I pull it out and flick it open. Beautiful home furnishing stare back up at me from the pages. Mmm, Mum has good taste. Then I catch the price list – ouch – and very expensive taste.

Chapter Twenty-Two

'So, what do you talk about in these sessions?' I ask tentatively as I sip my cup of tea at Sophie's house the next day after work.

Sophie shrugs. 'It's kind of about exploring our relationship and looking at our roles within it.'

'Okay,' I say, but I can feel myself frowning. 'Isn't it weird talking about such intimate things with a complete stranger?'

'It was at first, but she's helped us to look at our relationship from a different perspective.'

'How so?'

'We have to own the role we play and acknowledge our flaws. It's not like there's one specific reason why people cheat, Emma.'

'I guess.'

'People have affairs for a number of reasons. It's not always about the person they're cheating on. It can be very much about the person who's doing the cheating, and not really anything to do with the partner they're being unfaithful to.'

'I'm sorry, Soph, but how can it not be about the partner being cheated on?'

'It's not like people wake up one day and suddenly hate their wife or husband or whatever and decide to sleep with the next person they find attractive.'

She looks at me like this is the most obvious thing in the world, and I decide at that moment that it's probably better if I keep my mouth shut.

'People can stray for reasons that are purely about themselves; for example, a need for validation, a lust-based attraction to someone else, the thrill of the chase.'

I press my lips together, maintaining my silence.

'Sometimes it's a chemical reaction with someone you meet – it's pure science; you can't explain it. Or perhaps someone looks for something outside their relationship to fill a void that they didn't even know was there.'

My heart skips a beat. 'Is that what happened with you? Were you trying to fill some void between you and Matt?'

'Honestly, I can't really explain it. I love Matt, and I'm still shocked at my behaviour, that I could hurt him like that. I can't say for certain what made me do what I did. Yes, there was a chemical reaction, and maybe I had been feeling downtrodden and unsexy…well, un-anything for a while. I sometimes feel like a robot, just going through the motions. Not because I don't love Matt and Florence, of course I do, but because I'm trying to do a million things and doing anything for myself is so far down the list that I never seem to get to it.'

Hearing Sophie talk like this makes me feel sad. To me, an outsider looking in, she had the perfect relationship, the perfect family. She always looks amazing, and she always seemed happy. I guess you just never know what's really going on in a person's life, even when it's your best friend.

'And maybe sometimes things go too far,' Sophie continues, 'and they snowball, and people end up in situations that they never intended to get into and never believed they would. I'm not saying that there's an excuse for being unfaithful; I'm just saying that there are many reasons why people are.'

Sophie reaches out and touches my arm gently. 'You can say something, Emma. You're allowed to have an opinion on this.'

'Am I?' I say. 'I don't know.'

'Don't know what?'

'Whether I have an opinion, or if I should voice it if I did.'

'You think you're going to hurt my feelings?' Sophie raises her eyebrows at me.

I nod. 'I don't want to do that.'

'Emma, you can't say anything to me that I haven't already said to myself over the last few months. Believe me, I know what I've done, and you can't make me feel worse about myself than I already do.'

I swallow.

'But part of the therapy is that I have to forgive myself too,' Sophie continues. 'As much as Matt needs to go through the process and decide whether he can forgive me and move past this – and I have to somehow accept that he may not – I also have to forgive myself. Otherwise we can never move on; it will always be hanging over us.'

'I guess I can understand that.'

'But…?' Sophie prompts.

I shake my head. 'It's strange, Sophie. I had such firm and specific views on cheating and then…'

'And then it involved people that you love.'

'Right,' I say. 'And now it's not so clear.' I glance at my watch. Damn it, I'm going to be late. 'But we'll have to continue this conversation another time, I'm afraid. I have to go. I'm sorry.'

'Okay.' Sophie hugs me goodbye. 'See you soon.'

'What on earth are you wearing?'

It's forty minutes later and I'm sitting in the driver's seat of my car and watching, open-mouthed, as Simon clambers into the passenger seat. He's dressed from top to toe in orange and black Lycra. It's Thursday again already, which means one thing: it's running club time.

'And what is *that*?' I say, pointing to the bright-pink headband nestling just above his eyebrows.

Simon reaches up to his forehead. 'It's a head torch,' he states simply.

'Okay, I'll play along,' I say as Simon pulls the car door shut. 'Why are you wearing a head torch?'

He looks at me, bewildered. 'In case we get lost and it gets dark.'

'Simon, we're going for a five-kilometre jog, not a hike up Mount Kilimanjaro. Just how long do you think it will take us? And more to the point, how do you think we're going to get lost when we have a running buddy from the club who hopefully knows the route pretty well?'

'You may mock me, Emma, but it's better to be prepared.'

I watch Simon as he adjusts his headband. As much as I'd love to, I can't argue with that logic, so instead I shake my head and start the engine, and we head to the running club.

We arrive and I find a parking space. I get out of the car and stand there in a normal fashion. Simon takes a different approach: the minute he's out of the car he begins bending over, swinging his arms around and generally looking like a complete weirdo.

'I'll be inside when you're done,' I say, rolling my eyes and walking towards the building.

'It's important to warm up and stretch,' Simon calls after me.

I wilfully ignore him.

As I walk through the doors I bump, literally, into Declan. 'Oh, hi,' I say, blushing instantly.

This has to stop happening. It's not that I find him attractive (well, I mean, of course I do; who wouldn't?), but I feel old and wobbly around him and like he's judging my physique and my lack of fitness with a simple glance.

'Oh, so who's this then?' I hear Simon's shrill tone behind me and I cringe inwardly. I do love Simon but…

I note the look of surprise on Declan's face. 'Declan.' I smile. 'This is my friend Simon. Is it okay if he joins us tonight?'

Declan's expression returns to neutral and he holds out his hand to Simon. 'Of course. Nice to meet you, Simon.'

They shake hands firmly. I swear I see Simon having a swooning moment and I roll my eyes at him for the second time in about three minutes.

'Are you a regular runner?' Declan asks Simon.

'Absolutely.' Simon stands with his hands on his hips, trying, I imagine, to look serious, but that's impossible in his attire.

'Great. Grab some water then and I'll see you both outside,' Declan says, before heading out of the door.

I look at Simon and hold my breath, waiting for the inappropriate comment I know will come. He links his arm through mine.

'I see what you mean, honey.' He glances over his shoulder. 'Mr Hottie certainly gets the pulse racing and I haven't even finished warming up.'

'Simon,' I plead, 'can we just get through this run without you sexually harassing the running instructor?'

'Honestly, darling, I don't know what you mean.' Simon looks offended.

'I'll repeat what I told you the other week: you have a husband, and you're old enough to be Declan's dad.'

'I am well aware of that, thank you, Miss Prissy. I have no intention of doing anything other than enjoying a run this evening. I love James with all my heart. Although if I was young, free and single, I would of course attempt to woo Mr Declan out there.'

'He might be straight,' I point out.

'Really?' Simon raises his eyebrows.

'Really,' I say, rolling my eyes for the third time. At this rate, I'll have strained my eyeballs before the night is over.

'Oh, honey.' Simon shakes his head. 'You're so naive. Gay? Straight? People show you what they want you to see, not always what they are.'

I am lost for words.

As it turns out, Simon is a great motivator for achieving my quickest run time, not because he inspires me to perform at my best, but merely because I want to get around the circuit quickly and get the hell out of there (which translates to 'get Simon and his shameless flirting away from Declan'), so I ignore my screaming lungs tonight and pick up the pace.

'See you guys next week.' Declan grins at us as we finish our stretching, post-run. 'Great run tonight, Emma.'

'Thanks.'

'And Simon, good to meet you.'

'Yeah, you too.' Simon winks.

I grab his arm and practically frogmarch him towards the car. 'What *are* you doing?' I hiss as we stop in the middle of the car park once we're far enough away that no one can overhear us.

'I don't know what you mean.' Simon removes his head torch at last.

'You were chucking yourself at Declan all the way around.'

Simon wafts a hand at me. 'Don't be silly, babe, we were just making small talk.'

'That wasn't small talk,' I say. 'Small talk is, "Hey, where are you going on holiday this year?" It isn't, "Do you want to go to that new nightclub where there's a strip night?"'

'It's not a strip night, it's strip musical –'

'I don't care what it is.'

Simon folds his arms across his chest, a sullen expression on his face. 'Alright, missy, what's wrong with you? And it isn't just me chatting to Declan that's got you so wound up.'

I bite my lip and breathe out, feeling tension creeping in across my shoulders.

'Em?' Simon's hands move to his hips.

'Oh, God.' I put my head in my hands. 'Do you have time for a drink?'

'I'm not sure that alcohol is advisable after a run, but what the hell – looking at you, I think I'm going to need it. Come on.' Simon walks towards the car and I follow. 'But only if you drop the attitude,' he calls over his shoulder.

Ten minutes later, we're nestled in a corner booth in a fairly quiet pub near Simon's house. I take a sip from my chilled beer bottle and peel the corner of the label.

Simon takes a swig of his beer. 'I don't mean to be rude, Em, but I do have two boys that I'd like to get home to kiss goodnight in about' – he looks at his phone – 'half an hour, so can we move it along a little please, babe.'

'Oh, Simon.' I tear a chunk of the label from the beer bottle in one swift movement. 'I did a bad thing, a really bad thing.'

'Oh no, you didn't attempt to bake again, did you?'

'What?' I look up at him. 'No. Don't be stupid.'

'Thank God for that. I'm not sure I've recovered from your attempt at a lemon meringue pie.'

'Simon! I'm not talking about bloody baking. This is much more serious.'

'Alright, alright. Calm down. What did you do?'

I take a deep breath. 'I looked at Joe's phone.'

Simon stares at me, nonplussed. 'I'm sorry, hun, you're going to have to be a bit more specific than that.'

I roll my eyes for the fourth time. 'For God's sake, Simon.'

He frowns at me.

'A text message came through to Joe's phone while he was in the shower and I *looked* at it.'

'Oh dear, Em, you don't want to go down that slippery slope.'

'Are you listening to the words that I'm saying Simon?' I sigh emphatically. 'I dangled at the top of that slippery slope, and then I went down it head first.'

'Ah, right, I see – you actually did look at the text. I've caught up. That's not good. Who was the text from?'

I bite my lip. 'From his new co-worker, Karen.'

Simon looks at me expectantly. 'And what do we know about *Karen*?'

'We know that she and Joe are spending lots of time together at work; they're both working on the same project.'

Simon shrugs. 'That doesn't mean anything.'

'They seem to be having dinner together fairly frequently too. The text was her suggesting a new restaurant that they could try.'

'That still doesn't mean anything.'

'Really? There was a kiss at the end of the text.'

'Emma, babe, I love you, so I'm going to be honest.'

'Okay,' I say warily.

'You're freaked out because of all this stuff with Sophie. We all are. None of us expected her and Matt to be having issues, let alone that one of them would have an indiscretion.'

'An indiscretion?'

Simon shakes his head at me. 'Anyway, what I mean is that your underlying trust in human nature has been rocked and now you're questioning everything, including Joe.'

'Maybe.' I shrug. 'Maybe that's not it, though.'

'I'd say that it's understandable to have a wobble, but you need to get over it.'

'Get over it?'

'Yes, if you don't want to cock things up with Joe, which I'm assuming you don't.'

'Of course not.'

'Then you have to trust him.'

I down the last mouthful of beer.

'I'm serious, Em. You don't think it's hard for him working away too?'

I think for a moment. 'No.'

Simon tuts. 'He's away from his home, alone, in a strange city, living out of a suitcase in a hotel room.'

'Yeah, and? Get to the bit where this is difficult for him.'

Simon frowns at me. 'God you can be a pain sometimes.'

I stick my tongue out at him.

'And petulant.'

'Huh! Pot, kettle?'

'Okay, maybe I can be petulant too, but the focus here isn't me, it's you, and you need to start looking at things from Joe's point of view too. He's probably missing home, missing you, missing Mr Whiskers.'

'Banjo,' I correct him.

'And he can't wait to get home on a Friday night, back to the girl he loves.'

I look at Simon sceptically. 'Men really think like that?'

Simon rolls his eyes at me emphatically. 'We're not robots, you know; we have feelings too.'

'Okay.' I supress a smile. Maybe Simon is right. I should take his opinions more seriously in future and stop listening to that stupid devil tapping its feet on my shoulder.

'And that's a sign of sexual frustration, you know.'

'What?'

He nods at my empty beer bottle. I've absentmindedly stripped all the labels from the bottle and they're in a crumpled clump on the table.

Simon nods, giving me a knowing look.

Maybe I won't take his opinions more seriously after all.

Chapter Twenty-Three

What's that noise? I force one eye open.

Where am I?

I realise that I'm in bed and I can feel Joe lying beside me. It's Friday night, or very possibly the early hours of Saturday morning. It doesn't feel that long since Joe got home, we had dinner and we came to bed.

The bleeping persists.

I reach my hand out from under the quilt and retrieve my phone from the bedside table.

'Hlo,' I mumble into the receiver.

'Em? Emmie? Emmmmmaa?' Simon's voice slurs in my ear.

'Simon?' I whisper, glancing over at Joe sleeping beside me. 'Hang on.'

I fling my legs over the edge of the bed and awkwardly force myself to an upright position without disturbing Joe. I pull on my dressing gown and slip out of the bedroom, softly closing the door behind me.

'Simon. What's wrong?' I ask as I tiptoe down the stairs.

'Key.'

'What?'

'Key.'

'Simon.' I flick on the kitchen lights, nearly blinding myself in the process. 'What on earth are you going on about? What key?'

'Door locked. Cold.'

'*What?* Simon, are you drunk?'

'Yes.'

'And you're phoning me at' – I glance at the clock on the kitchen wall – 'two thirty in the morning because…?'

'Oh dear God, Emma!' Simon warbles down the phone. 'You have my spare key. I am stuck outsiiiide. I need to get inside. I'm freezing my balls off out here!'

'Where's James?'

'Away. Are you coming or not?'

I sigh. 'Yes, I'm coming. Let me put some clothes on and I'll be right there.'

'Hurry up. I need the loo too.'

'Simon, you are ridiculous!' I admonish him, before hanging up the phone.

I dash upstairs and pull jeans and a jumper from the laundry basket in the bathroom, where I discarded them only a few hours ago. They're a little crumpled, but I figure at two in the morning I shouldn't be seeing anyone I know.

'Emma?' I hear Joe's groggy voice calling me.

I open the bedroom door. Joe's propped up on one elbow with the bedside lamp on. 'What's happening? Is everything okay?'

'Yes.' I wave a hand. 'Go back to sleep. It's just Simon. The stupid arse is drunk and has locked himself out. He needs me to go over with my spare key to let him in.'

Joe rubs at his eyes with the back of his hand. 'What time is it?'

'It's two thirty.' I shake my head. 'I have no idea where he's been until now.'

'I'll come with you.'

'No, don't worry. You've had a long day. Go back to sleep. It's only a ten-minute journey. I'll be back before you know it.'

'Are you sure?'

'Yes.' I switch the bedside lamp off, plunging us into darkness. 'I won't be long.'

I head back down the stairs and grab my car keys from the key rack. It feels freezing as I open the front door and hurry to the car.

As I turn on the ignition, I curse Simon repeatedly. How is it that he's drunk and locked out of his house? He's forty years old, a father and a husband, not eighteen and still living alone.

Maybe I'm being too hard on him. I mean, it's not like I'm without a history of unfortunate incidents. I think back to the time I fell through the door of a coffee shop and starfished on the floor surrounded by the contents of my handbag, and the time I drunkenly slept with a guy who turned out to be dating Sophie, and then there's the fact that Joe and I only met because I knocked him off his bike with my car.

Okay. So, I'm not perfect.

I pull up outside Simon's house a short time later. It's in total darkness and Simon is nowhere to be seen. Great.

I climb out and pull my coat tighter around me as I walk up to the front door.

'Simon?' I call quietly, conscious that it's nearing three a.m. and I don't want to wake up half the street. 'Simon, where are you?'

A figure leaps out in front of me and I instinctively let out a blood-curdling scream.

'Jesus, Emma, it's me.'

'Simon.' I whack his arm none too gently. 'You nearly gave me a heart attack.'

'What took you so long?'

'Took me so long? I've been fifteen minutes.'

'Never mind that. Are you going to let me in or not? I thought I was going to have to pee in a bush!'

The look of horror on Simon's face is just too much to take and I can't help it, I start laughing.

'This isn't funny.' Simon hops from one foot to the other, which does nothing to make it less funny and just makes me laugh harder.

'Emma!' Simon growls at me.

'Okay, okay.' I unlock the door and Simon pushes past me – not very gentlemanly – and rushes into the downstairs loo.

I go through to the kitchen and fill a large glass of water from the tap. Simon reappears and bounces off three surfaces as he stumbles towards me.

'Drink this.' I hold out the glass. 'And then you need to get into bed.'

Simon giggles, his eyes rolling from one side to the other as he lurches from surface to surface, sloshing water everywhere as he tries to prop himself up.

'Okay, clearly you're not going to do this by yourself.' I take in a deep breath and exhale. Undressing Simon and putting him to bed isn't something I thought I'd be doing now we're in our forties; in our twenties maybe, but we're grown-ups now.

Simon has slithered over to kitchen table and is leaning over it at a dangerous angle.

'Come on.' I lift one of his arms. 'Let's get you upstairs.'

I usher Simon unsteadily from the kitchen to the stairs, realising that the height/weight ratio is not in my favour and that drunk Simon seems to be even heavier than sober Simon.

'One foot in front of the other, Si, come on,' I say as we slowly climb the stairs.

'I had vodka.' Simon chuckles.

'Yeah, mixed with tequila and some gin too for good measure, I'm guessing.'

'Not alt'gether, silllly billy,' Simon slurs.

I'm breaking into a sweat by the time we reach the top of the stairs and Simon seems to be leaning more heavily on me by the second. My shoulder screams under his weight and I practically shove him towards the main bedroom.

He flops heavily onto the bed, face down.

'Oh no you don't. You can't go to sleep yet, Simon,' I say, tugging off his left shoe.

Simon groans and kicks at me, but I persist.

'Other foot.' I grab his right shoe and wriggle it from his foot.

'Need to sleepy now,' Simon mumbles into the quilt.

'Not yet.' I roll him over and undo his belt.

'Hey, Emmie.' He laughs drunkenly. 'I'm not that kind of guy.'

I roll my eyes and unbutton Simon's jeans. He chuckles softly to himself as I battle with him to remove them. It's worse than trying to undress the manikins in the shop. Finally, the jeans relent and Simon is lying on the bed in just his boxer-shorts and t-shirt, his eyelids fluttering heavily as he mumbles incoherently.

'Okay, now you get to go to bed,' I say, manoeuvring him one way, then the other, until he's under the quilt. I tuck him in, like I imagine he and James do with the twins each night. I'm thankful that James isn't here to witness this.

'I love you, Ems.' Simon snuffles as I look down at him. His blond eyelashes fluttering, he looks like he did when we were kids, innocent and angelic.

I shake my head. 'I'll be back in a minute.'

I go downstairs and back to the kitchen, where I refill the large glass of water.

Hmm, Simon doesn't seem in a fit state to drink from a glass. I know – I open each cupboard until I find what I'm looking for, a tube of stripy children's straws. I choose a red one and grab the glass.

When I reach the bedroom I find Simon still babbling to himself.

'You need to drink this,' I say, putting the glass on the bedside table. 'Sit up a moment.'

'No. Sleepy,' Simon says, his eyes still closed.

'Okay, we're going to have to do this the hard way.'

I roll back the quilt and, ignoring protests from Simon, I reach my arms underneath his armpits and drag him up to a semi-seated position.

'Open.' I poke his mouth with the edge of the straw.

Simon opens his eyes and struggles to focus on my face as he reluctantly takes the straw between his lips. He takes a long drink.

'A bit more.'

He drinks again.

'Enough.' Simon wafts a hand at me.

'Okay.' I place the glass on the table before helping Simon back under the covers.

He snuggles down, his head lolls to one side and he begins to snore softly.

I look down at him, then glance at the bedside clock. It's three fifteen a.m. I desperately want to go home and get back into bed with Joe. I haven't seen him all week and we have precious hours together before he heads back down to London. But as I watch Simon sleeping, I know that I can't leave him. I love him – I mean, not right now; right now I'm really angry with him. But if I leave and anything happens to him while he's in this drunken state, I would never forgive myself.

So, instead of going back to my warm bed and my boyfriend, I go downstairs to where I left my handbag and I retrieve my mobile phone. I text Joe, hoping that his phone is on silent so that I don't wake him and he just reads this when he wakes up in the morning:

Still at Simon's. I can't leave him alone in this state. I'm going to have to sit up and watch him all night to make sure he's okay and he doesn't choke on his own vomit or something. I'm really sorry. I'll be home as soon as I can. xx

I switch my phone to silent, just in case, and go back upstairs to the bedroom. I slide gently onto the bed next to Simon, careful not to wake him.

My phone screen lights up with a text from Joe:

Not a problem. Do you need me to come over? x

I guess Joe's not getting much sleep either. I text back:

No, don't worry. I'm just going to sit here until he wakes up in the morning with a raging hangover. Then I'm going to kill him! Go back to sleep. xx

A moment later, the screen lights up again:

Okay. Love you. x

I close my eyes as I fight exhaustion, but then force them back open. I push myself into a more upright position and decide to read the news on my phone to keep me focused and awake. As I scroll through the reports it occurs to me that a lot of the 'news' isn't newsworthy at all and we could, I'm sure, live a long and happy life never knowing about any of it.

Thankfully, time seems to pass quickly, and it doesn't feel too long before I see a sliver of daylight through the curtains. Although maybe that's because it was nearly sunrise anyway when I got Simon into bed.

I look down at him, still sleeping peacefully, and I shake my head. What was Simon thinking? I frown. I don't think he's thinking at all at the moment.

I continue to read the news, now moving on to sports reports about teams I've never heard of and have very little interest in.

As the clock on my phone ticks over to seven thirty a.m., Simon stirs beside me.

'James?' he croaks as he pats the side of the bed. 'Is there coffee?'

'Wrong on both counts,' I say.

Simon opens one eye. 'Em? Is that you?'

'I'm your knight in shining armour.' There's a hint of sarcasm in my voice. 'Also known as the idiot with your spare key.'

'Shit.' Simon closes his eye and rubs his forehead with his hand.

'I'll make some coffee. I know *I* need some.'

I stand up and have to rub my legs as they're stiff from sitting in the same position for the last few hours. As I walk downstairs and into the kitchen I can hear the birds chirping outside. Simon really does have a lovely home – and a lovely family. Where did he say James and the boys are?

Simon has an even posher coffee machine than I do, and as I stand in front of it, I have to rack my brain to remember what to do with it. I randomly press buttons and the screen lights up.

'Come on, you stupid thing.' I curse it, pressing the 'large black coffee' button repeatedly.

'It won't work if you manhandle it,' I hear Simon say behind me. 'You have to speak to her nicely.' He comes up beside me, but I continue to stare at the machine.

'Watch,' Simon says, and he places a mug underneath the spout and presses two buttons. The machine springs to life and starts chugging loudly, before ejecting steaming coffee into the mug.

'There you go.' Simon hands me the mug and I silently take it from him as he proceeds to make himself a drink.

I take a sip of the red-hot coffee and watch Simon lolling against the kitchen worktop, now, thankfully, dressed in pyjama bottoms along with last night's t-shirt.

'Am I going to get the silent treatment for the whole time you drink your coffee?' he asks, propping his chin up on his hand as he watches his coffee being poured.

'I'm angry with you,' I snap.

'I see.'

'Do you? Do you really "see", Simon?'

'Em, it's a little early to be getting your knickers in a twist, babe.'

'Don't "babe" me, Simon.' I take a gulp from my mug, instantly regretting it as the scalding liquid burns a layer of my mouth off. 'It's a bit early because I had to come over in the middle of the night after you called me to say you'd lost your keys.'

Simon huffs. 'You're the only person who has a spare key.'

'That's not true,' I say. 'Your husband, James, has a key. But I'm guessing you didn't want to call him at three a.m. to get him out of bed while he was having a night away from you and your craziness, wherever he is.' My voice is a few decibels higher than I intended.

Simon scowls petulantly at me. 'Is that what this is about? That you had to come over here and let me in?'

'No, Simon, that's not what *this* is about. *This* is because you were in a very drunken state, and alone – anything could have happened to you.'

Simon slurps his coffee noisily. 'Don't be silly, Em. I'm a grown man.'

'Are you? Is that why I had to carry you upstairs to bed and undress you? Because you're a grown man?'

Simon purses his lips, then goes to say something.

'I'm not done,' I carry on before he can speak, and he rolls his eyes at me, which angers me even more. 'I have very little time with Joe at the moment, as you well know, and I've had to leave him in bed and come here to deal with you, and now I'm tired.'

'And grumpy,' Simon interjects.

I down the last of my coffee and discard my cup on the worktop, before scooping up my handbag, which I conveniently left on the breakfast bar. 'Sometimes, Simon, you can be downright selfish, and you need to grow up.' I turn on my heel and head out of the kitchen towards the front door.

'If that's how you feel, missy, then why did you stay here all night?' Simon follows me down the hallway.

'Because for some reason I wanted to make sure you didn't choke on your own vomit,' I call over my shoulder as I reach the door.

'Emma.'

I stop, with the front door open, and turn around to face him. Simon is standing in the kitchen doorway, looking hungover and pathetic. I shake my head at him and shut the door behind me.

The drive home is quick; there's not much traffic around on a Saturday morning. I let myself into the house as quietly as I can and slip off my shoes as I step inside, closing the door gently behind me.

'Emma?'

Joe's voice comes from the living room and I pop my head around the door.

'You're up,' I say as I see Joe on the sofa, legs stretched out, a mug of tea resting on his thigh. 'It's been a ridiculous night.' I flop down next to him. 'I'm sorry. Simon was in a right state when I got there. I couldn't leave him.'

Joe screws his face up a little but says nothing.

'You think I should have left him alone and in a drunken stupor?'

'I think Simon shouldn't get himself into that kind of state.' Joe's tone is curt.

I'm slightly taken aback by his attitude. I didn't expect this from Joe. I'm tired and don't want an argument, so I decide to go for a diplomatic approach.

'I'm not disagreeing with you on that point,' I say, 'but the situation is what it is. There was no way I could have left him alone. What if something had happened to him? He could have fallen and hit his head.'

Joe shrugs. 'I guess so.'

We sit there in silence. Joe drinks his tea. I wonder how, from doing what I thought was the right thing and being a good friend, I've somehow ended up the bad guy in a hostile conversation with my boyfriend.

Joe speaks first. 'How come you're the one Simon comes running to every time he needs something?'

I frown. 'Because I'm his best friend and I've known him all my life. Plus I have his spare key.'

'Right.'

'Right?' I exhale. 'Surely you're not jealous of Simon? Because that's what it sounds like.'

'Don't be stupid.'

'So now I'm stupid, as well as Simon, it would appear.'

'There you go again, defending him.'

'I'm not defending him. Why would I need to defend him? This is ridiculous!'

Joe stands up, so I stand up too.

'What's this really about?' I say, trying to calm my voice even though I feel like screaming.

'It just seems to me like every time one of your friends shouts, you go running to them.'

'So you're angry at me for being a good friend.'

'It just feels like they come before us.'

I shake my head and my hands instinctively go to my hips.

'We don't have that much time together at the moment and –'

'That's not my fault, Joe.'

'So it's my fault that I want to help my career?'

I wave my hands, exasperated. 'It's nobody's *fault*.'

Joe stalks around the room, and I'm bewildered. It feels like I've walked into someone else's life here, because mine was fine and dandy when I left the house six hours ago.

'Do you know what, Joe? I think I'm going to go back out the door, get myself some air and then come back when, hopefully, my kind, caring boyfriend has reappeared.'

Joe looks down at the floor, and I walk out of the room, slip on the shoes that I kicked off quietly only a few minutes ago, grab my handbag and leave, ignoring a strong desire to slam the door behind me.

I walk down the garden path and turn left. About halfway down the street I realise that firstly, I have no idea where I'm going, and secondly, it's about eight a.m. on a Saturday morning, so wherever I'm going probably won't even be open yet.

I pause and glance back over my shoulder at the house, wondering if the smartest thing to do would be to just go back. No, I can't do that. I've made my point. I've walked out and nearly slammed the door behind me. There's no dignity in returning within thirty seconds, even if it is the smartest thing to do. And let's face it, doing the smartest thing has never been my speciality.

Instead, I continue down the street, picking up the pace until I'm almost powerwalking. My momentum takes me to the bottom of the road and left, along the main road towards the town centre.

A man with a large Alsatian walks towards me, and we do that funny dance thing where he steps to one side and I step to the same side so we're still standing in front of each other, blocking the path.

'Sorry, love,' he says as he steps to the other side, and I instinctively do the same.

The dog seems to tire of our merry dance, and it leaps up at me, standing up on its back legs and practically looking me in the eye, its large pink tongue lolling from the side of its mouth. A gargled scream comes from my mouth, and the dog owner glares at me.

'He won't bite,' he says, sounding annoyed, as the dog proceeds to bare his teeth while his claws dig into me.

'Oh, good!' I shriek as I try to prise his paws off me, very conscious of his huge fangs.

The man tugs the dog's collar. 'Come on, Colin.'

Colin? Seriously?

The dog licks his mouth and locks his stare on me, before finally clambering down, and I make my escape and hurry down the road. This day is getting worse by the second: not only have I had very little sleep and an unexpected argument with my boyfriend, but I now find myself covered in dog dribble and shivering in the chilly morning air.

Then, further up the road, I see the best thing that anyone could see in this situation and I sigh with relief – it's a coffee shop and it's glowing with light, like a beacon calling to me.

I scurry up to the door and quickly go inside. It's quiet, as you might expect so early on a Saturday morning. A guy with a huge beard is sitting in one corner with a newspaper, and a man dressed from head to toe in Lycra (because he's been for a run, I hope, rather than because this is his usual Saturday attire) is sitting a few tables away, also engrossed in a folded-up newspaper. I head into the ladies' toilets to wash the dog saliva from my hands before walking back to the counter.

'A cup of tea, please,' I say to the barista, 'and a toasted tea cake.'

I hand over the money and wait at the end of the counter for my breakfast. A minute later I collect the mug of steaming tea and the plate with my teacake on, and I walk over to a comfy-looking chair next to the window.

I spread butter thickly on the warm teacake and watch as it melts, but as it turns out I don't have much of an appetite. I drink my cup of tea instead as I look out of the window. The sky is cloudy and a bit grey. That's just what I need, for it to chuck it down on me as I walk home.

But I'm not ready to go home yet.

I'm surprised by Joe's reaction. He knows how close Simon and I are. He's never reacted like that before, and this isn't the first time that Simon has unexpectedly demanded my time. Admittedly, this was the first occasion at two thirty a.m. (well, since we were both much younger and irresponsible, which is how I ended up in possession of Simon's spare key in the first place).

It feels like everything is falling apart at the moment. Joe and I feel…I try to think of the word, and 'disjointed' is the only one that comes to mind. We knew it would be a challenge, him working away, but it's more inconvenient and difficult than I thought it would be. I miss him when he's not here, but when he is home it feels like I have to spend every minute with him because he'll be going again so soon. And now there's Karen in the situation somewhere – maybe in my head, perhaps in reality, but somehow there regardless. I don't remember Joe and me arguing as much before, certainly not like this.

I take another sip of tea and pull off a bit of buttery teacake. As I chew it, I move down the 'everything is falling apart' list. The next name on it is Sophie. I haven't seen as much of her as I usually would, and if I'm honest, that's because I've been avoiding her a little. I know that sounds selfish. She's my best friend and she's going through a huge crisis, but I don't know what to do to help. I know that affairs happen, and maybe more often than we think, but I'm still trying to understand how this happened. How a seemingly happy couple with a lovely life have ended up torn apart, and how Sophie can claim that she loves Matt when she's had her head turned by someone else.

And then there's Simon. Bloody Simon and his histrionics. Some days I find it amazing that he has a husband and two children. He swings between being a responsible adult and a petulant teenager.

But I love him, and he's the first person after Joe that I look to for support. He's been there throughout my whole life and he's picked me up when I've been down more times than I can remember. I guess I'll text him later to see if he's okay.

I finish off my teacake – despite my earlier lack of appetite it seems that I was hungry after all – and I drink the last of my tea.

I watch as a few more people filter into the coffee shop. It looks like both Beardy Man and Lycra Man are in no rush to leave, as they're still flicking through their newspapers. I do want to leave, though; I want to go home. I don't want to sit here, staring out the window as my thoughts churn unhelpfully around my head. I want to sort things out with Joe. He'll be heading back to London in twenty-four hours and I don't want us to spend the rest of today being mad at each other.

I pick up my handbag and head for the door. Once outside I realise that I made an epic fail when I stormed out of the house earlier – I should have picked up my coat; it's freezing out here. What happened to the lovely warm weather we've been having? I guess that's the annoying British climate, unpredictable and ever-changing.

I wrap my arms around myself to keep warm and walk briskly, but before I make it to the end of the street the heavens open and big, fat raindrops splash on the pavement, bounce off my head and run down my face.

'Are you kidding me?' I mutter and I start to sprint, the icy cold shower increasing my usual running speed.

I finally make it home and run up the path to the front door. I fling it open, step inside and close the door quickly behind me. As I shake myself like a dog, rainwater drips from every part of my body. My clothes are soaking and suctioned to me, and as I glance in the mirror next to the door I see that my hair is plastered to my head. Thankfully, due to my early-morning jaunt to Simon's, I'm not wearing any makeup, so there are no streaks down my face.

Joe appears in the living room doorway. He looks at me, slightly amused for a second, then his expression tightens. 'Hi,' he says quietly.

'Hi,' I say back nonchalantly, as though it's perfectly normal for me to be standing here in this state. I was expecting a fiery confrontation; however, Joe appears much calmer now than when I left.

'You should get a hot shower,' he says. 'You must be freezing.'

I nod and bend down to remove my sopping shoes, before walking upstairs. Joe watches me, but says nothing more, although as I reach the top of the stairs and look back at him, a half-smile crosses his face.

In the bathroom I peel off my wet clothes and turn on the shower, increasing the temperature by few degrees. The hot water feels nice as it pounds onto my head – in much the same manner as the torrential rain, but whereas the ice-cold rain shocked my nerve endings, the hot water soothes. I've never understood those ice baths at spas. Who wants to steam themselves in a red-hot sauna only to then plunge their body into ice-cold water? It's a wonder more people don't have a heart attack while doing that. Sophie once told me that it's good for your body to go from hot to cold, that it helps to improve your circulation or something. How, I have no idea, but after my freezing rain experience, I think I'll give it a miss.

I get out of the shower a few minutes later and wrap a large, fluffy towel around my head before pulling on my dressing gown. I hover at the top of the stairs, unsure what to expect from Joe. Over the years we haven't had many arguments, and I hate it when we fight. I hate the confrontation and the whole emotional upheaval that seems to linger and take days to recover from, even once you've worked things out and agreed to move on. I can smell freshly brewed coffee, so I pad down the stairs and go towards the kitchen.

I find Joe leaning on a kitchen worktop. He looks up as I walk in. We stand facing each other, Joe's lips pressed into a thin line, me biting my lip as I wait for him to speak first.

'I'm sorry,' Joe says. 'I overreacted. I don't know what I was thinking.'

I exhale, and the cold grip around my heart that I hadn't even realised was there until this point slowly releases. 'I'm sorry too,' I say. 'I didn't mean to put my friends before us, before you. It's just that Simon can be very –'

'Demanding?' Joe raises his eyebrows.

'I guess so. And somehow I feel responsible for him. We grew up together, both only children, and he's like the little brother I never had. I know that sounds weird, given that we're the same age, but I feel this overprotectiveness towards him and an overriding need to take care of him, even when he's being a total idiot.'

Joe nods. 'I know that.'

'It's not okay for him to call me in the middle of the night but –'

'It's not really about Simon.' Joe shrugs.

'Oh.'

'It's everything.'

I swallow. 'Everything?' As in me? Is he fed up of me and leaving me for Karen?

'All this stuff with Matt and Sophie, it's messing with my head.'

'Right,' I say. Is it good that it's about them? 'How is Matt?' I ask.

'Not good,' Joe says.

'You never talk about it, and I never ask because, well, I thought you didn't *want* us to talk about it.'

'It's weird, what with Sophie being your best friend. I feel like we're...'

'Stuck in the middle?'

'Yeah.'

'You think I don't feel like that too?'

Joe looks at me with a surprised expression. 'I assumed you would be on Sophie's side.'

'Sophie's side? I'm not picking a side, Joe – *we're* not picking sides, remember? Whilst I may have feelings on the situation, neither of us knows exactly what went on in Sophie and Matt's relationship. I'm trying to stay supportive of both of them, but it's hard not to want to try to fix it.'

'I know. It's killing me seeing Matt so unhappy.'

'Do you think he'll forgive her and they can move past this?'

Joe shakes his head. 'I don't know. He wants to, he really does, but it's too raw. He can't see past it right now.'

'Sophie says they're at least communicating in the therapy sessions. She says that she's devastated and she's deeply sorry.'

'I'm sure she is. But Sophie must have known the risk of this happening when she was' – Joe clears his throat – 'doing whatever with that other guy.'

'She didn't sleep with him.'

'She crossed a line.'

'I know, and it's bad, very bad. But I can't imagine she was thinking at all. I think the situation snowballed really quickly and Sophie got carried along with it. She put a stop to it the moment she regained her senses.'

'That doesn't make it right.'

'No, but maybe it makes her human.'

Joe frowns at me.

'People do stupid things. She made a mistake, Joe, and she knows it.'

'Well, it's a pretty big mistake, Emma.'

'Do you think that Matt should forgive her?' I ask, although I'm not sure what the right answer to this question is.

'That's not my call,' Joe says, and I guess he's right. 'So, where did you go earlier?' he continues. 'You know, before your rain shower?'

A smile pulls at the corner of my mouth. 'I just walked and ended up in a coffee shop about half a mile away. After getting mauled by a huge dog.'

'Of course,' Joe says with a completely straight face. The ridiculous things that happen to me no longer surprise him.

'It was nice. It might become my new favourite place.'

'I see.'

'So, are we okay?' I ask, unsure what the answer to this question is either.

Joe nods. 'We're okay. It's just hard at the moment. I love what I'm doing at work, but I hate being away from home, from you.'

I'm relieved to hear this, but the niggling devil on my shoulder prods me. *Maybe this isn't really about Matt and Sophie. Maybe this is about you and Joe. And Karen.* I bite my lip, waiting for the angel on my other shoulder to jump in and say something positive, but she just purses her lips and files her nails.

'I hate it too,' I say.

Chapter Twenty-Four

'Hello, darling,' Mum purrs down the phone the following Monday evening. We haven't spoken since the huge delivery incident.

'Hi, Mum.'

'What are you doing next week?'

'Um, working, and maybe –'

'Joe is still away, isn't he?'

'Well, yes, from Monday to Friday, but –'

'Oh good, that's settled then.'

'What? What's settled?' I don't remember there being a discussion, or a negotiation.

'I need to pop over to sign some paperwork for the house. I'll come and stay with you. It will just be for a couple of nights.'

'Pop over? Are you in England?'

'No, silly, pop over from New York.'

'Right, of course,' I say, thinking first that you don't just 'pop' three thousand miles from New York, and then that I'd better hoover before Mum arrives.

'Wonderful, darling. I'll check the flights and text you later. It will just be me; Parker will stay in New York. We can have some girlie fun.'

'That sounds good, Mum.' I smile into the receiver, forgetting that she can't see me.

'Bye for now then.'

'Bye, Mum.'

I hang up the phone. Usually, my mother coming to stay relatively unexpectedly would send me into a spin, but I'm looking forward to the distraction, and like Mum said, it will be a bit of girlie fun. Things have felt pretty intense on a number of fronts recently and a bit of escapism is more than welcome.

'My mum's coming to stay for a few days next week; something to do with the house purchase,' I tell Joe when we speak on the phone the following evening.

'That's good,' Joe says. 'It'll be some company for you.'

'Yeah, I guess.'

'I know what you're thinking.' Joe chuckles.

'And what's that?'

'That you're going to have to clean the house before she arrives.'

'Ah, well, that's where you're wrong,' I say smugly. 'I'm thinking that *we're* going to have to clean the house before she arrives.'

Joe laughs. 'How did I know that was coming.'

Chapter Twenty-Five

As I walk into mine and Sophie's usual coffee shop on Wednesday lunchtime, I see Simon sitting on a large brown chair at a table in the far corner and I head over. He catches my eye, and for a second he looks contrite, but that quickly passes and is replaced with nonchalance.

'Hello,' I say as I reach the table.

'You can take that condescending look off your face,' Simon says.

'I don't have a condescending look.'

'Oh yes you do. You're looking at me like I'm a child who's been caught stealing jelly sweets.'

I sigh and raise my eyebrows. 'Did you ask me here simply to argue with me?'

'No,' Simon answers petulantly. 'I got you a flat white.' He gestures at a cup on the table in front of us.

'Thank you. See, was it so hard to be nice?'

Simon purses his lips.

'I assume that I have your permission to sit down?'

'I bought you a coffee, didn't I?'

'Okay.' I exhale and sit in the chair opposite Simon. I take a sip of my coffee. 'What's the attitude for? Shouldn't it be me giving you attitude after the other night, not the other way around?'

'Last time I saw you, you told me to grow up and stop acting like a teenager.' Simon huffs, kind of making my point for me.

'That's correct, and I stand by my comments.'

Simon scowls across the table at me.

'You were drunk and had locked yourself out of your home – a home, I might add, that you share with your husband and two children. I think under the circumstances what I said to you was both accurate and appropriate.'

Simon takes a noisy slurp of his coffee.

'Look, I don't want to argue with you, but you need to tell me what's going on with you, Simon.'

'Oh, Em, I don't want to fall out with you either.' His whole body sags. 'I'm so sorry I've been so snippy.'

'Well, that's one word for it.'

'You know me, I get defensive when I've made a complete dick of myself and I try to project my anger at my own behaviour onto someone else, namely you.' He wags his finger at me.

'I know that.'

'I've always been the same.'

'I know that too.' Simon hasn't changed since we were five years old and at school together. 'So are you going to tell me what's going on with you?'

He shrugs. 'I don't know what's wrong.'

'Yes, you do.'

He looks at me with a pained expression.

'I can't help you if you won't be honest with me. That's how this works, Simon. So are we going to talk things through like adults?' I ask tentatively.

Simon rests his chin on his hand. 'I guess so, babe.'

'Do I take it that your mid-life crisis is over? What's going on? Are things okay with you and James?'

Simon looks forlorn. 'Can we refer to it as my "micro crisis", please? I behaved like such a dick.'

'I wouldn't be quite as harsh as that.' I press my lips together to supress a smile. 'Maybe just a…' I try to think of the right word.

'A dick.' Simon sighs.

'Okay, we'll go with your word. So how are things?' I ask.

'Well, my stupidity has led me to realise what a wonderful man I married.'

I smile.

'After James found me hungover and feeling sorry for myself, we had a heart to heart, and I opened up to him about some stuff that's been bothering me recently. He seems, for some reason unbeknownst to me, to love me regardless and to have forgiven my hideousness.'

'James is a good man, and a good husband.'

Simon nods. 'He is.'

'But you already knew that, Si.'

'I know.' He takes a sip of coffee.

'So why, again, were you behaving like an idiot? Getting drunk, going to nightclubs, flirting with my running buddy?'

Simon finishes his coffee while I look at him and wait for his answer. The truth is that I already know why he was behaving the way he was; I can read him like a book. But the thing with Simon is that if you try to tell him, to reason with him, before he's ready to acknowledge the situation for himself then he pushes back and erupts.

'You'll think I'm stupid, or crazy, or both.' He fiddles with his coffee mug.

'Maybe.' I shrug and give a half-smile. 'Maybe not.'

Simon bites his lip. 'I got scared.'

'Scared?'

'I'm, like, a forty-year-old dad.'

'That's true.'

'I mean, how? How did I get a husband and two kids?'

I wave a hand at him. 'Well, the simple answer to that is that a man asked you to marry him and you adopted two babies.'

I drink my coffee as Simon pulls a face at me. 'That's not what I meant, Em, and you know it.'

'Look, Simon, I get it, honestly I do.'

He looks at me sceptically.

'Let me take a stab at this. You woke up one day and looked around you, and you couldn't believe that you were in your forties and in the role of a responsible adult with mortgage payments, a husband, and two children with more energy than you ever thought kids could have.'

He frowns slightly.

'You found yourself tripping over Spiderman toys in a daze while trying to get everyone ready for work and school, and you couldn't remember when you stopped going out until three in the morning, it just felt like a lifetime ago – and a life you'd lost.'

Simon stares at me for a moment. 'You haven't been taking mind-reading classes as well while Joe's away, have you?'

I laugh. 'You're no different from me, or Sophie, or anyone else for that matter – well, maybe Sophie.'

'Yeah, I only flirted a little with Declan the running guy.'

'You flirted a lot.'

'Really?'

'It was embarrassing.'

'Okay, moving on.' He swats me on the arm. 'You don't have children; you only have yourself to worry about.'

'And Banjo.'

Simon giggles. 'Oh yeah, I forgot that you've become a crazy cat lady.'

'Cats are great company,' I say. 'They listen to your every word and don't argue back. And when I say "listen", I mean look at you with disdain until you give them a treat.'

He shakes his head. 'Who are you?'

'I don't think you're in any position to make fun of me. It wasn't so long ago that you were calling me in the middle of the night in a very drunken state and locked out of your own home. I haven't managed *that* yet.'

'Sorry about that. That was the worst of the things I've done. And do you want to know what the really stupid thing about it was? I was thinking of James the whole time and wishing he was there with me. Clubbing was no fun without him.'

'See, Simon, *that*'s how you ended up married,' I say.

He looks at me, confused.

I cock my head to one side. 'You fell in love, and life on the whole is much more fun when you're sharing it with someone.'

'Oh.' Simon screws his mouth up.

'So what possessed you to try to break that?'

He shrugs. 'I'm an idiot. Sometimes I forget how good I've got it. I regress back to being a child, and I panic.'

'Panic?'

'Yeah, like things are going too well and I don't deserve to be so happy, so I do stupid stuff to ruin things.'

'Why on earth do you think that you don't deserve to be happy?' I say, astounded.

'Do you remember when I first told people that I was gay?'

'Of course.' Simon was so nervous about telling his family, although I think they already knew on some level.

'Well, all I wanted was to find happiness, to find someone to love me for who I was.'

'And you found that in James.'

Simon sighs. 'I know.'

'Although you did do plenty of research first.' I smile.

'Exactly. I slept with every gay man in a ten-mile radius.'

'And your point is?'

'I did all that, and I still found a perfect man who loves me. He knows exactly who I am, and he doesn't care.'

'That's true. James loves you just as you are.'

'And we have the boys, two beautiful boys. And they look to me for help and guidance. How do I live up to that? I have everything that I've always wanted. Nobody gets everything that they want. What if the boys get bullied because they have two dads? That'll be my fault for being selfish and wanting it all.' He hangs his head.

'Simon.' I take hold of his hand across the table and squeeze it tightly. 'Look at me.'

He looks up at me through his long blond eyelashes.

'You're entitled to want it all,' I tell him, 'just like everybody else. Happiness isn't something that only certain people who tick a particular box get to have. Happiness is there for everyone to achieve, regardless of sexual orientation, ethnicity, religious beliefs et cetera; it's a state of being. You're entitled to be happy as much as the next guy. James makes you happy, but I see how happy you make him too. I remember the first time I met him – although I use the term "met" loosely.'

'I remember.' Simon shakes his head and tuts. 'You very nearly scared him off.'

Years ago, I called in unannounced at Simon's flat, only to find Simon and James on the sofa – naked. It's an image that I've tried very hard, and unfortunately failed miserably, to erase from my memory.

'As for the boys, they have two parents who love them unconditionally, and that's special. You'll show them the value of loyalty and friendship.' I smile. 'And how to be strong in the face of adversity.'

'I guess so.'

'And how to tell their Gucci's from their Prada's.'

'Of course.' Simon grins. 'Thank you, babe.'

I smile at him.

'How is Sophie doing?' he asks.

I shake my head. 'I never thought it would be that easy to cheat.'

'How do you know it was easy for her?'

I frown. 'Because she did it. It would have been harder to resist it.'

'Maybe.' Simon shrugs. 'Maybe not.'

'I can't believe that you're justifying it, Simon. Sophie cheated on her boyfriend. She risked everything – and lost out big time.'

'You don't think that Matt will forgive her?'

'I have no idea. I mean, I try to be positive for Sophie, but I don't know if it's something that I could forgive.'

'It was a kiss, babe. It could have been worse.'

'I think it was probably one glass of Prosecco away from being worse.'

'What is it that you're struggling with the most – the fact that Sophie cheated, or that she lied to you too?'

'She didn't lie; she just didn't tell me.'

'Deceit is deceit no matter how you dress it up.'

'I guess. It just feels weird. Sophie and I tell each other everything, and I had no idea. I thought things were a bit tense because she and Matt were both tired from working full time and raising a three year old. Never in a million years did I think that Sophie was lusting after someone else.'

'What does Sophie say? I mean, I can't ask her; I'm not supposed to know.'

'She'll know that I've told you.' I bite my lip. 'Matt's moved out, so there's no hiding it anyway.'

'Where's Matt living?'

'With a guy he and Joe play football with. He couldn't stay with us. It would be too weird. Joe's away for four days a week, so it would have been me and Matt on our own.'

'Which would have been ridiculous.' Simon nods.

'Exactly.'

'Is that why you're mad at Sophie? Because it affects you and Joe too?'

'Wouldn't that make me horribly selfish?'

'No, it would make you human, Em.'

I look at him sceptically.

'Come on, how could it *not* affect you and Joe? Sophie is your best friend, and Matt is Joe's brother.' Simon swills the dregs of his drink around. 'Do you remember when you and Joe were first together and you broke up, and then you found out that Sophie and Matt had started seeing each other secretly?'

'I remember,' I say. 'So what's your point?'

'Don't hate me for saying this.'

'But?'

'But they had to work things out even though things were bad between you and Joe. It must have put some pressure on them.'

'That's totally different. Neither Joe nor I cheated on each other.'

Simon looks at me and raises his eyebrows.

'And nobody *asked* Sophie and Matt to start seeing each other.'

Simon snorts. 'You sound like a child.'

I tap my fingers on the table.

'You're right,' I say. 'I need to get over myself and be there for Sophie. She made a mistake.'

'Yeah, it's hard when emotions are flying high. You and Joe are stuck in the middle of this situation whether you want to be or not. Sophie knows that too; she's not stupid. I'm saying, try to remain open-minded.'

'I'll try.'

'Look, remember when I thought James was cheating on me a few years ago?'

'And it turned out that he was planning a surprise mini break for the two of you?'

'I didn't say that it was my finest hour, Em.'

I chuckle.

'What I'm saying is, it can happen to anyone, even if you think you're really happy.'

'Well, that's a heart-warming thought. Does this mean I should really worry about this Karen woman and Joe?'

Simon sighs. 'No, I'm not going over this again with you. You need to trust Joe.'

'Like you did with James? Didn't you track him on some stupid GPS app on your phone?'

Simon blushes. 'Enough about that.'

I chuckle.

'I'm just saying that you have no reason to suspect Joe really. Although I do admit that we're all capable of doing unthinkable things, honey, even me and you. I mean, not *me and you* together, I'm gay, but...you know.'

I roll my eyes at him. 'I'll bear that in mind.'

I arrive home exhausted from my discussion with Simon. I don't know if that's because of the topic of the conversation or because Simon pushes me more emotionally than anyone else, maybe even Joe. He's always been able to get the truth out of me, even if it's kicking and screaming along the way.

I'm conflicted, I know this. I love Sophie, but I don't know how to deal with the situation we've all been plunged into and...

Oh no.

I stare at my reflection in the full-length bedroom mirror.

Well, that's just great. You think you've had a good day and then you realise that you've been walking around all day with the back of your dress not fully zipped up. Awesome.

I vaguely remember thinking this morning that I needed to fasten my dress completely before I left the house, but in the rush to grab a croissant and my usual caffeine fix, I simply forgot to twist myself into an origami swan to reach the half-fastened zip.

Joe usually assists me with things like that. I hate the fact that I need a man, in a practical way at least. How can it be that in the twenty-first century a strong, independent woman needs a man to get into her clothes properly? What on earth are these clothing companies thinking?

Chapter Twenty-Six

The next week goes quickly. Joe and I are in regular contact by text, and it appears that normality in our long distance relationship has resumed. The day that Mum is coming to stay soon arrives, so I head to the airport to collect her. When I arrive I pull into the pick-up and drop-off area and glance at my watch. Mum's plane landed about forty minutes ago, so she shouldn't be long. She'll only have hand luggage for a couple of days' stay.

As if on cue, Mum appears through the automatic doors, pulling a wheelie case that I'm sure is far too big to have fitted in the plane's overhead lockers. I wave, and Mum waves back and starts walking over to me.

'Hello, Emma.' Mum flings her arms around me, abandoning her large suitcase as she hugs me tightly. 'It's good to see you.'

'You too, Mum,' I say into the cerise scarf wrapped casually around her shoulders, making her look 'photoshoot ready' as usual. 'Come on, we'd better hurry up and get moving; there's a long queue of cars behind us.' I glance at the line of cars snaking all the way to the entry barriers to the pick-up area. Several drivers are tapping their steering wheel, looking frustrated.

'They'll wait, darling.' Mum swishes a hand dismissively.

'They have no choice but to wait, Mum, but that doesn't mean that they'll be happy about it.'

'Everyone is in such a rush nowadays,' Mum says as she removes her scarf and slides into the passenger seat, leaving me to sort her suitcase on the pavement.

I open the boot and stare at the suitcase. I'm no scientist, but I'm going to take a wild guess that the laws of physics mean that this suitcase is too wide and heavy for my short arms to pick up and place sensibly into the car. I look at the car behind me and the driver raises his eyebrows and makes a gesture with his hands which I interpret to mean 'Get on with it then'.

I grab the handle with one hand and count to three before scooping the bottom of the case up with the other.

'Jesus, Mum, what have you packed? Rocks?' I mumble, trying to direct the suitcase into the boot.

'Did you say something, Emma?' Mum calls.

I give the case one last shove and with a loud clunk it settles itself into the boot. Getting it out at the other end may prove even more of a challenge, though, as it completely fills the space. I close the boot and walk back around to the driver's seat, ignoring the amused look from the driver in the car behind.

'What took you so long?' Mum asks as I pull on my seatbelt.

I refrain from answering that question with a smart quip as I start the engine and pull away into the traffic queuing to get out of the airport car park.

'Maybe the fact that your case weighs more than me?' I say once we reach the exit barrier.

'Don't be silly, Emma. It's just a few days' worth of clothes.'

That I doubt.

We finally make it out of the airport and are on our way.

'What is it you need to do while you're here?' I ask as I navigate down a country road.

'I need to sign some papers at the solicitor's tomorrow. It's not far; I'll take a taxi.'

'Sorry, I have to work tomorrow or I could have taken you.'

'It's fine, Emma. I'm not here to intrude on your life, just to grab a bit of time with my daughter while I can.'

We arrive home a short time later. I pull up in front of the house, and Mum climbs out of the car and stretches while I open the boot.

'You're going to have to give me a hand, Mum,' I say, looking down. 'This case is wedged in.'

Mum rolls her eyes at me, no doubt the first of much eye-rolling over the next few days. I realise that I do this a lot too, usually at Simon, so it must be a trait I've picked up from Mum. She walks around to the rear of the car, leans in and hoists out the case. Having placed it down on its wheels, she then proceeds to pull it up the path to the front door without any help required from me.

That figures.

I follow and unlock the front door. Inside, we're greeted by Banjo, who eyes Mum warily.

Mum stops in her tracks. 'What's that?'

'It's a cat,' I say matter-of-factly.

'I can see that, Emma. What is it doing in your home?'

'Mum, meet Banjo.' I reach down and rub Banjo between his ears, and he purrs. 'Banjo, this is my mum.'

The cat yawns widely and Mum rolls her eyes for the second time as she steps warily towards Banjo. He refuses to move and she has to manoeuvre the large wheelie case past him.

'Are you sure you'll be okay on your own for a bit?' I ask as Mum makes a cup of tea once we've dragged her case up the stairs and she's unpacked.

The running club has, unfortunately, changed its day this week, for some reason to do with the building that I can't remember.

'Of course, Emma, I'll be fine. I am an adult, and you're only popping out for a run. I mean, how long does it usually take you?'

Well, there are a number of factors that influence that, I think, namely how many lattes I've drunk that day; whether or not I've eaten a muffin that day; whether Simon talks to me all the way around; how hard it is to look like I'm not dying while jogging next to a fit twenty-year-old running buddy; and whether I'm trying to talk to Simon to prevent him from flirting with the twenty-year-old running buddy.

'Emma?' Mum looks at me while stirring her tea with some speed.

'Not long,' I suggest. 'I'll just pop upstairs and get ready then. We can eat when I get home.'

'Great.' Mum smiles. 'I'll take a look in the fridge, see what I can find to cook.'

I consider saying nothing, but realise that the truth is better than the fallout later when Mum has found very little in my fridge that could be classed as 'food to cook', more like just cheese and, well, more cheese, and some wine to go with the cheese. My online shopping routine, which Sophie gave me such grief about, has dwindled in Joe's absence and I've resumed my previous way of living off cheese and biscuits.

'Okay, Mum, I'm going to save you the trouble. I haven't done the weekly food shop recently, so there may not be much in there. Why don't we go up to the local pub when I get home instead?'

'Is it wise to drink after going for a run, Emma?'

'Yes.' I nod. 'Especially when you've been running with Simon.'

Mum raises her eyebrows at me.

'It's how I like to live my life, Mum – balance. It's yin and yang: running is good, alcohol is bad, therefore they cancel each other out.' I grin, pleased with my rationalisation.

Mum rolls her eyes at me and takes a drink of her tea.

'I'll go and get changed,' I say, defeated by that one simple reaction.

Upstairs, I strip off, fight to get into my sports bra (I mean honestly, who designs these things?) and pull on some grey jogging bottoms and a pale-pink t-shirt. As I pull my hair into a tight ponytail I hear the doorbell ring.

'I'll get it,' I call, coming down the stairs. 'It'll just be Simon.'

But Mum beats me to the door. She pulls it open and I see Simon standing on the doorstep dressed like a satsuma in bright-orange running gear.

'Simon, what on earth are you wearing?' Mum looks him up and down with an expression of dismay.

Simon glances down at his attire, then back at Mum, and I hide my smile. It's like we're ten years old again, when Mum used to comment on Simon's outlandish dress sense. Even back then he always had his own style and stood out from the crowd.

'You're never going out in public like that, are you?' she asks as I make my way down the stairs.

Simon looks perplexed. 'They're new,' he says. 'And what's wrong with what I'm wearing?'

'There's an age where men can get away with tight-fitting leggings, Simon, and forty isn't it. And what colour do you call that?'

'Orange,' Simon says, his tone heavy with sarcasm.

Mum sniffs. 'A bold choice.'

Simon opens his mouth, but I quickly intervene. 'We should get going,' I say, ushering Simon back out of the door. As amusing as this little exchange is, I fear that if it continues it will end in a cat fight.

Mum loves Simon, but she doesn't always 'get' him. She's never understood his need to express himself in every aspect of his life, from his over-the-top personality to his lack of social awareness.

Simon turns back around to say something further, but I shove him towards the car. He huffs like a teenager as he climbs into the driver's seat and I climb into the passenger side of the car.

'I don't know why she has to be like that,' he says as he turns the key sharply in the ignition and the car roars to life. 'I don't know who she thinks she is!'

'Um, my mother?' I struggle not to smile. 'When have you known her to be anything other than like that?'

Simon just looks wounded.

'She loves you, Simon, you know that,' I say, fastening my seatbelt with difficulty as he rams his foot down on the accelerator and the car lurches forward at speed.

'Well, she has a funny way of showing it,' Simon snaps.

'Yes, um, I understand that, but could we slow down a little, please? I'd like to arrive at the running club in one piece tonight.'

'Sorry, hun.' Simon slows the car down.

'I don't know why you worry about what she says.' I pause. 'Interesting choice of outfit, though.' I'm unable to hide my smirk.

Simon wafts a hand at me. 'Don't start. You sound like James.'

'What did he say?'

'He said that if I ever stepped outside the house dressed like this with him then he would divorce me.'

I laugh loudly, trying to focus on the road ahead.

'It's not funny,' Simon protests, which just makes me laugh louder. 'I told him, when he made those vows, he made a commitment.'

'For better or worse,' I say between laughs. 'Is this what they meant by "worse"?'

Simon huffs..

'Okay, okay, I'm done with the teasing.'

Simon looks at me, his lips pursed, before he turns his attention firmly to the road ahead, gripping the steering wheel, and this makes me laugh harder.

When we arrive at the running club, I watch as Declan does a double take when Simon climbs out of the car and strides towards him.

'Hi.' Simon waves as I follow behind. 'Are we ready to warm up?'

Declan nods, looking bemused. 'Sure.'

Tonight's run isn't too bad. I'm saved from trying to talk and run and breathe all at the same time by Simon and Declan running slightly ahead as I jog behind them. Declan keeps shouting words of encouragement over his shoulder as I amble along. I ignore him, for no other reason than I know my own body and it will not be coerced by anyone, man, woman or hot twenty-year-old running buddy. It's forty and it's stubborn.

We finish our run and stretch out (as always, very important, apparently, or I won't be able to get out of bed tomorrow, which doesn't sound like a bad thing at all).

Simon is in a better mood as he drives me home. The run appears to have dispersed his frustration from his earlier encounter with my mother. I hug him goodbye before getting out of the car and heading into the house.

'I'm back,' I shout, kicking off my trainers.

'In here,' Mum calls from the lounge, and I pop my head around the door.

'I'll grab a shower and be ready to go to the pub in ten minutes,' I say.

'Things happen, darling: situations change, people change. People make mistakes and do things they never dreamed they would.'

Mum takes a sip of her gin and tonic. We're perusing the menu in the pub and I've been explaining the current situation with Sophie and Matt.

'That's no excuse,' I say.

'I'm not saying that it is, Emma. I'm saying that life isn't black and white; in fact, most of the time it's varying shades of grey.'

Please don't let her elaborate on that, I pray silently. I think back to some of the situations that I've got myself into, unintentionally, over the years. I slept with Sophie's boyfriend (prior to Matt), although I didn't know he was her new boyfriend at the time. Sophie managed to forgive me.

'It's not the mistakes that define you,' Mum says. 'It's what you do next that counts.'

'Do you think people can get past an affair?'

'I think people can, but they both have to want to, and that's not as easy as it sounds.'

'I'm sure it's not. I have no idea what I would do, or what I'd *want* to do.'

'Well, in my opinion Matt needs to make sure that he can not only forgive Sophie but also not hold it against her for the rest of their lives.'

'That's the tricky bit, I guess, the broken trust.'

'And Sophie needs to forgive herself too.'

'Forgive herself?'

'Yes, if Matt *can* move past this then Sophie needs to be able to as well, or it will still hang over them both.'

'How do you go back to normal after that?'

'They'll get there, if they both work at it. Relationships are hard, Emma, and you have to work at them. It might not always feel like you are, but there is always a compromise, or a decision you need to agree on.' Mum shrugs.

'I suppose,' I say, feeling that normal is massively underrated.

As I get into bed later, my phone buzzes from the bedside table. A text from Joe flashes on the screen:

Hope your mum arrived safely. Have fun with her for the next few days. See you on Friday x

I text back:

Had a nice evening with Mum. Went for a run with Simon dressed as a satsuma! He doesn't change. See you on Friday night x

I wonder what Joe did this evening?

I open my eyes as the alarm clock rudely shrills in my ear. It's seven thirty a.m., and I'm about to roll over and close my eyes for another ten minutes when I remember that Mum is sleeping in the spare room. I slide out of bed, simultaneously rubbing my eyes and flattening down my scary hair, pull on my dressing gown and walk out onto the landing. The spare room door is ajar, so I pop my head around to see if Mum wants a cup of tea. The room is empty and the bed is neatly made. Did I dream that I picked my mother up from the airport yesterday?

'Mum?' I call, but I'm met with silence.

The bathroom is also empty. I head downstairs, nearly falling over Banjo as he appears from nowhere and winds himself between my legs. I have to go down one step at a time, sideways on, to make sure I don't end up head over heels.

'Mum?' I call again, wandering from the lounge through to the kitchen.

Nothing.

Then I notice a piece of paper next to the coffee machine. Where my mum has found a pen and paper, I have no idea. Then I realise – she probably carries this stuff in her handbag.

Woke early so headed out to pick up something for breakfast. Pop the coffee machine on and have a shower, and I'll be back shortly. Mum x

I go back upstairs and take a shower. I'm just finishing straightening my hair when I hear the front door open and close.

'I'm back, Emma,' I hear Mum call.

'I'll be down in a minute.'

I finish my hair, apply a bit of makeup and then go back down to the kitchen.

'I got cinnamon bagels,' Mum says.

'Great, thank you. I'll make the coffee.'

I take two mugs from the cupboard and start up the coffee machine as Mum toasts the bagels.

'What time do you need to be at the solicitor's?' I ask as Mum butters the bagels and I add milk to the coffees.

'Not for a couple of hours. I thought I might pop into town with you when you head into work and I can have a mooch around the shops before my appointment.'

'Okay, that's fine.'

We eat breakfast and I finish getting ready. Then, for once, I leave the house for work at an appropriate time, instead of fleeing in a whirlwind already ten minutes behind schedule. I park the car near the shop and hug Mum goodbye, and she wraps her cerise scarf around her neck and heads off towards the high street.

Jarrod seems in a slightly picky mood today. Maybe all is not well with him and his new love. I smile at him and decide to be kind, even though he's already being snippy about how I folded some sweaters. We all experience the rollercoaster of romance and it doesn't hurt to show empathy.

'I was going to put the kettle on while it's quiet,' I say about an hour into the morning as I walk over to where Jarrod is folding and rearranging some chinos.

'Sure,' he answers curtly.

I press my lips together and refrain from saying anything further, and instead I turn and walk back into the staff area and switch on the kettle. I make the drinks and take them back out to Jarrod.

'Don't put it down there!' he snaps, making me jump. I slosh half the tea down myself, but thankfully miss the spreadsheet he so clearly wanted me to avoid.

I bend down and put the mugs on the floor. 'I'll get a cloth.'

I head back to the staffroom, swearing under my breath, return with a cloth and try to wipe the tea from my top, without success. Great, I have a brown stain on my clothes and it's only ten thirty in the morning.

Jarrod takes the cloth from me and wipes the bottom of the cups. 'I apologise, Emma, if I made you jump. I was a little sharper than I intended.'

Was that an apology? This is unchartered territory for Jarrod.

'Um, that's okay,' I say. 'No harm done really.' If you discount the stained top and third-degree burn.

Jarrod sips his tea. Thinking that perhaps our relationship has moved forward slightly, given the fact that Jarrod has acknowledged that he might have upset me, I decide to take this opportunity to try to engage him in conversation.

'Is everything okay?' I ask, as Jarrod attempts to remove an invisible piece of fluff from his jacket.

He looks at me, slightly aghast, as though no one has ever asked him any kind of personal question before. 'Oh, yes, absolutely.' He frowns.

I nod. 'Right, only it seems to me that you're maybe...' I pause, wondering how best to say this. 'Distracted?'

He opens his mouth, closes it, takes a sip of tea, then frowns again.

Maybe trying to have a meaningful conversation was a mistake.

'Can I ask you something?' he says nervously.

I realise that I may regret this, but I smile and say, 'Of course.'

'You've been with your boyfriend for a while, yes?'

I'm a bit taken aback by this line of questioning. 'Um, Joe? Yes.' I nod.

'And, well, is he...' He clears his throat. 'The one?'

Now it's my turn to look uncomfortable.

'I'm sorry, Emma, I shouldn't be asking.' He gulps his tea.

'No, Jarrod, that's okay. I wasn't expecting that question, that's all.'

He holds up a hand. 'It's really none of my business. I shouldn't have asked.'

'Can I ask why you want to know?' And then I realise. 'Have *you* found the one?' I find myself smiling.

Jarrod blushes. 'I think so.' He shakes his head. 'I don't know, maybe.'

Now I see why Jarrod is on such an emotional rollercoaster. He's in love!

'Close your eyes,' I say. Jarrod looks at me like I'm mad, but then does what I say. 'Can you imagine what your life would look like without her in it?' I ask.

I watch the expression on his face. He squeezes his eyes shut tightly and a huge smile spreads across his face. His eyes open, and I swear there's a sparkle in them. I think that says it all.

'No,' he says. 'No, I can't imagine my life without Laurel.'

'Laurel? What a lovely name.'

Jarrod flicks his gaze to look over my shoulder. 'A customer is heading in.' He adjusts his tie, back to Mr Formality, and it appears that the moment has passed. The shop door opens and closes.

'I'll clean the mugs,' I say, taking Jarrod's from him as I drink the last of my tea. I nearly spit it back out as I turn to see Jarrod striding towards my mother.

'How can I help you today?' Jarrod asks. 'And what a fabulous scarf,' he says.

Oh no, no, no!

I hurry over. 'Don't worry, Jarrod, this is my mum.'

He turns to me. 'Oh.' Then back to Mum. 'Nice to meet you.' He holds his hand out and Mum takes it in hers. She looks him up and down while they shake hands.

Please God, do not let her offend Jarrod, especially when we've taken such a leap forward in our relationship only minutes ago.

'So, you must be Jarrod?' Mum says.

'You've finished at the solicitor's already?' I ask, trying to divert the conversation away from Jarrod.

'Emma has told me all about you,' Mum continues, ignoring my pleading look.

Jarrod glances from Mum to me, then back to Mum.

'She didn't tell me how dashing you are, though,' Mum says, and I breathe a huge sigh of relief.

Jarrod beams at Mum.

'Why don't you show me some of the lovely things in your store.' Mum links arms with Jarrod and he leads her over to the handbags.

I laugh to myself as I take the mugs to the kitchen. As I look back over my shoulder, Mum winks at me over hers.

After Mum has negotiated a deal on two handbags and a matching pair of shoes, we agree to reconvene at my house later. Apparently, Mum has some more shopping to do. I hope it's just window shopping, as I very much doubt that anything else will fit into that suitcase of hers.

'An interesting woman, your mother,' Jarrod says to me in passing later that afternoon as I rearrange the shoe display.

I have no response to that.

I arrive back home that evening to find Mum sitting on the sofa in the lounge. She's looking causal, in jeans and a pale-beige thin-knit jumper, as usual making the simplest of outfits look glamourous. She hands me a glass of wine as I take off my coat and discard it on the armchair.

'So, what's really going on, Emma?' Mum takes a sip of her wine without taking her eyes off me.

I fiddle with the stem of my wine glass. 'I don't know what you mean.' I didn't realise that the glass of wine was a bribe for information.

Mum raises her eyebrows.

I raise mine back at her.

'That's okay,' she says. 'We have all night.'

I tap a finger on my glass. 'Nothing's wrong, Mum. Everything's fine.'

'I hate that word.'

'What word?'

'Fine,' she says. 'People use it when they really mean that everything is not *fine*.'

'And what makes you think that I'm not okay?'

'I'm your mother, Emma, I know these things. You're overcompensating.'

'By?'

'By being overly chirpy.'

'So now I'm being too happy, so something must be wrong?' I shake my head and take a sip of wine.

'Emma?' Mum drops her head to one side and holds my gaze.

I bite my lip.

'Okay,' she says, 'I'll grab the bottle of wine, and then you start talking.'

She gets up from the sofa and places her glass on the coffee table. As Mum leaves the room, I inhale deeply and then exhale. She returns with the half-empty bottle of wine and places it on the table in front of us.

'Honestly, Mum, I don't know where to begin. There isn't one thing that I can say is bothering me. I just feel lost.' I take a large drink of my wine.

'Let's start at the beginning, Emma. Can I make some suggestions?'

I nod.

'Well, I think you've had a number of stressful things happen within a short space of time, and perhaps it's the accumulation of them that has left you feeling *lost*.'

I chew my lip.

Mum continues: 'You moved home, which is one of the most stressful things that you can do. Your boyfriend is working away, leaving you alone for long periods of time in a new environment. And your best friend cheated on her long-term partner, which is now making you question everything about your own relationship with Joe, as you feel vulnerable with him working away.'

My chest tightens as the truth of Mum's words grips my heart. 'What makes you think that I'm questioning Joe?' I ask.

'You trust Joe, of that I'm sure,' Mum continues, ignoring my question. 'But you're unnerved by the fact that Sophie has been unfaithful. You never expected it of her, so you're left wondering if anyone, and possibly everyone, is capable of that.' She looks at me. 'Am I close?'

Damn it. Mum has hit the nail right on the head. All this time my feelings have been bubbling away under the surface and I've done my best to keep forcing them down, deeper and deeper, because every word that Mum has said is right. I have been totally thrown by Sophie's actions, I have started to question my relationship with Joe, and I do feel vulnerable – and I *hate* vulnerable.

Chapter Twenty-Seven

'Remind me why we're looking at furniture again, Mum? You literally signed the contract yesterday and you haven't even got a moving date.'

I pat a cushion on a pale-grey sofa. It's the following morning and we're in a huge department store.

'We will, darling, it's just a matter of time.'

'Wow,' I say under my breath as I turn over the price tag. 'Isn't this stuff a little pricey, Mum?'

'Emma, I live in New York. This is *not* pricey.'

'Oh.'

'You should see what some of the shops in Manhattan charge for a throw or a decorative cushion.'

I think back to the décor in Mum's apartment in New York and remember a particularly eye-catching gold pillow on the spare bed when I last stayed there. I almost sneaked it into my roller-case before I left. If Mum didn't have such great attention to detail, I might have risked it.

'It was three hundred dollars.' Mum looks at me with a knowing smile.

I frown. 'What?'

'The gold pillow.'

'You spent three hundred dollars on a pillow for the spare bed?' I'm astounded. 'And how did you know that I was thinking about that?'

'I saw you admiring it when you came to stay. I was surprised that you didn't try to pack it without me noticing.'

I smile coyly. 'I wouldn't do that, Mum.'

'Of course not, darling.'

'Anyway.' I decide to steer the subject away from the gold pillow. 'What else are we looking at today, in addition to sofas?'

'We need to look at bedroom furniture.'

'I think I'll let you wander over to that department on your own while I look at curtains or something. I draw the line at helping you choose the bed that you and Parker will be sleeping in.' That would be so wrong; this is my mother we're talking about.

Mum shrugs, looking amused. 'Fair enough. I'll look at the bedroom department, then we'll head home, shall we?'

'Okay.'

Mum wanders off and I shake my head, still shocked at the three-hundred-dollar pillow. I daren't ask how much the amazing quilt on that spare bed cost. It felt like I was being wrapped in cotton wool each night.

I pick up a candle and sniff it cautiously. It smells like a warm summer evening to me, whatever that scent might actually be. I decide to buy it. This may be the only item in this department store that I can afford.

A few minutes later, I see Mum coming back towards me.

'I've picked up a brochure,' she says, waving a glossy magazine at me. 'I want to show Parker before I make a decision.'

I raise my eyebrows. 'I'm sure you can find whatever you want to show Parker on their website.'

Mum tuts at me. 'I like a brochure.'

I can't help but smile as I refrain from rolling my eyes at her.

'What's that you're buying?' Mum points at my hand.

'A candle,' I say. 'It smells expensive.'

Now it's Mum's turn to roll her eyes at me, and I realise that, despite our finances and level of acceptance when it comes to the astronomical cost of soft furnishings, Mum and I might not be so different.

We have some lunch, and then it's time for me to take Mum back to the airport for her flight home. After struggling to manoeuvre the huge suitcase – now even heavier thanks to Mum's purchases yesterday – into the boot of the car, we're finally ready.

'You should talk to Joe,' Mum says as I drive through the afternoon traffic towards the airport.

I don't meet her gaze. 'Maybe.' I shrug. 'I'm not sure what I'd say.'

'Just tell him how you feel. Honesty and communication are the foundations of a long-lasting relationship, Emma.'

Hmm.

'You know that I'm right.'

'Maybe,' I say. 'But that doesn't mean that I want to put everything out there.'

'You don't think Joe can handle your emotions?'

I bite my lip. It's more that I'm terrified of what he might say back. I haven't mentioned my fears about Karen being in the picture to Mum, or even Sophie for that matter. Somehow it doesn't seem appropriate to explain to my friend who has cheated on her boyfriend that I'm worried my boyfriend is cheating on me.

I pull into the drop-off area in front of the terminal. As we get out of the car, Mum takes hold of my arm.

'Just talk to him, Emma. You'll feel much better, I promise.'

I smile. 'It's been good to see you, Mum.'

'And you, darling.' Mum pulls me into a hug. 'It won't be long before these goodbyes are a thing of the past, Emma.'

'I know. I'll miss visiting New York, especially the Manhattan shops, but my bank account will breathe a sigh of relief.'

'There're lots of things I'll miss too, but I'm excited to be coming back to England. And I won't miss cab drivers honking their horns at three a.m., or nearly getting mown down ten times a day by all those pesky cyclists.'

I laugh. 'You say that now, but when you're sick to death of hearing owls hooting in the middle of the night and having to constantly drive around cyclists on the road, you may change your mind.'

A car behind us beeps its horn.

'I'd better get moving,' Mum says, grabbing hold of her large roller-case. 'Speak soon.'

She heads off into the airport terminal and I climb back into the car. I watch her walk through the revolving door until she disappears. What Mum said makes sense: I can't argue that honesty and communication make a good foundation. But Mum spent eighteen years with my dad and they didn't make it work. How honest was she with him, or him with her?

A horn blasts from behind me.

'Alright,' I huff, waving a hand dismissively at the car revving up my rear, and I move away from the drop-off area.

Back at home, I crash on the bed in my pyjamas. It's been an exhausting few weeks, both physically and mentally, but I have a plan for recovering. Tomorrow's Thursday, and I've arranged a day off work and booked an afternoon of spa treatments with Sophie, followed by an overnight stay at the hotel. I hope Banjo will be alright with a large bowl of biscuits and a bowl of water. I'll be back early in the morning anyway to change for work; I'm sure that he'll survive.

Chapter Twenty-Eight

I wake, alarmed to find that I can't move my head. It takes me a second or two to realise that Banjo is lying across the top of my pillow and his giant head is squashed up next to mine. I can hear his faint snuffling as he dreams; probably chasing a rabbit.

I try to slide my head slowly away from his, careful not to wake him mid-dream so he doesn't mistake me for his prey and gouge my eyes out with his long talons. Just as I think I'm free, a large paw taps the side of my face, and I'm reminded, not for the first time, that I've been demoted in the hierarchy in this house.

'Okay, Banjo.' (I realise that in the short time that Banjo has resided with me I've very quickly turned into a 'crazy cat lady' who not only talks to her cat but actually tries to barter with him.) 'If you get off my face,' I say, 'then I'll give you cat milk.' I feel the brazen lick of his coarse tongue on my forehead and take this to be an indication of a successful negotiation.

Five minutes later, as Banjo slurps his bowlful of milk, I pad around the kitchen with a mug of freshly brewed coffee, contemplating my current life. Here I am, in the house of my dreams, but living alone, with Joe two hundred miles away, potentially enjoying the company of another woman. I feel Banjo brush up against me and rub his face on the back of my calves. Okay, so maybe I'm not alone. I reach down and stroke the top of the cat's head, and he purrs loudly, before rolling over and licking his bum.

Charming.

As Sophie and I walk into the hotel reception just after lunch, I inhale deeply. I love the smell of the spa. It's instantly relaxing, and I know that I'll want to buy all of the lovely products that they use on me, despite it costing the equivalent of a month's mortgage repayment – but life is too short, and at my age I need to take care of my skin. Plus Joe isn't here to argue with me, and that's not my fault.

We're greeted by a small, very tanned young woman with amazing skin (I guess it goes with the territory of working in a spa). She smiles at us as we approach the reception desk.

'Hello, ladies,' she practically whispers, and I have to lean closer to her to make out what she's saying. 'Do you have a booking?'

'Yes, at two thirty,' I say at a normal volume. 'We have an appointment for a facial and a massage, and a room for tonight.'

'Of course,' the receptionist whispers. 'Have you been to the hotel or spa before?'

'No, it's our first time here,' says Sophie quietly.

We are each handed a clipboard with a form and a pen. 'Can you fill in your details and answer the medical questions, please? Take a seat over there.' The receptionist smiles again, and I barely see a wrinkle or crinkle on her skin. 'Then we can arrange for your luggage to be taken to your room.'

I glance down at the small wheelie case next to me, unsure that this qualifies as luggage.

Sophie and I walk over to two pale-grey sofas and we sit down and begin completing the forms.

'I'm so ready for this,' Sophie says. 'My shoulders feel like they're full of knots.'

'Me too. My lower back could definitely do with a bit of attention, and the bags under my eyes are now purple thanks to that stupid cat.'

'Don't give me that; you love Banjo.'

'I do, but I've forgotten what it's like to sleep through the night without being woken at some unearthly hour by a large paw patting my face.'

'So stop letting him sleep on your bed, silly.'

'Easier said than done.'

'No, it's not. You just put him in the kitchen at night and shut the door.'

'It is *so* not that easy, Sophie. If I do that then he simply yowls loudly with no intention of stopping until he mentally breaks me, and then when I let him out he looks at me like I've tried to kill him and he gives me the cold shoulder for a day.'

'The cold shoulder?' Sophie chuckles. 'I love animals, you know that, but you're crazy. You're passing human emotions on to a cat.'

'It's hard not to when I spend most of my time with him. He's Joe's furry replacement for the time being.'

'And what happens when Joe comes home and wants his side of the bed back from Banjo?'

'They'll work it out, and one of them will be victorious,' I say seriously, and Sophie raises her eyebrows. 'My money's on Banjo.'

Sophie laughs.

'Emma?' A male voice with a strong French accent interrupts us, and I look up. 'I'm Jacques.'

I stare up at the tall, toned Adonis who stands before me.

'You are, Emma, yes?' he says.

I look at Sophie. 'Um, yes, I'm Emma,' I say.

'You are with me, yes.'

'Oh, um, with you?' I can feel the colour rising in my cheeks as I take in the chiselled muscles on his arms.

'For the massage and facial.' He nods at me. 'Lucy will take your case to your room.' He turns to a petite blonde I hadn't even noticed was standing behind him.

'Ah, right.' I glance back at Sophie and she shrugs at me, looking amused.

I stand up nervously.

'You have completed the form, yes?'

I hold out the clipboard, not taking my eyes off him.

'Great. Please follow me.' Jacques smiles and he turns and leads the way down the corridor. I can hear Sophie softly giggling as I dutifully follow Jacques.

We enter the treatment room and I hover awkwardly near the door.

'You have had a massage before?' Jacques asks.

'Yes.' But not by a man, I want to add.

'I will do the massage first, then the facial, okay?'

'Okay,' I repeat. Can men do facials? This is the twenty-first century, I suppose, but still.

'So if you undress down to your underwear...'

Oh. Dear. God.

'And then lie on the bed face down and cover up with the towel, yes?'

I nod, my mouth dry. He wants me to strip off down to my pants (which, thankfully, are particularly large today) and lie down while he rubs oil on me. This is bad, this is very, very bad, and it's not going to be the slightest bit relaxing.

Jacques leaves the room, and as the door closes behind him I exhale and lean on the treatment table, looking up. Why, oh why, oh why do I get to be massaged by what is probably the hottest guy I have seen in, okay, maybe forever? I mean, I know that there are male masseurs, but it never occurred to me mine would be a man. I'm having a facial for one thing. What do men know about that?

Okay, breathe, Emma, breathe. You are stuck in this room now and there is no way out. Jacques is going to return shortly and expect you to be undressed and under the towel, not hunched over the massage table contemplating the hand that life has dealt you.

I stand up, shake my head and then get on with the task of undressing. I slide between the two towels on the bed wearing nothing but my pants, feeling incredibly vulnerable and unsure what to expect from the next fifty-five minutes. As I press my face into the pillow, I hear a knock at the door.

'You are ready for me, yes?' Jacques calls.

Although somehow it feels wholly inappropriate, I call back, 'Yes, I'm ready for you.'

I hear the treatment room door open and close and then him approaching the bed. It's like every sound is enhanced. The unscrewing of a lid, the squirt of oil, Jacques rubbing his hands together.

'Now, Emma,' he says above me, 'just relax and enjoy, okay?'

Relax and enjoy? Is he kidding me? I've never felt so unrelaxed in my life. As I feel his hands on my shoulders, I cringe and feel myself blushing rapidly. Thank God I'm lying face down so he can't see my bright-red cheeks.

As Jacques starts to rub my shoulders with expert hands, I realise that he might actually be the best masseur that I have ever experienced. My muscles respond immediately under his touch. I have a 'light bulb' moment: Jacques may in fact be gay, and so very uninterested in me lying nearly naked under his touch. In fact, even if Jacques isn't gay and is very much into women, that doesn't mean he finds me at all attractive. Plus, I'm sure that he's a complete professional, and just because he's a man and I'm a woman, that doesn't mean it has to be awkward.

I push all the stupid thoughts to the back of my mind and concentrate on enjoying the feeling of tension being massaged out of each and every muscle.

As it turns out, Jacques pays the most exquisite attention to detail, and the facial he gives me is possibly the best I've ever had too. I make a mental note to leave Jacques a five-star review.

'How do you know that he's gay?' Sophie asks, and takes a sip of her room-service champagne.

It's an hour and a half later and we're sitting on the double bed in our room wearing the complimentary bathrobes.

'I don't,' I say, topping up my own glass. 'But while he was rubbing his oiled hands all over my naked body, I liked to imagine, for both our sakes, that he was.'

Sophie giggles.

'Not because I think I'm some irresistible sex goddess he'd be instantly attracted to; more that...well, I never imagined any man other than Joe would touch me so intimately.'

'He's a masseur.' Sophie rolls her eyes at me.

'I know that, but you're still lying there naked with a complete stranger who's being paid to touch you. It's weird.'

'So you feel less weird if he's gay?'

'Yes, like when I share a bed with Simon. It doesn't feel weird because...Okay, I take that back; it does feel weird sharing a bed with Simon. Mainly because I've witnessed him using more products than me before he climbs into bed. Plus, I usually wake up with him snuggled up next to me.'

Sophie laughs. 'Or because you're both so drunk you don't remember getting into bed.'

I take a sip. 'That only happened once.'

She raises her eyebrows.

'Twice,' I concede.

I pour more champagne. It feels good having a girlie night, just me and Soph. It's been a while, and it's much needed on both sides.

'And now you're living with your new furry friend.' Sophie's already chuckling. I think the bubbly has started to take effect. I have to admit that I feel a bit tipsy myself.

'Oh, you wouldn't believe that cat. It's like he's taken over the whole house. He's huge, for a start; you need both hands if you're going to attempt to pick him up and last night he actually had his head on my pillow.'

Sophie lets out a snort, and we both end up in a fit of laughter.

'We should get some food,' I say as I regain my composure. 'Or we're both going to end up completely sloshed. Want to get dressed and go down to the bar?'

'Not really.' Sophie smiles. 'I think it would be much more fun to stay here in our dressing gowns and have a carpet picnic.'

'That sounds perfect,' I say, and I collect the room service menu from the bedside table. 'Order whatever you want, but make sure it comes with a side of champagne.' I giggle.

'Don't you have work tomorrow?' Sophie looks at me.

'I don't care,' I say. 'Jarrod is either Mr Nice or Mr Grumpy depending on how his relationship is going. He can have a day off and be Mr Quiet and ignore me while I'm marginally hungover.'

'Are you sure?' Sophie asks.

'Absolutely.'

Oh my God, how much did we drink last night? I prise my thumping head from the pillow and immediately place it back down in the imprint it has created.

'Emma?' Sophie croaks.

'Yes?' I roll over to find Sophie lying next to me, face down under the covers. 'What time is it?' she mumbles.

I reach out and fumble for my phone, hoping that I'm a creature of habit and I've left it on the bedside table like I do at home. Thankfully, I have. I press a button and the screen lights up.

'It's seven fifteen,' I say.

'Oh dear. What time do we need to leave for work?'

'Um, fairly soon,' I moan. 'I'll get in the shower.'

I slide out of bed and make my way to the bathroom in a hunched position and with only one eye open. I flick on the bathroom light, and instantly regret it as the dazzling spotlights burn my corneas. I squint at the mirror. I look decidedly less refreshed than I had hoped from my overnight spa stay; I'm guessing that champagne negates the benefits of an anti-aging facial.

I shove my hair into a bun on top of my head and climb gingerly into the shower and turn on the hot water. I quickly lather up shower gel and rinse, before grabbing a huge white fluffy towel and wrapping it around me as I go back into the bedroom. Sophie is still lying face down on the bed.

'Come on, Soph, you'll feel much better after a cup of coffee,' I say, nudging her leg.

'Liar,' she says into the pillow.

I open my mouth to argue, but she's right. It'll take more than a cup of coffee to shift a champagne hangover.

'Soph, you need to get in the shower,' I say, rubbing myself haphazardly with the towel. I climb into clean pants and find my bra, on top of the cupboard next to the miniature kettle.

Sophie rolls out of bed, huffing like a teenager as she stumbles to the bathroom.

'Why do I feel so bad? We didn't drink that much last night, did we?'

I glance at the two empty champagne bottles. 'Maybe it was the combination of massages and alcohol.'

'Hmm.' Sophie scowls as she closes the bathroom door.

I swipe a cotton-wool pad soaked with rejuvenating cleanser across my face and then follow with a brightening moisturiser –it will have its work cut out for it today, I fear. There's very little I can do with my hair other than spritz it with dry shampoo and pull the hair straighteners through it to try to tame it.

By the time Sophie emerges from the bathroom I'm dressed and just spraying perfume onto my wrists. With the number of products

I've used this morning to make myself appear human, I smell like a department store cosmetics counter.

'Shall I go and order breakfast while you get ready?'

'Good idea.' Sophie pulls a comb through her chocolate curls. 'I won't be long.'

I pick up a room key-card and, leaving Sophie to finish getting dressed, I make my way to the restaurant for breakfast, following the smell of toast and coffee.

'Good morning, madam.' The waitress smiles at me. 'Can I take your room number, please?'

'Fifty-two,' I say, patting down my hair, which, despite the dry shampoo and hair straighteners, feels like it's getting bigger by the second. 'My friend will be joining me in a minute,' I add.

The waitress leads me practically across the whole dining area, passing several empty tables on the way, until she reaches a table for four in the corner. Maybe my hair is scarier than I thought.

'All the food is on the buffet over to the right' – she points – 'so just help yourselves when you're ready. Can I get you some coffee or tea?'

'Coffee, please.'

As she heads away I take my phone from my pocket. It's seven forty. Oh, there's a text from Joe:

Morning, how was the spa? x

I type back:

Great. Really enjoyed it. Was good to spend some time with Sophie. x

The phone pings again:

See you tonight. x

I wonder what this weekend will hold for me and Joe. It still feels like we're on rocky ground and I can't get the thought of Karen being somewhere in the picture out of my mind. And while Mum's advice to be honest with Joe about how I'm feeling makes sense in theory, I fear what that will look like in reality.

'Please tell me that there's coffee.' Sophie appears from nowhere and sits down at the table opposite me.

'Of course.' I smile. 'It's on its way.'

'Good. Let's get some food.'

We eat breakfast – and by that I mean that I force down a bacon sandwich and a coffee while Sophie picks at some pancakes and fruit – and then we collect our luggage and check out.

I make a quick stop at home to feed and let out a meowing Banjo, and to change into something more appropriate for work than my jeans. He gives me an angry stare as I put a scoop of biscuits into his bowl, guilt-tripping me for leaving him alone overnight.

'It was less than twenty-four hours, Banjo, and I left plenty of food,' I say to him as he chomps on the biscuits.

I arrive at work and bump into Jarrod as I step through the door.

'Well, good morning, Emma,' he says, at me rather than to me.

'Hello, Jarrod.'

He looks me up and down. 'Are you hungover?'

I see Jenny hovering in the doorway to the shop floor, cringing.

'Of course not.' I quickly remove the sunglasses still perched on my nose.

'Then what's going on with your hair?'

Brilliant.

Chapter Twenty-Nine

At the end of what feels like a testing day, I arrive home and decide to freshen up before Joe makes it back. Although the Prosecco hangover has just about worn off, I feel like a quick shower will reenergise me.

I sigh before turning on the shower and climbing in. I stand under the hot water as it pounds onto my shoulders, seemingly forcing the weariness from my body. After a good five minutes, I step out of the shower and get dressed in clean jeans and a shirt, before touching up my makeup. Usually, I wouldn't be so bothered, but I feel like I need to look my best for when Joe gets home.

I've debated Mum's words in my head for two days and I've come to the conclusion that she's right: I do need to speak to Joe and tell him how I'm feeling. I need to get everything out into the open, my fears about Karen included.

I swish chocolate-coloured eyeshadow onto my eyelid, like makeup is armour that I'm applying to both give me courage and to shield me. It's funny how makeup can make you feel like a totally different person. I swipe rosy-pink lip gloss across my lips and press them together and apply a squirt of touch-up colour to the roots of my hair, before looking in the mirror. I look much better than I did half an hour ago when I first arrived home.

I hear the front door open and close.

'Emma?' Joe calls.

I glance in the mirror one last time before heading down the stairs. Joe's standing at the foot of the stairs, looking up.

'Hey.' I smile.

'Hey.'

'Everything okay?'

Joe's voice sounds a bit weird and I can feel my heartbeat quicken as I walk down the stairs to him.

Joe takes a second, then shakes his head. 'Sure. It's been a long week. Fancy a drink at the pub?'

'Oh, um, yes.'

'I'll get changed and we'll go,' Joe says. He goes to stride upstairs, but stops in front of me and gives me a quick kiss.

I watch him as he heads upstairs and into the bathroom, and I realise that I'm gripping the bannister. Something doesn't feel right; the knot in the bottom of my stomach is telling me that it's simply a matter of time before something bad happens. Maybe Joe is planning to break up with me. Maybe he's taking me to the pub so we're in public when he ends things and I won't kick off at him. Chris did that, all those years ago: I thought he was taking me to a posh restaurant to propose over a lovely meal, when in fact he was taking me there to tell me he was leaving me and that our two-year relationship was over. Is this history repeating itself?

'Ready?' Joe appears and the crisp scent of his aftershave is both comforting and unnerving.

'Ready.' I force a smile, and we head out of the house.

It's a few minutes into our walk to the pub before I reach for Joe's hand. He wraps his fingers loosely around mine.

'So you and Sophie had fun at the spa?' Joe asks.

'Yeah, it was relaxing – although not initially.'

'How come? I thought you were supposed to be relaxed the moment you stepped into those places.'

'In theory, yes, but not when the therapist carrying out your facial and massage is a man.'

'A man?'

'I'm pretty sure he was gay,' I add hastily.

Joe lets out a half-laugh but says nothing, and we walk the rest of the way in silence.

'What do you want to drink?' Joe asks as we walk through the door of the pub. It's a busy Friday night and the bar is jammed with groups of friends chatting and drinking.

'A white wine,' I say, and immediately regret my reflexive response, thinking wine might not feel so good on top of last night's champagne.

'A large glass?'

'Absolutely,' I say. Sod it, if Joe is breaking up with me then I'm going to need a huge glass of wine to drown my sorrows. 'I'll try to find us a seat.'

Joe edges between people to reach the bar and I stand on the spot and turn in a circle, trying to find an empty table. All I see is a high round table with no stools or chairs, but at least it's something to put our drinks on. I hover at the table, waiting for Joe to return. It seems to take ages before I see him walking towards me carrying the drinks. He puts them on the table and I immediately pick up my wine glass and take a drink. Joe mirrors me with his pint of lager.

Okay, that's a shot of Dutch courage, and with Mum's words echoing in my ears, I decide it's now or never. I open my mouth, but nothing comes out. My throat is dry, and I swallow, then try again.

'So how's Simon?' Joe steps in before my mouth makes up its mind whether or not it's turned mute.

'Simon?' Now it's my turn for my voice to sound weird.

'Yeah, how's he doing?'

'Fine, I think.' I frown.

'And your mum? Did you have a good few days with her?'

I feel like I'm being interrogated, gently I admit, but interrogated nonetheless.

'You know my mum, like a whirlwind,' I say.

'Of course.' Joe nods. 'Everything going through with the house for her and Parker?'

'Seems to be.'

'Good.'

It's like we're making forced small talk, which feels odd; in fact, this whole evening feels odd.

Joe takes another drink of his pint, and it's my turn to copy him now as I take a gulp of wine. I decide to play along with whatever charade we're doing and continue the chat.

'Mum's really excited about moving back to the UK,' I say. 'I'm not sure what she thought of Banjo. She was a little surprised by him.'

'Right.' Joe smiles.

'And she brought enough clothes for a fortnight's holiday,' I babble on. 'You should have seen the size of the suitcase.' I take another gulp of wine.

'I bet.'

'I don't know how she's going to get all of her stuff over here from New York. It will cost her a fortune.'

Joe looks at me earnestly and I stop talking. He looks like he's about to say something, but then he drinks the last of the lager in his pint glass.

'Joe?'

'Yes?'

I look right at him, into his dark-brown eyes, the eyes that I fell in love with, that make me smile, that have a sparkle in them when Joe's being cheeky, that I love to wake up to.

Joe clears his throat. 'Shall we have another?' He tips his empty glass in my direction.

I blink back a tear. 'Sure.' I swallow.

Joe heads back to the bar, and I glance around at laughing couples and groups of friends, all enjoying a relaxing Friday night. It's like Joe and I are in a bubble, completely removed from the rest of the bar, stuck in an awkward interaction.

Is this the end? Is this how eight years of a relationship come to a close?

I wipe a tear away with the back of my hand as it escapes down my cheek. My breath catches in my throat, almost choking me, and I gulp the warm, sweaty air.

I see Joe getting served at the bar and it takes all my inner strength to compose myself. Maybe the last few weeks have been building up to this point. Have I driven Joe away? Has he found comfort in the arms of someone else, namely *Karen*?

Joe makes his way back over to me and places another glass of wine and a pint of lager down on the table.

'I'm knackered,' he says, taking a drink. 'We'll get off home after this, okay?'

I nod and take a drink from my glass of wine.

Joe begins to talk about his mum and dad going on some holiday somewhere, but I'm barely listening, simply watching his lips move as he speaks. I nod and murmur occasionally, but I can't concentrate on anything that Joe is saying. Tonight, for many reasons maybe, is not a normal night and I can't pretend that it is.

We finish our drinks and make the short walk home. When we arrive, we head into the kitchen, where I feed Banjo and Joe puts the kettle on.

'We should have something to eat,' Joe says, but I have zero appetite.

'Maybe just some toast,' I say. 'With a cup of tea.'

'Sure.' Joe busies himself making the drinks while I take the bread from the cupboard and slip two slices each into the toaster.

'What do you want to do this weekend?' I ask as I butter the toast, glancing at Joe from the corner of my eye as he stirs the tea.

'Mmm, nothing in particular. I might go for a run tomorrow.'

'Okay.' I hand Joe his toast.

'So when does your mum think the house will complete and she and Parker will move?'

'Not long,' I say. 'Maybe a few months.'

'Right.' Joe nods.

We finish the tea and toast.

'I'll get ready for bed,' I say, putting my plate and mug in the sink, and I head up the stairs.

I go to the bathroom and close the door behind me, taking in a deep breath. As I look in the mirror I realise that I look defeated, and maybe I am after tonight. Leaning over the sink, I splash cold water on my face before removing my makeup and applying moisturiser.

When I go into the bedroom, Joe is already in bed with his iPad. I slide into bed beside him, and he puts the iPad on the bedside table and turns out the light.

'Goodnight,' Joe says as I turn away from him. It takes a moment, but then I feel him move close to me and drape his arm loosely over my shoulder.

It must be the two glasses of wine on an empty stomach, because I fall asleep the minute my head hits the pillow.

The next thing I know I'm opening my eyes to find the bedroom filled with daylight and the bed empty beside me. I feel an uneasy tightening in my chest as I push myself up to a seated position. For a change, Banjo is nowhere to be seen either.

I pull on my dressing gown and plod heavily downstairs. As I reach the coffee machine in the kitchen I see a handwritten note from Joe on the kitchen side secured under a mug:

Gone for a run. Left at seven thirty. Be back in an hour.

I glance at the kitchen clock; it's eight fifteen.

Hmm.

I turn on the coffee machine and stare out of the window at the garden, a view that I loved when we first bought the house. A feeling of emptiness washes over me. Last night was awful. Joe and I have never been so distant. I have no idea what the rest of this weekend will bring, and whether Joe and I even have a future after that.

My mobile bleeps from the kitchen table, where I left it last night before going up to bed. I grab the coffee mug from under the machine and take a slurp as I pick up the phone. Sophie's name is flashing on the screen.

'Morning,' I say, answering the call as brightly as I can manage.

'He's coming home,' Sophie says excitedly down the phone.

'What?'

'Everything's going to be alright: Matt's coming home tomorrow.'

'Oh, Sophie, I'm so happy for you.'

'We had our last therapy session yesterday and he's agreed to move back in.'

'That's great.'

'Don't get me wrong, I know it won't be easy, and it will take some time to get back to how things were, but I can't stop smiling. I've missed him so much.'

I'm smiling down the phone too. 'Just take it a day at a time, Soph, and you'll work it out.'

'I know, and I will never, ever do anything to jeopardise my relationship with Matt again. I'm so lucky that he's prepared to give things another go.'

'I bet Florence is excited.'

'We haven't told her yet; it's going to be a surprise.'

'Lovely.'

'So what are you and Joe up to?'

'Oh, um, I'm not sure. He's just popped out for a run.'

'Ah, well, maybe in a couple of weeks we can all go out to dinner together.'

'That sounds great.'

'Okay, well, I'd better go. Catch up next week over coffee or something?'

'Perfect.'

'Bye then.'

'Bye, Soph.' I hang up the phone.

That's such great news. I'm so happy that Matt has decided to give things another try with Sophie. When I saw him that day in the coffee shop, I knew in my heart that he still loved her, but forgiveness is a totally different thing. At least Matt is prepared to try to move past Sophie's mistake.

I hear the front door open and close, so I walk to the kitchen doorway. Joe is crouched down, removing his trainers. He looks like he's barely broken into a sweat. When I go running I return red-faced with sweat running down pretty much everywhere.

'I just got off the phone with Sophie,' I say. 'Matt is moving back home tomorrow.'

Joe stands upright. 'I know.' He brushes a stray hair from his forehead.

'Oh.'

'Matt told me yesterday.'

'You didn't say anything.'

Joe presses his lips together. 'Matt needed to speak to Sophie and be the one to tell her. If I'd said something, would you have told Sophie?'

'No.' I shake my head, but I'm not entirely sure that I wouldn't have.

Joe looks at me with a sceptical expression. 'I'm going to take a shower,' he says.

'Do you want me to make you a coffee for when you get out?'

Joe seems to hesitate for a moment. 'No, thanks.'

He walks up the stairs, and I go back into the kitchen and sit down to finish my own drink.

I hear the shower running above me, and I sit and stare out of the window again, watching a pair of blackbirds hop around the garden together. Relationships must be so much simpler for animals; humans seem to overcomplicate everything. It looks like Sophie and Matt will make it through, though, and Simon has got over his mini mid-life crisis, so where does that leave me and Joe?

As if on cue, I hear footsteps coming down the stairs. Joe and I need to clear the air. I need to bite the bullet and talk to him honestly, like Mum said. I stand up, take a deep breath and turn around.

My chest constricts to the point that I think I've actually stopped breathing. Joe is standing in the hallway fully dressed in jeans and a sweater and with a roller-case at his side.

'What's happening?' I croak.

Joe rubs his knuckles across his forehead. 'We need a break, Emma.'

'A break?' I gulp.

'I don't know what's going on with you at the moment, but I don't feel like you're happy.'

I'm stunned.

'You don't trust yourself, you don't trust me, you don't trust us.'

'That's not true,' I stutter.

'You hold back, Emma.'

'Hold back?'

'It's like you're scared to fully commit to our relationship.'

'I am committed to our relationship. I'm here, we're here, right now.'

'Physically, yes. Emotionally?' He shrugs. 'I don't know.'

I can feel my whole body beginning to tremble. This is Joe breaking up with me. All of the stupid things that have gone through my mind over the last few months, all the reassurance I've had from friends, from myself, that Joe and I are strong and will be okay – it was all in vain. I remember when Chris took me to that stupid posh restaurant to break up with me, I was angry and hurt – but this?

This is something else. I realise now that the way I felt about Chris was nothing compared to how I feel about Joe. Joe is the one, he's the one I'm supposed to spend the rest of my life with. This isn't just anger or hurt; the trembling in my entire body is complete devastation.

'Joe,' I croak.

'Emma, you know that I'm right. When we got engaged years ago and then you called off the wedding, I was heartbroken; I thought that was the end for us. But then we worked things out, and we've been stronger since.'

My heart leaps; there's hope – maybe this isn't the end.

'Don't you ever wonder why we've never gone down that route again? You've never talked about marriage.'

'You wanted to get married?'

Joe shakes his head. 'A wedding never bothered me. I wanted to spend the rest of my life with you. I was committed to us, marriage or not.'

Was? That's past tense. My stomach drops.

'But it's not just about how *I* feel and what *I* want, it's about you too, Emma. We have to both want the same things.'

'But I do, we do want the same things. I don't care about being married either. I love you, Joe.'

Joe shakes his head. 'I need to be sure. I need *you* to be sure. Look at your relationship with your friends.'

'My friends?'

'Yes, if one of them calls to say they need you, you go. It's instant, a reflex action. Your commitment to them is so strong; the bond you have with them is never in question.'

'Are you asking me to give up my friends?'

'No, Emma, I would never do that. I love how great your friendships are. You trust your friends, you're committed to them one hundred per cent. You never doubt them – but you doubted me, you doubted us.'

We stand facing each other, and as I look into Joe's deep brown eyes I remember the first time we met, the first time I looked into his eyes, the first time he kissed me.

'What does this mean? Are you breaking up with me?'

'I want you to take some time, take this week, and think about things. If we're doing this, us, forever, then I need to know that you are one hundred per cent in this, not holding anything back.'

'You think that I doubt you?'

'I know that you looked at my phone.'

Shit. How does he know that?

'The text from Karen? You saw it and freaked out.'

I run my tongue along my teeth. There's no right response. If I say I didn't read the text, then he'll know I'm lying. If I say I did, then he'll know that I looked at his phone.

I shrug.

'The reason I know you saw the text is that everything was fine that day before I got into the shower. But when I got out of the shower you were acting weird, and you said the one thing that tells me you're not okay when I ask you.'

'And what's that?'

'You said "I'm fine", which is actually a blazing flashing sign saying that you're not fine.'

Oh.

'Karen is gay, by the way. She has a lovely girlfriend, Selina.'

Gay? Is he kidding me?

'And you never thought to mention that?' I wave my hands in the air.

'And how would that go?'

'Oh, I don't know, maybe just drop into the conversation "by the way, my work colleague Karen has a girlfriend".'

'No, Emma, I never thought to mention that, and do you know why?'

'No.'

'Because it's not relevant to me. I couldn't care less if Karen is gay or straight, because I'm in a relationship with you.'

Oh.

'But you care, and Karen has certainly been bothering you, and this is exactly what I'm talking about. If you trusted me, *trusted us*, then *you* wouldn't care if Karen was gay or straight either.'

'Are you leaving me?' I can hear the tremble in my voice.

'I'm going back to London. We both need to think about what we want. We take this week, without contact, and we decide, once and for all.'

'Without contact?'

'Yes, we take time, we think, we decide, and then we talk again next Friday when I get back.'

A million thoughts swarm through my head and I will my brain to engage and force my mouth to open and say something, anything that will stop Joe walking out of that door. But instead I simply stand there, heartbroken, and watch Joe open the door and walk away.

Chapter Thirty

I don't know how long I stare at the closed front door before I finally exhale. Did that really happen? Did Joe give me an ultimatum and then leave? Is he actually going to cut all contact with me for the next six days?

I take my mobile phone from my pocket and press 'call' on Simon's number in my speed dial. He answers after two rings.

'Hiya, babe.'

I open my mouth, but no words come out.

'Em?'

'He…he left.'

'Who left?'

'Joe. Joe left.'

'Didn't he just get home?'

'He's going back to London. He says that I need to think.'

'Hun, you're not making any sense.'

'He said that I'm not committed to our relationship one hundred per cent, that I hold back, that I'm scared to trust us above everything else.'

'You think that's true?'

'I don't know.' I sit down on the bottom step of the stairs. 'Maybe? I don't know.'

'I know that you love Joe.'

'Of course.'

'Is this because of the whole Karen thing?'

'He knows that I saw that stupid text.'

'Oh.'

'Apparently, she's gay.'

'Oh, honey.'

'And Joe says that I worry about other people because I don't trust him.'

'And do you? Trust him?'

I hold my head in my hand. 'You know what, Si? I think I might just be the world's biggest idiot when it comes to relationships.'

'How so?'

'If I'm honest and I look at myself deeply, then I have to admit that Joe might have a point.'

'I'm listening.'

'Well, all this looking at reasons why people in their forties break up...'

'Oh God, not this again.' Simon sighs dramatically down the phone.

'I'm being serious, Simon. Maybe I wasn't trying to figure out what might go wrong with me and Joe. Maybe I was trying to figure out what happened to my mum and dad's relationship so that I wouldn't repeat it.'

'Oh, I see. That kind of makes sense, hun.'

'What if I'm scared to fully commit because I'm scared I'll get hurt if it doesn't work out? And why would it work out? If my mum and dad couldn't make a relationship work, then how can I? I'm a combination of both of their genes.'

'You're overthinking things, Em. You're not your mum, or dad. You're in control of your own destiny.'

'I guess.'

'No, not guess, actually in control.'

'So what are you saying?'

Simon tuts. 'Honestly, babe, for a really smart girl you can be a complete dumbass sometimes.'

'Thanks,' I say through gritted teeth. 'That's really helpful.'

'What I'm saying is, do you love Joe?'

'You know that I do.'

'And do you want to be in a relationship with Joe?'

'Of course.'

'Right now?'

'Yes.'

'And always and forever?'

'Oh God, Simon, you're right. I am a complete dumbass.'

'What are you waiting for?'

'I love you. I'll call you later.'

I hang up the phone and glance at the time. Then I quickly check the rail network website. The next train to London leaves in twenty minutes. That must be the train that Joe will get on.

I take the stairs two at a time, fling my dressing gown on the floor and pull on last night's jeans and shirt, minus a bra and pants, but right now that really doesn't seem important.

I grab my keys and run out the door to the car. I jump in, jab the keys into the ignition and practically wheel-spin away from the kerb. Traffic is heavy for a Saturday morning.

'Come on, hurry up!' I shout at the queuing traffic in front of me as we shuffle along the ring road.

Sixteen minutes.

Why are you so stupid, Emma? Why did you let him walk out of the house? Why didn't you get him to stay? Why didn't you tell him that you *do* love him and want to spend every day with him for the rest of your life? That it's you that you don't trust, not him; that you don't trust yourself not to cock everything up – and now you have. Now you've let Joe think that you aren't in this for real and he's getting on a train to London to give you time to think about what you want.

'I don't need time, Joe. I know what I want.'

Fourteen minutes.

For God's sake. I press my hand down on the horn, which I realise is futile, but with nothing more productive to do, I press it again. This earns me a rude hand gesture from the driver of the hatchback in front of me.

Nine minutes.

Finally, I reach the entrance to the train station car park, and I swing the car into the opening, nearly taking the corner on two wheels. I steer into the nearest vacant space, not giving a damn about parking straight, and I jump out and run towards the station building.

Six minutes.

I dash between people milling around until I reach the screens showing the arriving and departing trains. My eyes dart up and down the list until I see Joe's train. Platform eight – great!

Four minutes.

I resume my sprint, catching the elbows of people in my way but barely offering an apology as I run on. When I reach the footbridge to platform eight, I take two steps at a time on the stairs and nearly upend someone's takeaway coffee, and I hear an expletive as I push past three people strolling along the bridge with giant roller-cases. I mean, who strolls in a train station? People who aren't crazy-stupid and trying to stop their boyfriend getting on a train in order to save their relationship. No time to think about that now, Emma.

Whoa!

The world begins spinning, and then I hear a crunch and an excruciating pain shoots up from my knee. I let out a loud scream and find myself face down on the cold, tiled floor.

'I'm so sorry. Are you okay?' I roll over to find a tall man leaning over me, an apologetic expression on his face. 'I didn't see you.'

'Never mind,' I gasp, the air knocked from my lungs. 'No time.'

I push myself up onto my knees and nearly keel over again with the pain in my left knee. I glance at my watch – two minutes until Joe's train leaves.

Shit!

Somehow I get to my feet and half-run, half-hobble across the footbridge. I stagger down the stairs to the platform.

Where is it? Where's the train? Is this the wrong platform?

I see the screen hanging above. The train to London is showing, but 'Train departing' is flashing across the screen. As I look up ahead, I see the final carriage of a train in the distance and my heart breaks.

I hunch over, resting my hands on my knees as I try to catch my breath. A big, fat tear runs down my face and plops off the end of my chin. I don't have the energy to lift my hand to wipe it away. I'm spent, emotionally and physically; adrenaline fuelled my sprint across the entire train station, but now I've crashed and burned.

I really thought that I'd make it, I thought I'd get to Joe in time. But he's gone, and what if I've lost him forever?

I squeeze my eyes shut for a second as tears begin to well, then breathe in deeply and exhale. Opening my eyes, I force myself to stand upright.

'Emma?'

I do a full one-eighty-degree swivel.

Blink.

My heart's in my throat.

Blink again.

'Is it really you?' I stare at the dimples I fell in love with, the dark-brown hair swept to one side in a 'lazy bedhead' style that works, and those deep brown eyes, locked on mine. 'But your train left?' I turn and point feebly into the distance.

'I didn't get on the train.' Joe's voice draws me back around to face him.

'Why?'

'What are you doing here?' Joe steps towards me.

Right. Why am I here? This is my moment. This is the moment that made me drive like an angry person, sprint across a train station and fall flat on my face on the floor.

'Um, right, yes, well,' I fumble, and Joe studies me, no expression on his face at all. 'I was an idiot. I was stupid. I didn't know what I had until...' I can hear the quiver in my voice. I breathe in, then out. 'This isn't coming out how I wanted it to.'

Joe shrugs. 'So for once, Emma, say exactly what you want to say.'

I nod. 'It's me that I didn't trust, not you, not us – me.' I take a step towards Joe, so I'm not quite within touching distance but close enough to smell the crisp scent of his aftershave. My heart thuds loudly. 'I think subconsciously I was holding back because I was scared that things wouldn't work out somehow, that somewhere along the line things would fall apart. Like it was in my DNA and I was destined to be crap at relationships because my mum and dad didn't make it work.'

Joe's eyes are fixed on mine, but he says nothing.

'All that stuff about Karen was me being stupid, and looking at your phone was bad, very bad – I will *not* do that again. But my love for you was never in question. I *do* love you, Joe, and I promise that from this day forward I will not allow my hang-ups to override my common sense. I will commit, I *am* committed one hundred per cent to you, to us, to our relationship, and I'm sorry, sorry for everything.'

I bite my lip, waiting for Joe to say something.

He cocks his head on one side and a hint of a smile tugs at his mouth. 'That's pretty much what Simon said.'

I frown. 'What?'

'Simon. He said…mmm, let me think of his exact words. That's right, he said, "She's had an epiphany and come to her senses. Don't be too hard on her; I don't have the drinking capacity to be her emotional crutch if you dump her."'

'Simon called you?'

I'm going to kill Simon.

Joe glances at his watch. 'About twenty minutes ago.'

Hang on a minute. 'That's why you didn't get on the train?'

'That's why I didn't get on the train.'

A tear trickles down my cheek, and Joe reaches up and gently wipes it away with his thumb. 'I know that you love me, Emma. I just needed to know that we both wanted the same thing, that we were, *are* both in the same place. I've felt you pulling away from me recently.'

'I have never loved anyone like I love you.' I gulp, a second tear escaping down my face. 'And I can't imagine my life without you in it.'

'Good.' Joe cups my face with his hands. 'Because I'm not going anywhere; I'll be here with you always.'

'Forever?'

'Forever.' He leans in and kisses me, a warm, safe, passionate kiss that feels like home.

Joe pulls away. 'Well, I mean, I have to go to London; I have work on Monday. But I'll be back.'

I can't help but giggle, and Joe laughs too.

'Maybe you could get the train on Monday instead?' I say.

'I'm sure that can be arranged.' Joe wraps his arm around me and we slowly walk from the platform.

As we leave the train station, I feel a sense of calm wash over me.

The last few months have unnerved me, challenged me and in many ways tipped my life upside down, but now it feels like I'm back on solid ground, and right here, tucked into Joe's warm embrace, is exactly where I should be, where I need to be, and where I'll stay, always and forever.

Epilogue

Here we are again, my birthday dinner. In forty-eight hours, I'll turn forty-one.

I smooth down my bright-pink dress and apply a matching lip gloss.

Why when people told me that time goes quicker as you get older did I not believe them? It doesn't seem two minutes since I was turning forty, and now I'm *in* my forties.

'Emma? The taxi's here,' Joe calls up to me.

'Coming.' I grab my matching clutch bag and, after one last look in the mirror, I head downstairs.

'You look hot,' Joe says, pulling me into his arms and pressing his lips against mine. 'Maybe I should take you back upstairs.'

'I thought you said the taxi was here,' I whisper as Joe nuzzles my neck.

'Mmm, maybe.'

'And we have dinner reservations,' I say, 'and hopefully six of our friends waiting for our arrival at the restaurant.'

'So? They'll wait.'

I giggle. 'Come on, we'll be late.'

Joe takes my hand and we go out to the taxi. We arrive at Luciano's a short time later. We're greeted and led to the table, where Simon, James, Jenny, Scott and, thankfully, Sophie and Matt are already seated.

Sophie looks stunning. Her chocolate curls are full and bouncing, and the glow that was missing from her cheeks while she and Matt were apart is back, now that time is almost a distant memory. Matt sits by her side, looking content as he lovingly brushes a loose curl away from her face.

Jenny looks refreshed and happy as she and Scott chat with James.

'Happy birthday, babe!' Simon jumps up and flings his arms around me. 'Drink?'

'Yes, please.'

Sophie hands me a Cosmopolitan, and I smile and take a sip as we sit down.

'I'm starving,' I say as I peruse the menu. 'Let's order, then we can all catch up.'

The waiter comes over a few minutes later and we all order our food.

'Right,' Simon says the minute the waiter has left the table. 'Come on, birthday girl, make a speech.'

'A speech? No.' I shake my head.

'Come on, Emma.' Joe smiles at me. 'I think a speech is most definitely in order.'

I look around the table at seven smiling faces.

'Okay,' I concede, 'but I'm not standing up.'

I reach for my Cosmopolitan and take a large gulp, suddenly feeling a little emotional. I swallow, then begin.

'Although I can't quite believe that on Monday, I'll be forty-one years old, I wouldn't want to change a thing. I couldn't think of anything worse than being in my twenties again.'

'I don't know,' Simon interjects, 'I had more spare time and more energy, and hangovers went away with a paracetamol and an energy drink. Now it takes three days to recover from one night out.'

Everyone laughs.

'But we wouldn't be where we are now,' I say, 'and I wouldn't have you all in my life.'

'Plus your dress sense was a little iffy back then.' Simon giggles and James elbows him none too gently.

'That's not to say that being in your forties doesn't present some challenges. It's been an interesting year, but we've all made it through, and I for one am looking forward to the next year. So, thank you for being such good friends. I treasure our friendships and love you all.'

I raise my glass, and everyone follows suit.

'To us.'

'To us,' everyone choruses.

The next day, the day before my birthday, I'm sitting on the side of the bath and contemplating what a funny year it's been.

I always thought things would get easier when I turned forty, that somehow we would all be older and wiser and make less mistakes. As it turns out, Sophie made the biggest mistake of her life in her forty-first year. She made a stupid decision and nearly lost everything that she held dear to her. Thankfully, she got a second chance, and I'm pretty sure she will cherish each and every day with Matt now.

Simon and James grew as a couple, and after much reflection Simon conceded that he's much happier now as a husband and a father than he ever was as a single guy moving from man to man without a care for commitment. None of us thought we would see the day he settled down, let alone became a responsible parent. But people surprise you; in fact, sometimes they shock the hell out of you.

But that's what happens when you grow up without even realising it. You make stronger commitments, take on bigger responsibilities, but you're also susceptible to making grown-up mistakes. Life is fragile, and one wrong move can see it come crashing down around you.

Joe and I have been tested this year too. Our relationship was put under pressure by him working away. Even though it was only for six months, it felt like my world was disjointed and a little off-kilter every day, until he returned and equilibrium was restored. I admire anyone who can survive a long-distance relationship – it's incredibly hard. I had always thought that Joe was my soulmate, but the time we spent apart from each other really proved that to me. He really does make my world complete.

Perhaps my biggest lesson this year was that secrets test loyalties, whether you're keeping someone else's or your own. Also, sometimes there is no right answer. You have to make a call, but if it all goes wrong, all you can do is hold on to all the pieces and hope that there'll be an opportunity to put things back together.

I guess the conclusion I've drawn from the last twelve months is that you can plan everything, but things can change in an instant, for better or worse, and you just have to adapt. Oh, and that my mother is right: honesty is the best foundation to build your relationship on, however hard that might be.

I think one of my biggest strengths may be my ability to adapt to circumstances that aren't within my control. When Mum and Dad separated when I was sixteen, I adapted to living in two different houses, experiencing life in two different environments, but I was fortunate that their love for me was never in question.

I adapted to Chris unceremoniously dumping me over a posh dinner in a restaurant when I thought he was going to propose. Admittedly, my 'adaption' did include drinking my body weight in wine, but it's part of the healing process, isn't it? You can't just bounce back overnight when your feelings have been squished to a pulp.

And now, *almost* at the age of forty-one, I'm going to have to adapt again.

We're going to have to adapt, both Joe and I.

Life really can change in an instant, but this time I know it's for the better.

I glance down at the plastic stick in my hand and read the word 'Pregnant' again.

I just hope that Joe feels the same way.

Thank you for taking the time to read my book; I hope you enjoyed it. If you did, I'd really appreciate it if you could take a moment to leave me a review on your favourite retailers' website.

Thanks!

Sasha Lane

About the author:

Hi, I'm Sasha,

I love anything books, along with cats, wine, yoga, and jogging when I find the time. I write Chick Lit novels with a twist! They're Chick Lit style with a hint of darkness. I write in first person as I find it much easier to get into character and tell their story that way. I try to create characters that are just everyday young women so hopefully readers can find something about their personality or life that they can relate to, and fall in love with them as much as I have while writing about them.

Other titles by Sasha Lane:

Girl, Conflicted

Girl, Unhinged

Girl, Unconventional